Praise for Christ.
The Best of Our Past, the Worst of Our Future

'Christi Nogle is one of my favorite new voices in horror. Her fiction is by turns devastating, horrifying, and beyond beautiful.'
Gwendolyn Kiste, Bram Stoker Award-winning author

'Just as you think you have a handle on what a Christi Nogle story might be, you turn a page and are surprised anew. Enigmatic, surreal yet shockingly visceral, often rooted in a deceptively familiar domesticity turned nightmarish, these strange and unsettling tales unfold in lyrical prose that belies their savagery.'
Lynda E. Rucker, Shirley Jackson Award-winning author

'An astonishingly original collection of dark tales – mysterious, haunting, challenging and disturbing, written in crystalline prose as compressed as poetry. Read and then reread and be doubly rewarded!'
Ramsey Campbell, author of *Fellstones*

'Christi Nogle takes readers on a dark yet wondrous journey through perils, horror, and thrills in this extraordinary debut collection. Behold the timelessness of these lives, these tales!'
Eric J. Guignard, award-winning author and editor, including *That Which Grows Wild* and *Doorways to the Deadeye*

CHRISTI NOGLE

PROMISE

A Collection of Weird
Science Fiction Short Stories

This is a **FLAME TREE PRESS** book

Text copyright © 2023 Christi Nogle

FLAME TREE PRESS
6 Melbray Mews, London, SW6 3NS, UK
flametreepress.com

US sales, distribution and warehouse:
Simon & Schuster
simonandschuster.biz

UK distribution and warehouse:
Hachette UK Distribution
hukdcustomerservice@hachette.co.uk

Publisher's Note: This is a work of fiction. Names, characters, places, and
incidents are a product of the author's imagination. Locales and public names
are sometimes used for atmospheric purposes. Any resemblance to actual
people, living or dead, or to businesses, companies, events, institutions, or
locales is completely coincidental.

Thanks to the Flame Tree Press team.
The cover is created by Flame Tree Studio with thanks to
Shutterstock.com. The font families used are Avenir and Bembo.

Flame Tree Press is an imprint of Flame Tree Publishing Ltd
flametreepublishing.com

A copy of the CIP data for this book is available from the British Library
and the Library of Congress.

1 3 5 7 9 8 6 4 2

HB ISBN: 978-1-78758-813-4
PB ISBN: 978-1-78758-812-7
ebook ISBN: 978-1-78758-814-1

Printed and bound in Great Britain by Clays Ltd, Elcograf S.p.A.

CHRISTI NOGLE

PROMISE

A Collection of Weird
Science Fiction Short Stories

FLAME TREE PRESS
London & New York

To my writing friends, writing groups, mentors, and mentees.
You inspire me every day.

CONTENTS

COCOONING

Six months ago, we were doing planks and push-ups and eating perfect at every meal. Now me and Donny are lucky to make it around the block a couple times after dinner. That's it for the day – and only on the weekdays, just so the dogs don't get too hyper while we're at work.

It's fall. Feels good to let go.

Leaves are taking over the yard. There's poo to clean up if anyone cared to look, but we don't look. We're too busy streaming horror movies and eating pasta and cinnamon rolls all weekend. Donny must be sneaking Halloween candy, too, because the bag's going down. We can turn the lights off and go to bed at eight on Halloween for all I care. Might be nice to have a good snuggle.

We're so cocooned, it takes us a week to notice it's not just us, that there's something up in the neighborhood. One day I put towels over the bathroom mirror and take the hanging ones out, and just a few days later everyone's big mirrors are leaning against the trash cans.

It reminds me of when everybody got flat-screen TVs and dumped all the thick ones on the curb. Those blocky TVs were more than useless. They rubbed you the wrong way, like the mirrors do now.

It's just too dark in the house to see things right. That's what I tell Donny. When it's dark and you look in a mirror, things seem to crawl and shift. Or if you've had a drink or three, you might think you look extra sexy – or when you try to cut your own hair, all the motions are off. Mirrors are strange. They've never been exactly right, and now they're a little more wrong, is all.

And we don't need them. We feel how strong and tight our bodies are getting. We feel our nails and our hair growing thicker and stronger, the lines in our chests and hands smoothing out. The spots on Donny's arms are just a memory.

Mister and Gracey sprawl and snore at either end of the sectional. We make calzones, shortbread, big breakfasts for dinner. All winter we feel warm and full and good.

*   *   *

Donny's the first to think we might be gone to heaven, but he's the first to let go of that idea, too. He moves on to other theories that the guys cook up at work. A lot of those guys live in our neighborhood, but some of them don't, which gets them all wondering about things like how far it's spread, but there's nothing on the news about it. Nothing online.

Oh, we still work and shop for groceries and pay the bills. Everybody keeps eating and pooping, that's for sure. Everything's easier than it should be, though. Work goes fast, me and my friends have a nice lunch every day, the appliances don't blow out, pay lasts the month. Nobody's got car trouble. We don't get any unexpected calls from our parents.

Donny's moved on to other theories, but I think we just might be in heaven – up until Donny catches his thumb on the truck door. The nail turns black and keeps hurting him. That wouldn't happen in heaven.

*   *   *

We figure something's coming, and finally in spring some gals in rubber suits come and ransack the house. One of them keeps us on the couch the whole time and says how after the rest is done, she'll turn the couch over and go through the batting. They keep saying how gross the dog hair is every time they lift something up. It's maybe the most humiliating thing to ever happen to me. They make fun of Donny's comics and his books. They make fun of our food.

The dogs are kenneled up. They bark awhile, but they settle when Donny uses his big voice, squeak under their breath for a bit to let you know they're still nervous.

They're stuck in these cages, but they still want to protect us. It's pitiful.

It takes hours. I finally beg the one gal into letting us sit on the back porch awhile 'cause it's so nice out. There are people on the patio across the way, and we see the ones in suits rushing around their outbuildings. Some wear green suits, some pale pink. Donny presses the side of his leg against mine and rubs my knuckles.

He thinks we're going to die. It never occurred to me, but I see in his face he already went there. I don't know. When they're finished, I don't think they'll just go – I'm not stupid – but I don't know what'll happen.

I say, "I was thinking we ought to get chocolate chip mint and pink peppermint and put a scoop of each on top of a brownie and then make Cara's ganache recipe. I think it's dark chocolate and butter. Or whipped cream?"

"Keep going," says Donny, and I talk about topping it with toffee chips and salt and black walnuts.

"Your yard's real pretty," says the gal who took us out back. She walks a little away, tips her helmet up and spits on the ground, and Donny and me squeeze each other's hands because that means it's not something that'll kill you. She wouldn't take her helmet off. The old guy to the north of us whispers over the fence, "What do you know?" But she's coming back, so we don't answer.

"I said real pretty," she says.

The grass is patchy but soft and bright. The crocus bed is up and some of the tulips. "Thanks," I say.

She rocks back on her heels and says, "Yeah, I really like what you've done with all the dog shit."

I get that rush to grab her by the scruff and drag her off my property, but I can't do that, and that's what finally makes me afraid. She's slouching back, smirking, looking from side to side. The chemicals pumping through my blood turn to poison, and I'm cold all through.

The gal takes out a compact. She pushes her helmet back and she's gorgeous, so gorgeous she has a boy's haircut just to rub it in. She checks her mascara. "Gets hot in the suit," she says, and, "Hey, you want to use this?" She gestures like she's going to throw the mirror to me and chuckles and goes inside.

They leave us outside for two minutes and know we won't run. There are too many of them.

When they move us to the van, Donny has my hand. He's saying, "Where are our dogs?" He lets go of me, pulling toward the house, but a man comes on one side of him and a bigger gal on the other. They put him in the back row of seats and I slide in beside him.

The dogs whimper from their kennels in the back. We poke our fingers through the bars and pet their noses. We see the vans sitting in driveways all the way out of town.

Then we're on the highway for a good half hour, just complying our butts off.

Compliance is key, they told us back at the start of this thing, so we love on the dogs and keep holding hands and answering their questions. Anyone can see I'm complying a little better than Donny, who's starting to quake. He asks questions of his own and they don't answer.

Out past Hammett, the gal in the shotgun seat says she's hungry, is there anywhere good to eat?

"Well," I say, and not ten minutes later she's coming out with sacks of chicken-bacon-ranch sandwiches and nests of garlic fries and small-size drinks for everybody. I taste something in my drink, but Donny doesn't. He's too nervous to eat, but he's grateful for the root beer and drinks it down. I sip on my diet cherry pop and eat a few bites of sandwich before I go out, but before that I feel his hand go slack in mine, and I'm happy he won't be nervous anymore. My arm feels heavy where I'm resting it on the kennel, and then I can't keep my eyes open. I concentrate on the motion of the van building speed for the freeway.

* * *

"Don't open your eyes," Donny says. "Just lie still." I do open them – how can someone wake up without doing that? – but I can't see much of anything. I close them again and remember what happened.

We're spooning in a bed that's softer than we like. I'm the little spoon.

"I've got such a headache," I say.

He feels my eyes to make sure they're closed. "It's the stress," he says, and hugs me to him and then rubs my shoulders too hard. I hear the dogs breathing on the floor.

"Where are we?" I say, and Donny whispers for a long time about the room and what he saw earlier. He says the room is plain and white, about twenty feet square.

"The dogs?" I say.

"The dogs are fine – don't they sound fine? Here, puppy," he says and makes a smoochy noise. Gracey jumps up to us. Now she's the little spoon. I sink my hand into her rough poodle coat.

Donny says there's a table with padded chairs like in a motel room, and that's all the furniture. It's not entirely dark – a blue nightlight hangs mid-ceiling.

Oh, and there are mirrors on three of the walls. Big mirrors like on TV, the kind that have people watching from back of them.

We move in and out of conversation, in and out of sleep. We talk for the first time about how all of this started, a crawling in the mirror, just when it was dim or dark. We saw things there that we didn't like seeing. That's why we covered up the medicine cabinet. Just that one at first, then the one in the hall. But it wasn't really that noticeable, was it? We didn't like mirrors, and we maybe felt a little bit better than normal, was all.

I keep thinking the sun will come up, but after a while, Mister starts to squeak and then Gracey is pawing at me. Somebody makes a skunk fart. It's still dark, and Donny finally says there's no window, just another big mirror behind the bed.

"Good morning," calls some man through a speaker. "OK if we walk the dogs now?"

"Why are we here?" yells Donny.

"We'd like to go outdoors too," I say.

"OK to walk the dogs now?" he says, and Donny must nod, because the dogs are running toward a sound off to the left, and then they're gone from the room.

"There's a restroom behind the bed on your right. Feel for the door," the man says from the speaker. "Feel free."

And a gal comes on. "You ought to take a shower, too." I catch the first cackle of a bunch of people before she turns the speaker off, and it's quiet again.

★ ★ ★

The light is blue, very low. We're fine if we keep our eyes down. No mirror in the bathroom, so it feels more normal in there. Sometimes we make it in the shower and sit on the floor afterward, not wanting to go back to the bedroom.

There's plenty of water, but they aren't feeding us much, just vending machine sandwiches twice a day, once in a while a candy bar. They leave it on the table by the door when we sleep. They sent in bleach one time in a paper cup with a straw, another time gasoline. I screamed and beat on the walls when they first sent in things like that, but now I just flush it. I don't like it going into the water supply, but it's that or let it stink the place up.

I thought they were doping the dogs, but Donny says no, the dogs are just depressed because we aren't doing anything. With no TV and no light and no good food or walkies, I've pretty well soured on the cocooning myself.

I want to move now. I get down and do some push-ups and try to do some plank moves and burpees and things like that. It's tough with no music to keep going. It starts to burn, and I've got nothing but the burn to hold on to, but I keep at it, longer and longer.

One time I stand by the door and beg them to take the dogs away somewhere. My parents' place if they can, or just somewhere. Even a shelter. They're cuties; they'll do all right.

Donny tells me no, stop it, the dogs are better off here. He pulls me back on the bed and shushes me with his hand. But there's nothing wrong with the dogs. Whatever's going to happen to us doesn't need to happen to them.

We're not stupid. We know we've been infected by something – some alien thing or some government thing. An experiment, an attack, it makes no difference now.

Things like this happen. It just feels unfair to be the ones it's happening to.

Donny wonders if it was in the food. Or a meteor that came down near town. Or it came on the little feet of mice.

He sleeps more than I do. He says he has no hope anymore, though he'll feel hopeful for me if I say he should, and I say of course he should.

Donny has a good ten years on me, harder years too, and I've always assumed I'm headed toward a life without him. We don't have any kids, just the dogs.

"It was noticeable, if we'd've cared to notice," he says.

"Maybe," I say.

"We just wanted to stay happy as long as we could," he says.

★   ★   ★

One time when Donny's sleeping, I look into the mirror long and hard. Couldn't explain why, not if you tortured me. I spoon behind him until I'm sure he's out, then I stand and open my eyes.

At first it's just a shifting, shimmering movement too small to notice. My face – I know I'm holding it still – but it's moving slightly, crawling around the jaw. Then the mouth smiles and stretches tight, the motions just enough to bring on that alarmed feeling that made us cover the mirrors in the first place.

I start to see some things about my insides. Movements under my skin: muscles, heart, ribs. I lift my arm and see the motions at every point – all these arms stuck in the air between the place where my arm was and the place where it is. And a big dark cave where my guts ought to be.

The mirror's telling me something true that no one else can see.

I'm hot and weak when I finally look away. I go on my stomach for the cool floor, not far from Mister. After a while, I feel cool and slide closer to him. He's a husky-border collie mix, soft fur smelling of dander and the dirt from outside this place. I hug him into my belly and he sighs. I close my eyes.

He's a special dog. Always so cute, his black and white patterns partly ordered like his mom's were and partly wild like his daddy's. Ice-blue eyes. He was always special 'cause of his looks but later it was 'cause he was so smart and good.

I worried about him all the time when he was a puppy. I'd jump in and save him from every little thing. That's why he's such a baby now. Paranoid, Donny says.

I swear I can almost read Mister's mind sometimes, and my goodness, he's unhappy now, restless and stir-crazy and hopeless. He thinks he did something wrong and we're punishing him.

In the space between my belly and his back, I feel something I've never felt before – something between warmth and bubbles popping. I hug him real tight and keep thinking I should let go now. I really should, but…there's less and less of him to let go of.

I'm on my back now, pushing his jaw down into my chest. I see clear as day – my body from the waist down, my abs, white boxers, thighs all blue in the light. From my ribs up is the white fur, a furry paw sticking out near my sternum. His jawbone under my hand – and then just my chest bones under my hand. He's gone!

He's not, of course. He's part of me now.

In the minute it took to take him into me, he never fought, never made a peep. I feel him waking up now, and he doesn't panic. He doesn't struggle. He's warm and safe inside me and knows it. He's energized, plotting because he knows a lot more now, and he still wants to protect me.

He's grateful. I'm grateful too, at first, but the feeling starts to come that I've done something wrong. I don't care about the people behind the mirrors, but I don't want Donny to know.

I want to run. I've never felt caged in my life until just this second.

Donny's still asleep. I rush to the shower. The water wakes him up, of course, and he's asking why I'm in there, and I say I got too hot. There's only a little blood, a couple dark drops that the water washes away.

When I sleep, I dream that I ate Mister, every bit of him, bones and fur and teeth and gristle, watching myself in the mirror the whole time. I dream that when I went into the shower, I left a slick of blood I had to lap up afterward, but that isn't what happened at all.

★　　★　　★

It's a bad time for Donny and me. I keep worrying the people behind the mirrors will say something about what I did with Mister, but they never do. I tell Donny they let the dogs out and then he just didn't come back in with Gracey and maybe they sent him someplace better.

Donny paces. He's mad at me 'cause I was the one who told them to send the dogs away.

He won't let Gracey out again. He cleans up her messes with toilet paper and flushes them and swears at the guy on the speaker.

A bad time. Once, he hurls something into the mirrors. He peeks – just for a second – and says there's no room behind the mirror. I happen to have my eyes open when he says it, and it's true. Behind the broken glass is just a wall.

★　　★　　★

With Mister inside me making me stronger, I look in the mirrors anytime I want. My hair is different in the mirror, eyes glowing pale blue. My head has that tilt, and if I look a long time, Mister's face comes in more. It's good to see him.

Donny doesn't say I'm any different. When I pull pieces of my hair around to look, they're dark and plain, same as always.

One time I'm looking in the mirror and the door opens. Donny's asleep and even if he was up, he wouldn't look. It's the gorgeous one with the short hair, wearing a doctor's coat, leaning in from a bright hallway. She smiles, and the second I start toward her, she clicks the door shut.

Another time she says through the speaker, "Why didn't you do this earlier?"

"Do what, you crazy bitch?" Donny yells even though he knows I don't like that word.

★   ★   ★

Gracey's scratching at the door and Donny jumps up to drag her to the shower. He's trying to train her to go in there so he can hose it down. She whimpers.

"Just let her outside," I say. "Maybe they'll take her someplace better."

Donny puts his face right up against mine. "They killed Mister."

"They didn't," I say.

I can't remember the last time we had a real blowout. I usually try to make up right away; I'm doing that now. Please, you're right, and please calm down, on and on like that. I smell that Gracey's done her business and rush in to take care of it. I don't know if my cleaning it up will make him madder, but probably not. It'll probably soften him. The stress-poo is so nasty, but I wipe it with the toilet paper and water and hose off the shower and clean it all again with a little dot of shampoo.

I wash my hands and feet and dry them before I come back into the room. It's to the point in the fight where if Donny pushes, I'll start getting real mad, but if he lets go we can make up. And he's dying to let go. I see it. He's on the end of the bed. He holds out his arms, and I go to him. We hold each other. His face is in my belly, and I start to feel warm tingles there. I'm looking sideways into the mirror and see his eyes are open, looking straight up at me.

"What the hell are you doing?" he says.

I move away and come around the bed, get under the covers. Gracey jumps up and tucks into a ball between us.

"What were you doing?" he says.

"We can take Gracey someplace better," I say. She hasn't been groomed forever, and I have my hands deep in her rough fur. I don't know what Donny thinks I'm doing to her, but he starts to pull her like he's booting her off the bed. I'm already falling into her, covering her with my chest and arms.

"Come, take part of her," I say, but he's off the bed now, just watching. It's fast and clean as can be, just a few drops of brownish blood on my T-shirt and the covers and that rush of thankful feeling again.

I'm frozen there in the rush of her. Everything's frozen in place.

"I'll get this cleaned up," I say, and I go off to scrub the bedspread before the stain sets.

When I get back, he's at the end of the bed, head in his hands.

"What do you look like to yourself? In the mirror, I mean," he says.

I don't answer 'cause he's still mad. The room feels cool with no covers and nobody to curl up to. I do a few squats, turn to the mirror. If I just glance and don't focus, I think I see what Donny sees, me like I've always been but better. Everything tight, skin clear with good color, my plain dark hair somehow glossy. I close my eyes.

"If I look long and hard, I see what we're becoming," I say.

"You're making it happen faster," Donny says.

It's true. Whatever life we thought we'd enjoy just a little while longer, it must be over now. Gracey's just beginning to wake up in me, and I'm already hungry for something more. We ought to be out in the streets now. This rest has done me good, but some kind of struggle is what I need. Some kind of work.

"You should be looking, too," I say. "It isn't bad." I'm thinking of the two of us breaking out together.

"How will we ever get home?" he asks.

"We won't be going home," I say, "but as long as we're together...."

He's heartbroken. He's thought about dying but he hasn't thought about living and not going home. We're all made up, just like that, but he's ruined.

He's like Mister was before I saved him. Sad and mopey, all the will gone out of him.

★   ★   ★

It's hard to touch Donny now without taking him. The fluttery warm feeling starts six inches ahead of the touch, like static. He says he has nothing – no one but me, no home. His hope went a while ago, and now he can't even touch me.

I should take him. "Can you?" he asks.

He's nice enough to pretend the thought hasn't occurred to me.

"If it happens, I want you to look in the mirror right after," he says. "See if you see me." He's scared, but he's not the type to delay things. He takes off his T-shirt and moves me to his lap.

I take my shirt off, too, and all at once I'm thinking how much bigger he is – and how he must be hungrier than I am, and I'm scared. I feel his arms around my back and we're kissing lightly, chest to chest. The last time we tried it in the shower, not too long ago, we couldn't find my opening. It's gone. I have my whole hand reaching around in my boxers for it, but it isn't there. Still, the static feeling stops, and the tingly bubbles-popping feeling doesn't get stronger, and there are still two of us. We're grateful. We make out for a while and do a couple of things, take another shower and spend a long time getting dry.

We sleep right after. I'm the little spoon, but I'm on his side of the bed, which makes me think, as I drift off, how that never happened before.

I dream of eating him all up, of course, just like with Mister. I never had that dream with Gracey – she brought doggy dreams like the ones you imagine when you see them yipping and wiggling their feet – but I have the same nightmare all over again for Donny. Gnawing up the bones and licking all over the floor. It's so gross and goes on such a long time, and when I wake, I feel that guilt all over again, that I've done something wrong. I'm alone on the bed, and Donny isn't in the bathroom. I'm pacing around, thinking they took him and then knowing…it was me. I took him.

I have the guilt again, but it isn't fair 'cause I don't feel him inside me. No good feeling to push back the hurt. I'm about to finally lose it, and then I look into the mirror.

I focus until the being there shifts and shimmers. It isn't me exactly, or Gracey, Mister or Donny, but it's something of all of us, with a gaping cave in its belly. And it reaches – not close to the ceiling, that would be an exaggeration – but it reaches higher than it has any right to.

My arms and legs, if I look down at them, if I'm honest? They're not mine. They're Donny's. It was him that got me.

Only I don't think of it that way, not at all. I think of it this way: we're strong now, and good. We'll tear apart the corner of the room – the corner where the door is – tear with our teeth, with our claws. Just as soon as I think of it, we're doing it. Splinters in our mouth, something chalky. We're whining as we squeeze through the opening.

We smell the outdoors and long to be there. But before we go, we take a right turn down a bright hallway.

We pass a kitchen so bright our eyes sting, smelling of food and drink and people, and more of the dirt from outdoors – oh my God, the things we smell! Our mouth is dripping wet, and we come to the end of the hall.

The gorgeous girl stands by a locker, turns and gasps, and this time it's not a dream: we take her neck in our sharp teeth. We shake her, one two three, and drop her just as a man runs into the room. We take him by the neck – and our mouth tastes the two distinct flavors of their rich salty blood. It's the most sensation we've ever experienced. We test the flesh of his cheek and find it tough and tender, like nothing so much as sucking at our own wound. With a bit of guilt, we let the meat slip out of our mouth.

We turn toward another man, much older. We know this one is good. Is it his scent or his wakeful eyes? The way he holds his hands in surrender? We take this one in that other way – so fast, just a pressing into him and the rush of him waking into us. He is grateful, and he too is hungry.

★   ★   ★

The city outside is a small one, deserted at twilight. We know this place. It occurs to us that we have a good car parked forty feet away. It will feel better to walk the streets, or run – how long since we've run?

The people are all holed up behind curtains. A glowing cartoon-character blanket hangs on a window many floors up. It means that room never had a curtain. It means the people are hiding from something.

We aren't curious. After all, we've been commuting to work all through the crisis and listening to NPR just about three hours a day – not to mention what we learned through the observations and consultations at the center, not to mention what we learned from friends and family. We know what the scientists know, and we know what their kooky relatives know, and none of it is good, but it doesn't make any difference.

In any case, there is always someone who thinks he can sneak out after curfew – or if there isn't a straggler, well, doors are our playthings.

It doesn't matter what's happened because we'll all be together, so many of us now, getting stronger and smarter. We'll do our work at twilight, and it will warm us through the cold hours.

Sometimes, in the days to come, we'll feel that we might have done something wrong, but we'll tell ourselves, "No, we've done right," and list all of the ways we've been right – indeed, righteous. The voices will be so good and so strong – and so many – that we'll believe them.

Sometimes we feel sorry we can never go home again, but the word comes to us, *hiraeth*, a name for that feeling. We have known the word for many years, we heard it on a radio show, learned it from our grandmother, a word we just recently learned. The many beasts in us, those who never knew language until now, they find this word especially poignant. And so, when we think of home, we think of hiraeth and a memory of our nests and our mates and our littermates warms us. We mourn for our lost homes as we celebrate the new home we've taken in our selves.

Our body, when we glance in a mirror, is Donny's fine middle-aged body, shirtless and sweaty, his grizzly beard and thick salt-and-pepper hair grown to his shoulder blades. When we look longer – and by now we have to stand before a mirrored skyscraper at dusk to see our height – we are something else entirely.

LAUREL'S FIRST CHASE

My daughter and I came upon a yellow tent in the rocky stretch of western forest. She might have thought the camper must be somewhere near, about to come upon us – or she might have thought he was lying inside. What pleasure, to read in a tent through the last few hours of daylight, to put off the gathering of wood and laze inside!

He had done that for a while. He had lain inside on a soft green nylon sleeping bag and read his adventure story, but he was not doing it now. Still, it might have seemed so to Laurel if she could not see the fall he took on his fateful trek for wood.

I saw clearly. I saw the sun at noon in his memories and the sun at three o'clock with my own eyes. I apprehended that his death would not come until dusk. He was close enough I could feel how he'd suffered at noon and how the suffering changed by three o'clock, the richness of it, the almost-ecstasy. I felt how it would sharpen by five and ebb soon after.

If I'd not had Laurel with me, I might have gone to his side. He might have mistaken me – or pretended to mistake me – for a good Samaritan and begged for my help. Or he might have asked me to take a rock to his head. I might have obliged or not, depending.

I wondered, could Laurel feel him at all? I was initially certain that she could not.

I unzipped his tent's flap and we kneeled inside. I watched her face as she talked about how lovely the light was through the tent walls and how pleasurable it might be if we had books of our own with us. (She said that with her hand on the bag where the man had tucked his little adventure novel.)

She said we could lie here and read and think about gathering wood, but we would not gather wood. We would lie here and feel the dark coming on and keep reading. We could laze here, dreading the coming cold but keep reading.

So she saw all of this but could not see the rest. Or could she see the rest but not bring herself to say it?

She talked more and more frantically.

I thought it must be true: she saw something but was too afraid or too shy to say what she saw. When I put my hand on hers, she jumped up.

"Let's see more of this place," she said.

We would wander for an hour or more before circling back to the tent. By that time, the next camper would be in his position.

★   ★   ★

"Once?" she asked.

"Once we had a home here. Once a sort of town stood nearby, a road, a—"

"No." She laughed.

No? I rapped on the boards of a cabin. The cabin was not there, but I saw in her face how the sound came to her.

"We were...homesteaders? Farmers," I said.

"That's ridiculous. There were never any farms here," she said, rushing ahead. "I want to go home soon," she called back.

It was only four or four-thirty in the afternoon, but a campfire took shape up ahead. I walked a long rocky clearing behind my daughter, wondering if she saw the coming fire or anything of the night ahead.

I admired her height, the fine gold threads in her darkening hair. Her gait was still awkward, though she moved swiftly. I felt how aware she was of me behind her, felt her refuse to look back.

She swept her hair to the side and touched her neck. A month ago, it was, I saw a ball of flesh in that spot while we were finishing yard work. I twisted the skin, and before she could react, pinched it off with my fingernails.

"Ouch," she said. "What the—"

I flung the thing into the grass. "I think it's called a skin tag. I got it for you."

She touched the drop of blood. "Thanks?" she said.

Now she walked across the clearing, fingering that spot on her neck. Laurel would not look back at me. A second Laurel walked beside her for a moment, and this one did look back, but in an instant, it was gone.

I stopped and watched her reach the end of the clearing, saw her walk between two stunted pine trees, shift to the right to move around another. All I caught was the red of her shorts, and then she was gone.

I drifted toward the camper who had just arrived. He was going to be the one to start the fire. I thought at first that he was already walking in a spiral around the camp. I thought he had gone looking for the missing man.

I came closer and saw he was not spinning any spiral. He was only thinking of doing so. He stood beside the other man's cheap yellow tent and looked out into the trees, thinking how a man could move in a tight spiral and find someone who was missing if he cared to do so, then thinking that he would do that very thing soon now, any minute.

I came even closer.

I felt around inside his mind and took out a catalog of numbers and dates. He weighed one-hundred and seventy-eight pounds and held at twelve percent body fat. The numbers for cholesterol and such were good numbers. I knew because they had a prideful reddish glow. He had paid 349,000-some dollars for his home, 36,988 for his latest truck.

He had begun hunting at age eleven, and along with the ages that marked the first of each animal he killed, I found the totaled numbers of kills. Along with the numbers of kills was the sharp white flood of emotion for the first kill. That one was not the only kill that mattered to him, but it was one of a precious few. He thought of these as diamonds.

He was a good man.

He thought of his meaningful kills as diamonds, and the time he passed the diamond to the one who would be his second wife? He thought of that moment as a small flawless pearl. The birth of his boy was a grand and yellow jewel, uncomfortably intense like a direct view of the sun.

The boy was too small to be hunting, but the year in which the man would take him for his first kill was set in a calendar in the man's mind. He was already deciding on the place and imagining how the weather would be on that day. There were dates on the man's calendar for his next truck and other milestones to come such as the forty-fifth birthday and the fiftieth birthday, and the year in which it would be reasonable and necessary to take his wife on a cruise. He dreaded that year.

There were deep, pure emotions coloring all of the tables and dates.

He was sure he was a good man.

I thought for a moment of leaving my daughter to him. How happy would she be if I told her to go to him and say, *I'm lost. Can you help me?*

But I knew she saw. And we were mostly in agreement. All that was left was to put my hand on hers and say it was time.

I needed to find her first. I felt her around me but all dispersed, in several places at once, stronger and brighter here and fainter there. A swarm of my sweet Laurel.

I didn't pursue her. *Let her play her games for now*, I thought.

I watched the man pitch his impressive little plum-red tent, watched him take out an ultralight hiker's stove and miniature cooking gear. The price tags and advertising copy seemed to hover over each item as in a catalog, and how inordinately pleased he was to find the large rock with its flat top for meal preparation! I felt a little pang of pity for him then.

In his mind, he spun his web around the camp. He might find and save the weaker man, be a hero, but wasn't he already hero enough in his mind?

He began to bore me. The perfect posture, the wasteless motions of cooking and eating and tidying up. I wandered away.

As I wandered, image-memories came unbidden. A small fierce creature hunting on the forest floor, a ball of flesh the size of an orange in my hand, a girl in an art book with arms swept up growing branches, growing leaves.

"You remind me of her," I told Laurel. She closed the book and never asked why.

★   ★   ★

I found my daughter curled against the base of a tree, face dirty and leaves in her hair. She'd sighted him, must have.

"If he came upon you now, you'd catch him easy," I said.

"I don't know what you're talking about," she whined.

"It would be cheating to do that – no doubt – but it would work," I said.

"What," she said, not like a question but like the start of some question. Her breath hitched.

"Are you really crying?" I asked, amused. I came closer, and she cringed back against the tree. Tears came all muddy down her cheeks. I wanted to touch her face and feel the heat, but I didn't dare touch her.

We'd gotten too close, was that it? She sensed how good he thought he was.

After a time, she said, "Can we go home?"

"What home?" I said. Did she mean the house up in Bend? Was she missing her little pink room, the garbage I let her keep in it? The constant pretending to be human?

I will not go back there, I thought fiercely and was surprised by the thought.

Dusk was falling, and just across the creek, the weak man was finally ending. We were silent while it happened and shared, I thought, a meaningful look.

She crawled toward me, hoping to feed. I shook my head.

★   ★   ★

The man wallowed in shame, thinking how he ought to have searched instead of just imagining it. He sat before the yellow tent, called, and checked inside. He stepped inside without his shoes and came out again, reshod himself. He rifled through the other man's bag for a long while and then arranged the items back inside. There was nothing in the bag that surprised him or answered a question he had. He unzipped the tent again and set the bag inside. He rocked back up onto his feet, zipped the tent flap, and began gathering wood.

The shame he felt for not searching and the shame he felt for snooping in the bag were sweet and pure and equal in intensity.

★   ★   ★

My daughter squatted at the edge of a creek with a stick in her hand when I came upon her. Better. At least she was not crying.

"What are you doing?" I said.

"I'm hungry," she said.

"Me too," I said.

"I'm trying to catch a fish."

I thought of how I might have caught a fish when I was small – easy, with no second thought. Catch the watery sweetness of it in my mouth and move on to the next with no reflection, no delay.

I'd done her damage, raising her all these years. I'd made her less than she could have been.

She leaned in and poked her stick in the shallow water. She sighed and leaned back. "Stop watching me," she said.

"Do you see the fire yet?" I asked. It was so bright and beautiful, just a half hour away from starting and a hundred yards south. I was thinking like the man now, and I wanted to tell her how strange it was to be seeing things in his way, in yards and compass points and calendar squares. I tried to show her, but she was closed to me. It seemed she had always been closed.

I said, "The best time will be when he's still at the fire, before he gets sleepy. He'll be strongest then. He'll give you a good chase."

She stared into me.

"Or you could go and tell him you're hungry, but you know that wouldn't be fair."

She scrunched her nose, dropped her stick and rose, crossed her arms. "I can smell the fire," she said.

"Can you smell the man?" I said.

Laurel nodded. When I approached, she did not shy from me. I took her hand. Her cuticles were raw and red, the nails coming loose.

★   ★   ★

We watched the fire for a time. The man was still, but the images in his mind were painted in the dark sky above him: bird kills and deer kills and chases after wild, elusive creatures that never existed. The image of a weaker man crept close with all the weight and dread of a ghost, and receded, and went round in a spiral of smoke above the fire.

The man upended his flask above his mouth and then brought out a bottle.

"He drinks to get sleepy," I said.

"I know," said Laurel.

"It's time, or past," I said.

"It's too late now," she said.

"Not necessarily."

She cried again but not for the same reason.

"The things he values are of no value," I said.

She seemed about to open to me, but then the man thought of his little toddling son. The boy seemed to play and coo around the edges of the fire, and she was never more opaque than at that moment.

"Tomorrow?" I said.

"I can't," she said. She walked away again.

★   ★   ★

The man was a long while at the fire. He expected to sleep there instead of in his tent, but sleep could not come while he sensed me so near him. He went, he lay down comfortably enough in his sleeping bag, but something was wrong. His life began to look terrible to him.

He saw his son growing up without him. All he wanted was to be with his son, but he had come here. It wasn't even hunting season, just a camping trip, self-indulgent. His life nothing but restlessness, aimlessness, and vanity.

He had not even tried to save the man. He felt he had been placed here – in this place, this life – only to save the man, and he had failed to do it.

He knew himself to be a morsel in the center of a web, saved by a spider. He knew his hands would not move, and even if they moved, they would not be able to unzip his tent. He would not be able to try.

I imagined the kill. He imagined it with me. I was that close.

Before a kill, the fingernails loosen from bloody cuticles, the forefinger and middle finger only are needed. The organs my daughter likes to pretend she does not have push out. Long, noodly things. They stretch up and into his nostrils. She takes only what she needs, leaves him empty and beautiful.

I waited for Laurel to return. The man pretended to sleep, and then he did sleep.

He dreamed of taking a new puppy on the playground equipment to desensitize it to new sights and sounds. A montage of happy moments playing on the swings and slides. He walked a playground bridge, the anxious puppy behind whimpering – falling – but when the man looked down at the ground far below, it was no puppy there, but his son. The man shrieked and jumped in his sleep and then was still.

He knew.

He was paralyzed. It was cruel to keep him in stasis, but Laurel was nowhere to be seen or felt. I lay inside the yellow tent for a time. I built up the fire and waited. I slept.

★　　★　　★

I woke to hard steps on a wooden floor. Laurel stood one foot off the ground, ten or twelve feet from the fire.

"You've found one of the cabins," I said.

She nodded. "He's still here," she said.

"I told you I'm not taking him," I said.

She held my gaze. She finally believed.

I saw shimmers of firelight on the walls of the cabin and when I squinted, the rough outline of the woodstove and the little iron bed far back. It was the cabin where I'd taken my first family.

The image came of a little rounded seedling coming up from the forest floor, a little animal growing more ravenous as it gorged on small birds and rodents, a troll-like creature stepping onto the front step of a cabin already seeing itself stepping out, days later, a girl.

Laurel thought of it too. It was the most curious, magical thing. I didn't know what had caused it, but there had been a change in her.

"I've never known anyone else like us," I said.

"And who are we?" she said.

Our imaginations played over the sights of the animal hunting in leaves and the book with the sculpture of Apollo and Daphne. Our imaginations spiraled farther out among the stars, and that felt true to both of us, but we didn't know which one we came from or why we'd come – or why we'd been flung – down here.

The strands came out of Laurel's fingertips now, not just the first two fingers but all of them. "In the morning," she said, and I felt her hunger.

I felt the man tense in fear. He was exceedingly strong to break that level of stasis. He cried out, just one sharp bark, and Laurel scattered into pieces and ran from me once again.

I released the man into a wholesome, natural sleep and followed.

★   ★   ★

My daughter and I frolicked those last few hours. That's all I can call it. We laughed for the first time in so long. She let herself go for once, entirely. She unspooled like an anemone, rose like a tree and bent down into the earth. I felt my own body relaxing into the creek and that sweet slack feeling overcome me, like taking off a corset.

I thought of putting on a corset for the first time, and all the other moves I had made toward this life we'd been living. I thought of all the balls of flesh I'd dropped quaking to life on the ground.

We played through the trees, we relaxed, but our minds never wandered far from the man.

He slept. He turned in his sleep. He woke slowly.

"He's strong enough to run now," Laurel said. Her nostrils flared. She smelled him.

"Let him start," I said.

It wasn't long after that I saw him crouching, looking into the trees. I said, "Now."

We followed his frantic movement up and down the dark, steep hills. We stumbled, drunk on the mix of fear and hope that colored the figures in his mind. He didn't think of the weak man or of his son now; he thought only of himself, and I thought that would make things easier for Laurel.

He kept track of sights along the way and estimated from them how much farther to the car. He walked quickly but would soon break into a run as the trees thinned, and when he did run, she would chase in earnest.

Or so I thought. She ran, but she never did catch him. She stopped short and watched him stumble over rocks and sprawl out into the highway.

We watched him rush to his truck, watched the inevitable shaking fumble with the keys. His truck backed out and pulled onto the highway.

"His little boy," she said when I caught up. "I couldn't."

"It was the delay, was all. And he was too old," I said. "It wouldn't have been a challenge." I rubbed her shoulders.

We walked on, a mile and then two. My spirits were low. I thought, *This girl is going to kill me.* I thought how this had been her one chance and that ever after she would want to keep feeding from me, and that we'd have to go back to the sad little house and never be free.

It was just dawn and brighter every moment, but then I saw. We'd move down the road another hour until we sighted a new walker, this a much younger man, too thin with reddish stubble on his head and face, his silver backpack glaring in the sun.

I'd expect her to turn her head and pretend not to see him, but my daughter would brighten.

"This one," she'd say. She'd start at a trot and build speed.

I'd keep my arm around her shoulders until then, feeling so proud. When the time came, I'd watch her chase him on the road and veer back into the forest.

FINISHERS

I'm always a little excited and nervous when Mother unwraps a new package. Sometimes under the wooden lid there is a folder with photographs, perhaps also a storage disk with video references. If so, Mother's body seems to grow heavier on the instant; her shoulders pull down. It will be a challenge to get everything right. She will labor for weeks and worry, and even so, the robot will most likely keep coming back to us for adjustments.

Sometimes there is no folder, but the body under the foam peanuts and plastic is a chill russet-pink instead of the standard green-gray. This indicates extra mechanisms in the pelvis. There will be extra steps in the molding process of its 'bottom', and I won't be allowed to watch some of her work. Mother looks on this kind with distaste, and I am glad they don't come very often.

The best is a greenish body and no folder. This is Mother's opportunity to practice her art. And I'll get to help!

She'll turn on the robot right there in the foyer and we'll walk it back to our quarters, spend the evening with it, get to know what idiosyncrasies it already has. Mother says this is what any sculptor does – look at the stone, look at the wood, and see what form or character is suggested there.

Most bodies are the same. They're between five-eight and six-two, all broad looking to me. Mother calls the most common type the mesomorph. There is a softer, rounder sort called the grande and a wiry one called the straw. There was one, once, as small as Mother, and another one broader than our bedroom door, another with massive bowed thighs. All of these are rare, though. Most are the mesomorph.

To sit and have dinner with a new greenish mesomorph, one with no folder, is a rare treat. It doesn't yet speak, but soon we stop calling it 'it'.

We call it he or she or they, as we like. The robot becomes a person to us.

"Did you see how she leans just a little to the right?" I say.

"Oh yes," says Mother.

"And her waist is a little wide, isn't it?" I say. It isn't – she has just a standard mesomorph form – but something in the way she sits suggests someone self-conscious of a waist that is a little bit wide.

"Her legs are long and beautiful, though," Mother says. I love how her face brightens when we get one like this. It's the only time she looks the way she used to look when I was little.

The first step is brutal. If Mother wants an extra few centimeters of leg, arm, or torso, the body will need to go into the stretcher. Every other change from the standard form can be accomplished with the suction molds, but not this one. I am allowed to watch, but I am too cowardly. I decide I must attend class today but ask Mother to please call me before she does anything more than the legs.

She waves me away. Her face is grim again.

I used to love going to class. It's not actually going somewhere, I know that – especially these days – but it feels, or used to feel, like a trip.

I go into our bedroom, take off my clothes, and put on my bodysuit. I step up onto the platform with its school desk and treadmill. I pull the bodysuit hood over my head and turn it on, and what used to happen, back when I was small, is that my robot body would open its eyes and I would open the door of its cabinet and walk into the halls of a real school somewhere in the Midwest. If I was just on time, there would be children and teachers in the hall, and I would stand on the treadmill and walk toward my classroom.

It wasn't perfect, the navigation. There was always a delay when I made a turn. I would have to turn my robot body and turn off its movement, then move my actual body so that I could keep moving forward on the treadmill. I had to always be aware of where I was in both spaces, or I was a mess.

Once I was at my desk, though? Oh, it was heaven. Some of the children were there in body and some were there as I was, but I couldn't tell the difference. I raised my hand over and over, and my wonderful teacher called on me. He loved me.

He is the same teacher I have now, but not the same. His slender body is the same. His loud purple shirt, his smile. But he is not the same.

The children there in body could always tell who was a commuter (or who *wasn't real*, in their words). They cornered me on the playground one day early in my first year, all wanting to touch me to see what I felt like. I was afraid at first – I hadn't touched anything in the school except for my own desk and chair – but it felt wonderful to have all of their hands on me. It felt like touches on a foot that's fallen asleep.

Sensations are soft and strange in the robot body. When it's windy, you don't feel the wind the way Mother said you once could, back when you could go outside. You don't feel it in every root of hair, but you can feel the wind.

I went into the school bathroom once, and a girl said, "Why are you in here? You don't need to be in here." I had come in wanting to look in the mirror, of course. I knew I wouldn't look like me, but still I was surprised to see the tall child with her black curls and her wide violet eyes – surprised and delighted. I didn't like to think of what would happen when noon came and this pretty face closed its eyes only to open them moments later when another child in some other part of the world logged in for the afternoon classes.

Now it's all different. There is no bathroom because no one in the whole school is there in body – not the teachers, not the students. It's not safe for them to travel there, we're told. The air is too bad now.

The school isn't even there in body anymore, come to think of it.

My teacher looks like the teacher who used to love me for my enthusiasm, the one I loved in return. But I have no enthusiasm, and he is not the same person.

I never raise my hand. I pretend to sit at a desk, I pretend to listen until he lets us go, and I log off. There is a socialization period after class that isn't strictly optional, but I don't want to meet anyone this way. Anymore, I don't like the way it feels when they touch my shoulder. I can't abide the dead looks on their faces.

★ ★ ★

The new robot has a name, Eleanor, and she already has her long beautiful legs by the time I get down to the basement. I lay out silky light brown hair and a deep olive spray for her skin, but we're not quite there yet.

Mother chooses an unusual nose form, long and curved with flared nostrils. She attaches the plastic mold to the suction tube, presses it to Eleanor's face, and turns it on.

A deep chugging, glugging sound and then the gasp of release and now, instant character.

We laugh at how much the nose changes things. We agree now that the eyes will be wide set, hazel, with long, arched brows. The upper lip will have a curl; the lower lip will be medium-full. I set out all of the molds for the face and choose a small, youthful breast mold.

"This OK?" I ask.

"Perfect," says Mother.

"Why do robots have nipples, anyway?" I say.

She chuckles but doesn't look away from her tools, doesn't respond. I have asked this before.

She will freehand everything except the face and breasts with a suction blade and a rounded buffer. She's planning for a narrow backside to go with the wide waist.

You'd think because Eleanor is green, we won't need to think about any more detail than that, but it's not so. Eleanor might want to wear a bikini sometime. Mother has to give her backside some texture, but just a bit. We don't want to detract from those masterpiece legs. We have to decide what her abdomen looks like – wide, yes, but firm or a little bit slack? Will she have a prominent collarbone? Will her ribs show at the top of her chest?

By bedtime, it's not all done, but it's all decided. I can see Eleanor clearly in my mind and know that Mother sees her even more clearly. I bet that when I get up in the morning, she'll have already put away the molds and all the suction tubing, and Eleanor might already stand all olive-brown and ready for the detail work.

★   ★   ★

When I was ten or twelve and we were arguing, I told Mother, "I used to think I might be a robot, you know. I cut myself to see the blood, to know that I was real."

I wanted her to feel sorry about that. Instead, she laughed into her glass of whiskey.

"Is it funny?" I said.

"You think when they cut themselves, they don't see blood?" she said.

That struck me. They must, I realized. They must have a filter running in their minds somehow, so they always see what they're supposed to see.

★ ★ ★

"Your attendance is improving," my teacher says. We're all alone in the virtual classroom for a conference.

"Yes, and all by my own choice," I say. My arms are folded, legs kicked out into the space between us.

"You don't like school very much, do you, Mary?" he says.

"I'd rather work," I say.

He looks through a folder on his desk. "That's right," he says. "You're an apprentice...hairsetter? Is that right?"

"I'd say I'm a master hairsetter by now. I'm apprenticing at full finishing."

"Full finishing?"

"Everything – sculpture to hair to voice, customs even, *portraits*."

He doesn't chuckle, but he looks down. "Everything. Well, that's sweet. I didn't know there were any workshops like that around anymore."

"Our workshop is underground," I say. With a port into the foyer that we've never known how to open. The company that brings us the raw forms also brings us our paints and food and liquor, and one day soon they might decide that such artisan work is not worth the cost anymore, and then they might drag us screaming from our burrow – would they? – or seal us up inside. This is a fear I might have once shared with my teacher, but not now.

"That's very sweet. Quaint," he says.

"But?" I say.

"But," he says. "Well, you already know what I'm going to say, don't you?"

And of course I do. He is going to say that I need to make something more reasonable of myself, study something modern, join a company and perhaps live as company people do in a smaller, bleaker hole than the one I'm in now.

But there would be community, common feeling. Maybe a chance for love.

It breaks my heart how much this teacher looks like my teacher I loved. I remember how he walked us out the playground gate one time, just the ones of us who were there remotely because it would have been too great a risk for the others, and he showed us some of the town outside the school. He pointed to all of the wrong around us and explained why it was so. He told us we might be the ones to make it right again.

I remember the terrible things I saw, but I remember too the blue and aqua and pink of the sky. I remember touching trees with my sleep-tingling hands.

This teacher now, he just wants me to have a mind for something that will keep me from being obsolete before my time, and that's nice, but it's not enough.

★   ★   ★

Eleanor has rosy lips already, an oily T-zone, a thick tumble of tawny hair but no hairline. I miss class and spend the day and night rooting each hair of it individually, then each eyebrow hair, each eyelash. I want to do the hair on her arms, but Mother says it's too late and that I have to go to bed, and that I have to go to class. She says I must sleep and that when I wake up, Eleanor will be all finished.

I think of all the places Eleanor still has to go – because she is a special one, made to move through the world on her own. She will need much education and much testing, and then she will go off to do some job in the world. In the outside. I fall asleep trying to imagine it but cannot imagine much besides the wide bright sky.

★   ★   ★

Eleanor is gone. It was deadline, and we didn't get to do all we wanted with her voice. It was low and husky as we'd imagined, but not quite right somehow, and yet it was deadline. We consoled ourselves talking about how someone else might decide on an entirely different voice for her and how we could not control everything. We dressed her in a white satin slip and boxers and walked her to the foyer.

"I guess this is goodbye?" Eleanor said. She clasped her hands and held her arms down in a V, and we shut her into the foyer without a word. We cleaned up the workroom, ate and slept.

Now we wake. We eat again, loll around for half an hour. By the time we return to the foyer, there is a new box waiting.

"Let's start in the morning," Mother says.

"Don't you think…" I say.

But she's nodding. "We ought to at least open it," she says. She takes her pry tool out of her pocket.

"We should at least look," I say.

"So we can dream on it," she says.

"Of course."

She lifts the lid, and we both let out a sigh. A folder. A pink cast to the flesh beneath the plastic.

"How old are you now, Mary?" she says.

She knows my age; she must. I don't say anything.

"Time for the birds and the bees."

We have dinner with the folder, not the robot. He is still in his box, still under his plastic.

Thankfully, there is no drive with videos. He is a custom but not a portrait, you see. He is a new individual, like Eleanor, so we won't have to have the same precision as we would with a portrait.

He is a mesomorph, like Eleanor, like most of them. His colors and his dimensions are spelled out. Mother points to one particular detail and explains how we'll open the cabinet of molds that has always been closed to me, and how the telescoping bulb in his pelvis will make it raise and lower, swell and deflate after it's molded, and I giggle all the time because of course I already know all of this, but still, it will be kind of cool to see.

The robot is only a him because that was decided in the folder. All of the pink ones have the same shuddering mechanisms inside.

*   *   *

"Do you want to keep doing this forever?" Mother says.

"Yes, of course," I say and mean it. I have him sprawled on the floor and am half under his leg, rooting the hairs of his inner thigh, and I still have the chest and everything else to do. The folder specified all of it. I've never had such a boon of hair work before, and Mother says she isn't sure, but I've planned how to root the hairs of his thatch and treasure trail and butthole, which are all supposed to be lushly furred, and I have not thought about going to class at all.

"Have you ever thought of going out, seeing something of the world?" she says.

I did once long ago.

Nothing Mother ever said, nothing from my teacher, nothing ever suggested that I would be able to step outside the foyer door, and so I stopped thinking of it, and now I would do anything rather than let my thinking go that way again.

"No, of course not," I say.

I notice Mother has a glass of something clear.

"Is that water?" I say. "Can I have some?"

"It's not water," she says. Her face is cold and angry.

"Maybe we ought to go to bed," I say.

"I've been thinking what a shit life this is," she says.

"I'm sleepy," I say, and I pull myself out from under the robot's heavy leg.

"And how just about anything else would be better for you," she says.

*   *   *

"I know you're here," my teacher says. "I would not be seeing you if you weren't logged in. You know that, right?"

This is not a conference; this is class, and the other students are all looking on. His expression is cold and angry.

"Say something!" he says, and then there is some sort of glitch. His body slackens and a second later, he bounces back to the lectern saying, "Now let's get on with this lesson."

"Oh wow," a boy beside me whispers.

"What?" I say.

"They took him out. It's another teacher now."

"It's not. It's autopilot," says another student.

I don't care. I have just the hood of my bodysuit on and with my hands, by feel, I am rooting the hairs in the backs of the robot's thighs. We won't make the deadline otherwise, and the feel of it is addictive.

Mother is sleeping. She'll be angry that I'm doing this but relieved when we meet the deadline.

If we don't do what we need to do, maybe orders won't come. Maybe groceries won't come. Maybe the foyer door will never open again.

*   *   *

Mother and I fight. We make up. We fight again on a deeper and more satisfying level. I fold up the bodysuit and place it far in the back of my closet for good.

*   *   *

The hairy robot is gone. He stood politely in his satin boxers until someone opened the foyer door. He said hello in his soft deep voice, and they probably gave him some clothes to wear, and some shoes, after they looked him over. They led him out and a moment later brought in another box and closed the door.

This box is twice as broad as a normal box, one and a half times as high. A folder lies inside.

Mother is already thinking how we will cut this one's belly open. She's thought of this even before it arrived; she's been waiting for one like this.

She's thought of how we will take out great masses of filler foam and make a place where I can curl with my knife. I will get one chance to see the world.

Like a waking dream, an image of my old teacher crosses my mind. He speaks of the Trojan horse and all the other adventures of Odysseus.

While Mother and I work, we speak of what will happen. What will I see out there? Will I be caught, brought back here? Or might I even flee back here, finding the world too hot or cold or poisoned? If I come back, will Mother still be here?

But her face stays hopeful. The doom and disgust do not cross her face again, and so I cannot go back on this.

"If you return and I'm still here, will you know it's really me? What if they swap me out?" she says. I've thought of this. I'm brought back screaming, brought back in a wooden box, weak and drugged and chastened but glad to be home – only it isn't home. My mother I loved is someone else, or no one.

But I say none of this. Instead, I laugh and say, "Oh, I'll know *you* from the liquor on your breath."

She laughs, takes another drink.

But what if they seal up the port? What if they starve her inside?

I can't go. I know I can't. It's just something for us to fantasize about, isn't it? Yet we have removed the foam filling and hidden it in a corner cabinet deep behind the pots and pans. We have sculpted out a place inside just as though we really are doing this. I have practiced curling there and practiced the shallow, shallow breathing. Like meditation, like going someplace else.

"Aren't they watching us work? Aren't they watching us all the time?" I say.

Mother shrugs. She doesn't know.

Only after the space inside is ready for me do we work on the sculpting, the coloring, the crinkled copper hair. We have stopped talking of the future. We do the finish work more lovingly than ever before, but we're sure to stay on track for the deadline.

A FULLY CHAMELEONIC FOIL

The new saleswoman set up in the park. Her kiosk built itself from the new brand of metamorphic foil she was selling and had more foil hovering above its front to make shade. I went with a group of kids after school when she first set up, and she ran through her spiel even though she had to know we didn't have money. Hoping for word of mouth, I guess.

She passed out one-inch samples, which felt like thin, slippery plastic and looked like aluminum. When she began a new operation on her watch, all of our squares folded themselves into tiny silver cranes, which flew off our hands, settled back, and unfolded again. There were oohs and aahs, then groans when she said they wouldn't do anything without the watch. We put the samples in our pockets.

"The most obvious use is anything you might need a screen for – movies, for example, or use it as a wall or a fence." She stood out away from the kiosk and messed with controls on her watch. The piece of foil, which was about three by four feet, hung in midair like a TV screen, then stood close to the ground like a fence.

"It is fully chameleonic," she said. With that, the texture turned from crinkled space blanket to dry gray wooden boards.

We weren't too impressed. Being kids and all, we didn't see much need for fences.

"For the TV screen, would you have to project on it some way?" a kid said.

"Oh, I'm sorry," she said, and she put it back in the air and started playing a cartoon of a red bird. The picture was bright and clear even in the daylight. That did wow some of the kids.

She touched her watch and the foil folded up into a tight package maybe two inches square, which she plucked out of the air and tucked into her shorts pocket. She stepped back into the kiosk and brought out a much larger package. This one looked to weigh ten pounds, the way she was holding it.

"A serious investment, this is what we call the full sheet." She tossed it into the air and it unfolded itself far above our heads, above the wispy trees. It was maybe a quarter the size of a football field.

"Many more possibilities here," she said. The foil began to fold itself into the shape of a simple house, just a roof and four walls. It turned in the air so we could see all its angles, then unfolded and refolded into a smaller, more complicated design that had little rooms sticking out the sides and a lot of angles to the roof.

"Let's go out to this clear space," she said, and we all walked out to where there were no trees overhead. The house began to lower. She helped one of the kids come closer to the rest of us, and the house came down tight to the grass. It was dark inside, but then the walls began to glow with all the intensity of a movie screen. The walls were brick – no, they were shiny tile now, some sort of seashell.

"Abalone," said a little girl. "My favorite color."

Windows appeared, and through them we saw tall mountains and trees on all sides. The other kids were gasping, running from window to window. The scene outside changed to palm trees and a white beach. The windows changed to red and blue and green pieced glass. I just stood at the center. I must have sighed because the saleswoman came close to me.

"Not impressed?" she said. I noticed how tinny her voice was. It had an echo or something. And the inside of her mouth was silver.

"It's just, the floor is still grass," I said.

"We could go get another piece and make the floor."

"Sure, that would be cool."

"Would it?"

"I guess."

"There is one thing more to show," she said when the house had risen up and unfolded and re-tucked itself into a tidy bundle.

"What?" said the little girl who'd been so impressed with the abalone.

"You'll never guess," said the saleswoman.

I might guess, I thought. I kept my eye on the watch she set on the grass beside her foot. She began the slow process of unfolding then, first the legs and then the torso, arms, and finally the head. Everything that hadn't been showing stayed silver so that the foil, when she unfolded, was a horrifying crumpled mass of shattered glass, part of an eye on one shard of it and a part of a mouth far below, shards of green shorts and shards of leg skin, and so on. It reminded me of an especially ugly tie-dye.

The abalone girl was crying, whining, "Put it back."

A few adults had come in from the edges of the park. They grinned as the sheet rose high into the air where it had room to finish pulling taut. All of the bits of flesh and clothing color faded, leaving a silver reflection of us filling our sky. If the full sheet weighed ten pounds, this had to weigh a hundred or a hundred and fifty.

I took up the watch then and saw that it still had a list of operations to run. No doubt it would make her fold up again. Eventually, she'd put the watch back on and try to make some sales.

It was easy to see how to end the programs, just hit backspace again and again.

The sheet dropped, draped over treetops. The little kids were screaming and sniveling in the dark, the rest of us laughing as we found our way to the edges. I heard some older kids went back to loot the kiosk later. Me, I thought about keeping the watch, but I ended up just tossing it in the little duck pond at the edge of the park on my way home.

WHAT DO YOU SEE WHEN YOU'RE BOTH ASLEEP?

All I wanted was to be able to tell Wallace (((I'll be back in nine hours, same as always. Your job is to watch the house))) and have him understand it. I told him as much every morning, of course, but still he pined for me. He wouldn't use the dog door, eat, or drink until I returned. It hurt to watch him pace on the webcam, not to mention how my constant watching was interfering with work.

I resented this difficulty. In other ways, I was finally living the dream – slow baths, weekend-long sessions with a book on the chaise, ice water from the refrigerator door – but I couldn't enjoy our newfound fortune if Wallace wasn't happy.

I feared he'd bite the hired dog walker. She thought a lot of her dog skills and didn't want to give up, but after six weeks we agreed.

"Medication is what he needs," said Don in the cafeteria when he caught me checking on Wallace again. If I'd had forty-five minutes for lunch, I could have gone home, if just for a hug, every day.

"We tried meds. The vet didn't think they helped," I said.

"Couldn't you get a communications system?" said Patty.

"Those just translate neurotransmitter signals, or hormones? Something like that," I said. The messages were nothing more than (((I love you I love you I love you))) when he lay beside me and (((panicpanicpanic))) when I was at work.

"No, but I mean one of the new ones," said Patty. She brought out a tablet so we could browse new tech for the rest of lunch.

★   ★   ★

It was strange at first, like seeing colors you haven't seen before.

You're supposed to train for several months before it's safe to use full-time. One-hour sessions where you share sensations – eat the same foods, walk side by side so you see the same things.

Wallace loved this. I didn't need a system to see that.

I narrated, as was the plan: "Trees, road, Shiba Inu, woman, man, child. Car, truck. You hear me, Wallace? Truck, car, hurt bad. Truck scary." The dot in my right eye was supposed to ensure he learned the word. I focused the dot on the speeding truck and brought up memories of hurt and fear I thought he'd relate to. The time a yellow jacket stung his ear, the time he cut his foot.

He stared at me intently, like a cat tracking mice through a grassy field.

He sent back the image of the time I cut my finger on the dog food lid, the blood spurting out in the sink. I knelt and rubbed his ears. (((Smart boy))) I said.

*   *   *

(((Home safe))) I said to Wallace just before work. I called up images of puppies in a blanket, reading by the fire, the pleasure of licking breakfast plates.

(((Home you))) he said. He whimpered, ducked his head, and wagged.

(((House home, house me))) I said. I felt it, too. The house was me.

(((House-----Home, You))) he said, and it was beautiful, like a poem. A green lawn like at the dog park, a single oak tree on the left to stand for *house* and another tree far separate to stand for *home, you* and around that tree Wallace circled. He worshipped there.

*   *   *

I woke in the night, Wallace making underwater sounds from the floor. His feet twitched. Slowly, quietly, I turned on the app. I closed my eyes and tried to go where he was.

LEXIBLE OFF-TIME

Pertinent Excerpts: Filename 'Journal', Profile Number 515263646

Day 22, Subjective Time

I'm getting to the point where I'm starting to be judgmental about the objects in the house. This feeling is unpleasant and reminds me of when I was a teenager, walking through my parents' house with a friend, feeling that suffocating protective shame about the poor parts. Old paneling, stained carpets.

But this place is not poor. Quite the contrary. I suppose the things seem a little vulgar here. Showy, false. I stare at a tumbler before pouring water: heavy Mexican glass with a spray of rainbow freckles on its rim. I turn it, peer through the colors, forget to get water, head right back to work. The velvet fainting couch, the patterned carpet just a blur on my way to the desk.

Turning away from all that surrounds me and back to the work is so easy now.

I'm locked in this place – chose to be locked here so I could finally write my father's biography. The book is just chugging right along, but whenever I take a break, I start to grow unsettled.

It wasn't supposed to be *just* like this. I was supposed to be able to communicate, for one thing. Anytime I plugged the laptop in under the white button on the front door, I was supposed to be able to call out and get some kind of automated assistance. I've tried that over and over. It never works.

A slap on that white button if the laptop isn't plugged in? That's supposed to pull me all the way out. That I haven't tried. I don't dare.

I suppose that feeling of shame about my parents' house came on so strong because I was just at that right stage of development for it. I was

* * *

We run, he and I, through a vast wheat field. A rabbit m
but we can't see it, only the movement of it in the wheat. V
long time and fall to panting, catch the scent of water. We n
scrub to a wide river and drink. Water runs cool on my hand

(((Home, house))) I say. (((Hungry)))

Wallace only stares, panting. With an exhausted sigh, he fi
and walks me up the driveway to our house.

Inside are shadows, malevolent movements of light, a great e
Cold dread. Spooked, we walk out quickly, but even the
sinister, people leering and calling us to the fence, crashing garba
revving engines.

(((House without home, without you))) he says.

(((Your job))) I say. (((Brave dog)))

(((You I love you I love you))) he says. He brings up images o
weeping. Because he can't cry, himself, I suppose.

* * *

And I was cruel then, in the dream. It became vague upon waking. I
couldn't remember all that we said, but I recalled how I showed him
house, home on the left side of the park, *house, home* and all that meant: *heat*
and *food* and *ice water, chaise* and *book, work* and *money* and *people, friends*
– and the good Wallace was on that side too, the brave boy standing
guarding it all. On the other side of the park was only the poor pacing,
pining Wallace. No one circled around him. No one worshipped there.

We struck an understanding, then, made a true communication.

That morning I woke to find he'd finally used the dog door. He
lay curled in the lawn's back corner, tail held over his nose to keep out
the chill.

just old enough to be seeing myself from the outside. A kind of second consciousness hovered outside me, judging.

Here, there's a stain on the bathroom counter that won't come out. A blue-black semicircle. I thought – if I even thought about it when it happened – that the next time I slept and woke, it would be gone. Now, I rub on it with a soapy washcloth. I rub it with an alcohol-soaked cotton ball. Nothing moves it.

I take the treasure chest out from under the bed, light the yellow candle, light the blue candle. Nothing helps.

★   ★   ★

Day 30, Subjective Time

I spent the morning with Dad right before the Off-Time appointment. He was feeling well, so we walked in the backyard and looked at all the little green shoots coming up. We sat at the table, had coffee and scones, worked on a crossword together. He kept asking if I felt well. Maybe I looked grim, but I smiled and said, "Just fine, thanks." I gave him that look that said I thought he was being weird and embarrassing. Guess I never grew out of that adolescent stance.

He thought I was going out to get my hair done. I asked again if he thought I ought to cut it all off and go gray. Again he said I couldn't think of it; didn't I always get compliments on how rich and glossy it was? We always said the same things to each other. It gave us comfort.

He was soon back to bed. I went into the room that used to be a guest room but where I now lived full-time. I closed the door. I still had to finish scanning the last of my notes and photos.

Cross-legged on the bed, I worked robotically for an hour, photographing and then cropping each piece. Dad with his family on the porch of the old farmhouse. Dad on the road, in the mountains, on the beach, up in the air getting his pilot's license. There were images from his time as a famous artist's lover and others from his own exhibits and poetry readings. He'd had A Life. I wanted to document his adventures, his feelings about them, what he'd learned. The letters and interview notes were already saved to my Flexible Off-Time Profile Inbox, the hard copies safe in the file cabinet here beside my bed. When the last batch of photos was done, I compressed the folder and sent it to Off-Time.

Their logo caught my eye again – a white clockface on a rainbow background that read violet, indigo, blue and so on, instead of the expected order of roygbiv. That backward order always unsettled me a bit.

I suppose everything about the place unsettled me. It was just on the edge of the new mall, but it had that taboo feeling to it – like a tattoo parlor or a cannabis-plus dispensary – an edgy feeling making me wonder if nice people went there. It wasn't at all clear that people like me were allowed to take time off from life.

Aunt Carol showed up right on time. She let herself in quietly. By the time I'd come out of my bedroom, she was finishing the crossword Dad and I had started.

"Thank you for this," I said, giving her a little hug from behind.

"You do so much, Vickie. You deserve this," Aunt Carol said. She knew I was headed to Flexible Off-Time. Someone had to know. She knew where I was headed, but she probably thought it was for a vacation.

And then I drove off. Nervous, hyper-aware of every little thing on the drive, the little shoots coming up in other people's yards, the funny and repellant bumper stickers on other people's cars.

I showed up early, sat waiting in the sterile Off-Time lobby across from a little old lady immersed in a magazine.

"Your first vacation?" she looked up to say after a while. She reminded me of my sorely missed mother. Her hair was pewter-colored like mine was at the roots.

"Retreat – writing retreat, but yes, my first," I said. "Do I look that nervous?"

"Don't worry," she said. She picked up her purse and came to sit beside me, touched my shoulder. "You'll be able to pop right back out. If it's terrifying, if it's disorienting, you pop right back out. You can try again later – even tomorrow if you want. I did that the first few times. I spook easily, you know. I dropped in and hit the white button right away."

"That's good to know," I said. I knew it already. I'd dutifully read all the guides and online reviews. The social media posts of authors talking about their novels and screenplays created in Off-Time. I'd spent an evening digging into that one alarming news story, too, and yet I persisted with the plan.

It felt like an informed decision. I'd signed the forms, but more importantly, had *read* them. I was that kind of person.

"If you hit the button *right* away, you'll have to make another appointment. They charge a little something – nothing to speak of – but they can probably get you in again tomorrow, or next week. No harm, as long as you hit it right away," said the warbly little old lady.

I didn't want to chicken out and have to make another appointment. "What happens if you wait a long time before you hit it?" I asked, though I already knew.

The woman was glad to share: "The longer you're under, the longer it takes to get out. If you've been in there a week and push it, who knows? It might take almost a day to get out – or feel like a day, you know. Subjective time."

The little old lady and I kept talking for a while. She was a caregiver, too – for an aunt now. She'd done it for her father and mother not so long ago. She understood.

"I'm completely occupied with him," I said. I wanted to be with him for every good moment he had. When he slept, I had my remote work. I had the house to keep. If I wanted to write, if I wanted to think even, it was only in snatches. No way to concentrate.

The lady nodded. "It's like having a new baby."

I bristled a little at that, but then the Guide appeared. I wished the old lady well and followed the Guide back through a hall into a small room, where I was ushered to a white reclining chair.

My Guide was a fleshy young woman named Merrie with strong perfume. At first it struck me as baby powder, but as she worked around me arranging things, more and more layers came out. Rose, coconut, butter, jasmine.

It was like being at a hairdresser. I remembered hearing somewhere that busty hairdressers get better tips.

The Manager, Rich, came in and went over the final form with me. The subjective time estimate for my retreat was two weeks, but I was to understand that was only an estimate; it might seem a little longer or a little shorter. The actual time-in-chair would be no longer than fifteen minutes.

I went over the papers more carefully than he was expecting and might have smirked a little, thinking of that news story where the woman had thought she was going in for two weeks and then said it felt more like four weeks. She'd kept a detailed journal and was able to make a good case for how the subjective time had gone. People seemed to agree she was being unreasonable. She received a small settlement, but complaints had been minimal after that, the reviews positive. Off-Time added their disclaimer.

I signed, of course. Rich rushed away looking more smug than I liked.

"Did you choose your controller?" Merrie said.

On a shelf behind her were arrayed the treasure chest, pill bottle, joystick, and sack of runes.

The joystick with its rainbow of buttons caught my eye again, but I said with finality, looking away from her freckled cleavage, "The chest."

Merrie turned around and brought down the plastic treasure chest. "That's my favorite too." She probably said that no matter which one you chose, but it made me feel good nonetheless. She settled it in my lap and brought out her phone. The lights dimmed.

"You want to keep your controller out of sight to help with immersion. Put it under your bed if you like," she said. Merrie's eyes had seemed narrow because she'd kept smiling, but now her smile fell, and they looked huge and black. She opened the treasure chest, revealing candles in green, yellow, orange, red, violet, indigo, blue, and the black candle-shaped lighter.

She said, "Green stands for sleep. You need to sleep during your vacation – I'm sorry, your retreat. You'll need more sleep than you usually get. We recommend keeping to your normal sleep pattern but adding a long nap before dinner. Any time you should sleep and aren't able to do so, you take a green pill – I'm so sorry, I mean, you light the green candle. It's a magical object. It will make you sleep."

Merrie's stomach rumbled loudly. "I'm so sorry. It's almost lunch," she said. I caught a hint of sweat under the perfume.

"The yellow candle will change the tone. Tone means temperature, light – even perceived weather. If you're uncomfortable with the surroundings, light the yellow candle. It's a magical object. It will make things look and feel better. It will make your environment match the mood you wish to have."

When Merrie's stomach rumbled a second time, I said, "I've read everything. You don't have to—"

"I do. It's required."

She went on through them all. Orange for a sense of reality, red for a sense of love, violet for something they called 'meta-game' – a puzzle or a mystery, I gathered – indigo for focus, and blue was for calm.

Merrie grew quiet. Her guts were quiet, too. The room had gotten darker without my noticing, and I'd begun to feel very sleepy.

"Are you ready to lie back?" she said. I nodded, and the chair moved slowly under me.

I was lying on the reclining chair in the dark room, and then I was lying in my bed here. Simple as that. It felt – not real, but not like a dream either. Nothing was as sharp as it had been. My range of vision felt narrowed. I moved the treasure chest off my lap and swiveled to the edge of the bed, closed my eyes, breathed deeply. The breathing felt real. The air smelled of open windows and clean laundry.

The bedroom was much like my own at Dad's house. I stood and walked into a central area with an open kitchen, a lounge area furnished with a velvet couch and soft chenille blanket, a large worktable in the center of the room. On the desk were an e-reader and a laptop. I checked these as soon as I found them to see that all the notes and photos had gone through. Seeing they had, I sighed and felt calmer.

The environment appeared to be everything I'd asked for. I remembered the old lady in the waiting room talking about disorientation, and it was there for sure, but not as strong as I'd feared.

Weeks before, I'd taken an hours-long survey. I remembered choosing these tumblers, this couch, this plain suburban window view. I opened the fridge and found it filled with my favorite comfort foods including a strawberry cheesecake and a plate of fried chicken legs.

(If I had that day to do over now, I know I'd spend it on eating and nothing else.)

Out the window, someone walked a dog, and a little breeze ruffled the trees. I heard the soft sounds I'd chosen: wind chimes, distant birds, the light hum of the refrigerator.

I knew I couldn't go out on the street, but I could go out and walk around the perimeter of the house and all of it should hold up, though it wouldn't be quite as real as what was inside. A little quiver of nausea ran through me.

I did think about hitting the exit button, but I didn't do it. There was the fee and the hassle of rescheduling, of course, but the main issue was doubt. Would I ever get up the nerve to come in again?

I ignored the strange feeling and did exactly what I'd hoped to do: sat down at the work desk and wrote for subjective hours until my stomach (or subjective stomach) rumbled loud as Merrie's. I ate the chicken legs cold, washed my hands and face, went to bed. The windows showed moonlight and silver clouds, and the sounds had changed from birds to crickets by the time I lay down. Sleep came fast, as it should.

⋆　　⋆　　⋆

Why am I thinking about this today? Today is day 30, marking twice the time I was supposed to be here. I've matched the lady who settled with Flexible Off Time.

I'm thinking, too, how I tolerated the feeling of nausea, disorientation, dread. I must have tolerated it so well because it was not so different from the way I often feel, in the world we all agree is real.

⋆　　⋆　　⋆

Day 36, Subjective Time

I try to move that stain one more time. It disturbs me. You see, I don't go to the hairdresser, haven't in years. I tell Dad I'm going to the hairdresser just to have a reason to leave. I'll color it myself while he's napping and then have a nurse or Carol come so I can walk around town, maybe go to a bookstore and try to write for an hour.

I always color my own hair, and though it was barely in need of it when I sat down in Merrie's chair, after a time the gray grew out further and began to bother me. I was supposed to be in for two weeks subjective time. If that had been real time, then it should have been quite ready for the color, but why should my hair grow at all, in here?

I tried to fix it first by lighting the yellow candle. Somehow I thought that 'tone' might be the problem, but the yellow candle changed nothing, which got me wondering if any of them changed anything, really. Only the green and the blue seemed to have any effect – but then how to know if they really worked or were just placebos? When I lit the blue one, at least at first, I seemed to calm. The green one seemed to make me sleep, but after the doubt arose, both the green and the blue became unreliable.

But in any case, I was checking my roots out in the bathroom mirror and – because I forgot sometimes that this was simulated life – I reached down under the sink and brought out a box of color. I mixed it, applied it, lived in the rich chemical stink for twenty-five minutes (an undertone of root beer in this particular brand), rinsed vigorously and conditioned with the tiny tube of premium conditioner, rinsed again, and went on the back porch to sit in the virtual sunlight until it dried.

The laptop went with me. I was trying to write around the clock because I knew the two weeks had run out or were running out. I'd never slapped that white button, but at the end of my time, it would not matter. They would bring me out after fifteen minutes in-chair.

But who would bring me out? Merrie had been headed to lunch. If two weeks was fifteen minutes, then an hour was about sixty days.

If there was a mistake, if I was under for an hour, for two months, how bad would that be? I could finish the book.

I was right around fourteen days in at that point. The writing was going more slowly, but I'd already done so much. It felt I'd passed whatever point of inevitability I needed to. What wasn't written was planned. I could present this book to Dad before he died. I would have time to read it to him, or if not that, at least I could present him with the fact of it. His life had meant something, my life had.

But so many things in here did not work. The candles, the food, the very yard. Sitting out on the back porch trying to write, I avoided looking at the back corner of the yard. This part, unseen from the window, had never been finished. The grass and sky pixelated, shimmering around its edges before fading into dark gray.

I'd tried the yellow tone candle on it, tried the orange reality candle, the violet meta-game one that I never understood. I'd tried simply wishing and willing it to seal. Nothing.

After a time, my hair was dry. I went inside and ate soup right out of the can, lit my green candle and eventually slept.

When I woke, the empty soup can was gone. A clean new can of soup stood in the cabinet as it should. But the bottle of dye was still perched on the edge of the sink, the blue-black spill circling around it on the white tile.

The stain is *still* here. I've tried to clean it a hundred times, but it's still here, and the pewter line is showing at my roots again.

★   ★   ★

Day 44, Subjective Time

The food was fucked up from the very first day. That first plate of chicken wings: I ate them, and they were supposed to be back again in the fridge once I'd slept. The chicken legs *were* there the second day, but they seemed tougher, drier. I ate them again. They were back the next day, tougher. I didn't eat them. The next day they were tougher. The next day they were cracked. I threw them in the garbage along with the cheesecake now gone to thick jelly. They came back. The milk turned after a time. I dumped it down the sink. It came back but was still turned. Same with the cheese, same with everything in the fridge besides the ketchup and maple syrup. I cleaned the fridge thoroughly and lived with the smell of it all day even though the garbage bag was set out on the back porch. I slept, and the smell was gone, the garbage bag gone, but the food had come back to the refrigerator again, all still turned. The cheese was entirely green.

I wrote out my other complaints in this journal, but looking back through it now, I see I never explained what happened with the food. Maybe it just didn't seem as important as the other things.

I suppose I started keeping the journal only as a kind of proof of subjective time. Not for a lawsuit — I had no claim, as I'd never even tried the white button — but I thought these mistakes might add up to a partial refund or that at the very least, the feedback could be used to improve the Off-Time service.

Most days, it's something like, 'Woke, worked (3,500 words), can of SpaghettiOs, slept'. I hope that's enough proof, though I doubt it.

I'd come to expect sixty days, Merrie's lunch. This brought me back to the work. Soon I had finished a draft of the book originally planned, the chronicle of my father's life. Soon I had inserted all of the photos, captioned them, added the appendices with his full letters.

I saved the completed manuscript, copied it, and began editing, but as I began, I realized I had no intention of editing. I was expanding the piece, weaving in my own story with my father's. It was becoming something new and very different from what it had been.

I had placed my worktable in the center of the living space, in defiance of something Stephen King had said about how we shouldn't make work the center of life. I worked incessantly now. The green candle had stopped having any effect.

And then the thought occurred, much later than it probably should have:

Is this book even saving? So much isn't working in this place, and is the file transfer part of what's broken?

A panic came, some subtle premonition of the panic to come. Desperation. A sense of injustice.

I'd have never written this book without Off-Time — I'd never have managed the uninterrupted stretches needed to arrange and shape things, only half-hour snatches at best. I'd needed this time and now I came to wonder — not always, but in those spaces where I was focused on the back part of the yard, when I was contemplating what can of food to open – if it was all going to be wasted.

★　　★　　★

Day 71, Subjective Time

Perhaps a week ago, I finished my second draft of the biography at just over a hundred thousand words, which is a respectable length for a novel. I don't know if that's long or short for nonfiction, no way to look it up. Questions lingered about how to go about publishing, but on the other hand, it was just what I thought a publisher might like to see. Dad was far from a household name, but his story surely linked into those of the famous. The times he'd lived in were popular ones to dream about. Something bittersweet too in the idea that a daughter who'd had such a quiet life could write with such energy the odyssey of her father. It was as sentimental and earnest as one would imagine, and yet I fancied that it added something new.

I saved it (presumably) and made my copy. What happened after that is hard to think about now. It was as though I suddenly became much more intelligent and insightful – with a *real* energy, a focus so intense it made my previous work feel plodding. I began the rewrite thinking this would be a copy just for me, where I could place the challenging thoughts that had come to mind as I'd written that safe version.

The fact that it might not be saving? Well, that only added to my candor.

My father's life had not been all roses; I'd made that clear in the safe version. His relationship with the famous artist had been quite abusive. He'd had a better life with my mother, but he'd taken her death hard. I elaborated on painful times in his life now.

I added critiques, questions: Why did our house and everything around us have to be so dated and poor? Surely I was very unlike him, but why did he have to value my qualities so little? And there were good things, too: cuddling up to his strong body when I was so small, taking his hand to lead him around the yard just – what? – an hour ago. Maybe less.

Memories of my own, which had felt beside the point while I wrote that safe copy, were coming to the foreground – were, in fact, the only parts of the book that still seemed real.

Just past one hundred and fifty thousand words now, the work feels like something no one's ever dared before. Complex, labyrinthine, precious. Dangerous.

The first copy goes from something I would have defended with my life – it's amazing how the feeling changes so quickly – to a 'rough draft'. I consider deleting it and am almost brave enough to do just that.

What am I doing? Overwriting his life with my own. It feels good and just.

But the quality of the work is different, the labor more taxing. I am back to sleeping and taking naps as Merrie advised. No need to bother with the candle. The sound of rain comes; the windows still show a dry moonlit night.

More and more, I catch myself staring into nothing. Laptop on my crossed legs on the sofa, staring in the direction of the worktable.

Long subjective moments on the back deck staring past the pixels into the crawling gray.

★   ★   ★

Day 90, Subjective Time
Some of the cans are missing from the cabinet.

★   ★   ★

Day 110, Subjective Time
And now there are things moving in that far corner of the yard. You don't catch them when you stare, oh no; you catch them when you *aren't* staring.

Nothing came back to the cabinet today. Yesterday it held nothing but a packet of instant potatoes. I mixed them up and ate at them over the course of the day. When I woke this morning, the packet was gone. The dregs of potatoes I'd left in the bottom of the mixing bowl were gone, the mixing bowl clean in its cabinet.

I suppose there is no need to eat in here, but it feels dangerous not to. Like a last thread tying me to my previous life. The refrigerator has not smelled for a long time. Today I cracked it open and regretted doing so.

I think back on the conversation with the little old woman in Off-Time's lobby. She must have been a plant. Is that what you call it? An employee of Off-Time paid to prey on the naïve? All the good reviews, all the paperwork just to trap me here. But there's no reason to trap me.

I mean, I suppose she received a commission for it, but what reason would there be for Off-Time to trap me? I'm not anyone. They'd get no value from it.

I have been taking a long hot bath every day, sometimes twice. This afternoon, when I wiped the steam from the mirror, everything behind me was gray and edged in pixels. I gasped, swung around, but by the time I had turned it had reset. Blank blue walls and the window. I pulled up the blinds. A woman walked a nondescript dog. Trees riffled in a breeze.

Had someone turned off the background for a moment? Why? Just to make me feel delusional?

Whenever I'm not writing, these cyclical paranoid thoughts seem to take over, and then my thinking takes another leap: Off-Time was trying to silence me or exploit me somehow, and now my quest would be to break the chains. This felt exciting.

I thought again of the Off-Time rainbow, how it didn't go in the right order. Was this a clue to a reversal of some kind? Or a signal – that in some reverse realm, the rainbow went the other way. Were there other clues?

I toweled off and dressed (must write about the clothes soon – I realize I haven't put anything down about them) and when I came into the main room, the violet candle was burning on the workroom table. I hurried to it, blew it out. I picked at the wax pooled around its base, leaving a berry-colored ring.

Meta-game. I told myself that the paranoid and self-aggrandizing thoughts – conspiracy theories, really – were down to the lighting of the violet candle. That I hadn't remembered lighting it was a function of how very tired I was.

No one could work like I had been doing and not have the effects catch up. I lit the green candle, cuddled up to a pillow, and drifted into sleep.

★   ★   ★

Day 121, Subjective Time

Backyard, staring into the corner. A voice comes, just a string of syllables I don't understand. At a certain point, I catch three words I recognize: "Konnichiwa? Hola? Hello?"

"Hello?" I say, sitting up.

"Hello," it says. It sounds neither mechanical nor animal. The sound a stone or a piece of wood might make if it could speak. The word seems to come from no particular place, though I stare into the center of the gray in hopes of seeing something.

"How far have you come?" it says.

I have no answer. "Where are you?" I say, but its answer is much too quiet to make out.

It's gone. I call to it for a long time before I go in to sleep.

I felt no fear while it was talking, but now I dread the idea that it might return.

★   ★   ★

Day 138, Subjective Time

Today, once more, I devoted my day to rereading the book. It nears three hundred thousand words. While rereading, I added some two or three thousand more.

I recalled a pneumonic trick from far back in school. You build a house in your mind, a dwelling of many rooms and much complexity. Each bit of the space corresponds to a bit of the speech or manuscript. In mapping the house, you map the manuscript. You memorize its ins and outs.

And so I keep mapping the thing out in my mind; I keep glancing at the white button. If you've been in a week, it might be almost a day before you're pulled out, the little old lady said. I do the math. I've been in long enough that it will take three more weeks, once I've pushed the button.

Or, if my subjective time is so very different from average, maybe it will feel like ten times more than that, or a hundred.

Is it possible to memorize this book much more than I already have? I get up and before I can rethink, slap the white button, slap it again, hold it down.

I sigh, light the green candle, cuddle up to my pillow again. The sheets and the clothes are not clean each morning, as they used to be. They're greasy and smell of an old person's scalp.

There's no more water.

* * *

Day 168, Subjective Time

I don't remember when the candles stopped refreshing. They work now, though they are all but nubs. The red one is my favorite. It brings feelings – and in a dark enough room, the sensations – of love. Yellow is my second favorite. It can make things change even more than they said. It can change the view to mountains, desert, a fantasy cityscape high in the air. It can change me. My hair can be pink if I want, my body young – or large and soft as Merrie's, or different in a thousand ways. It can be entirely gone!

The white button should have worked already. I push it again every time I think of it.

The back of the yard shimmers. Sounds and words come from it, but I do not go back there anymore.

The manuscript nears five hundred thousand words.

* * *

Day 286, Subjective Time

I have not been writing, here or on the manuscript. I have been too busy!

But I want to get down this thing about the clothes before I neglect it again. Not that it's very important, but it's been nagging at me.

Back at the beginning, I would wear a bright, comfortable sweatsuit all day. There were six of them: green, yellow, orange, red, violet, indigo, and blue. I could choose whichever one depending on my mood, or I could wear the same one for a month. They weren't magical objects and didn't change anything, but sometimes I'd associate them with the candles – put on green if I was feeling restless or violet if I was feeling bored. Sometimes I'd change into the white nightgown before bed; sometimes I'd just wear the sweats. It didn't matter, though, because whatever got left on the bathroom floor came back new and clean in the closet when I woke up.

At some point, that stopped happening. Sweatsuits left on the floor would still be on the floor tangled with the bath towel, smelling of mildew and bodily funk. My sweat on them, smears of food. I wore all six until they were visibly dirty and then stood before the tub.

"Well, shit," I said to myself. "Guess it's laundry day."

I forgot where I was again and when I reached under the sink for the Woolite, there it was. I drew a blue zigzag of it over the clothes and breathed in the new scent. I poured in water and agitated the load with my arms, then once they tired I moved the laundry with my feet.

It was a disaster. Even before I rinsed, I caught the mistake. The violet, indigo, blue, and red had bled into the other colors, leaving ugly brown stains. At the time I thought that the yellow, especially, would be unwearable (I have, in fact, worn it dozens of times since). Nothing to do but wring them out and hang them over chairs on the patio. The empty back spot made its sounds as I was out there.

The sweatsuits were wretched once dry. Hard, stained, pilly around the armpits and crotch. I don't know if this was before I started hitting the button or after – timelines are becoming confused – but it must have been one of the things that made me want to go home. To have clean machine-dried clothes again, to wear them places, even out to get groceries, would be such a pleasure.

Will be, I should say.

The manuscript word count climbs two or three or four thousand words each day. I can't read it anymore. The narratives go in too many directions. In completion, it has been ruined. Bitterly I tell myself, *Well, at least I saved multiple drafts.*

I never needed Off-Time. If I'd been more disciplined, the book could have come together and been a better book for having been written in the light and bustle of the real world. I count up the wasted minutes staring at the phone or television in that other life. I could have saved up those minutes, kicked myself into focus, made it work.

The candles are gone, wicks are gone anyway, and the lighter ran out of gas. I sometimes rub on a piece of wax, but it helps nothing.

Panic is coming, a little more each day. What's the worst that could happen here? It is grim, far more so than anything that could have happened in the world. Ceaseless panic. No end.

And that is when the voice – *voices*, now – in the back of the yard grow louder.

"Hello? Hello? Can we help? We can help."

Plug the ears with wax, then – green and blue wax for sleep and calm.

Do not sleep, do not calm.

Try to write.

Try to undo the damage I've already done to the book.

Write in this journal.

Try to sleep.

Open the cabinet doors looking for anything to eat, anything to distract. Pretend to forget I'm in a simulation and reach in both expecting and not expecting to grasp some can or pouch of food. Open the fridge again; regret it again.

The voices get louder. Hear them even through blue-green wax: "You're the first to get so far, the first to reach us. We have been calling to all of them, but you are the first to hear."

"Leave me alone!" I yell. I go to the furthest point from the backyard and look out the front windows to the nondescript woman and her terrible dog. The scene is flat. The medium is degrading.

"We see you. Your dwelling is open to us," they say.

"Come close," they say.

"Open your—" and there is another word, but it is garbled. "Open your _____ to us."

Cry. Like a petulant child, scream, "Leave me alone!"

Scream a wordless scream and do it again. One good thing about this place: you can scream all you like.

Take in the long silence after the screams.

"We will wait," they say.

★   ★   ★

Day 290, Subjective Time

What is the _____, anyway? I thought they meant the heart or the eyes as metaphor for the soul, and then I thought, *No, they mean the brain.* If the dwelling can open to them, then might the brain open as well?

Of course, *my* dwelling must be part of my brain.

★   ★   ★

Day 345, Subjective Time

The manuscript stands at seven hundred thousand words, and it is perfect. I will not touch it again. I start new things now and abandon them. I smack the white button anywhere from twelve to fifty times per day, but I have transcended the worst of the panic. I exercise enough to feel tired, sleep, and start new books I will never finish. This is my life.

Today when I went outside, the back corner was roiling.

"Are you there?" they said, now with a British accent. "We thought we might have missed a call. *Were* you trying to call?"

"I was calling, but not for you," I said. I haven't spoken to them since that time they made me scream.

"Oh, you *are* there. Please, please wait a moment," they said. They shaped the gray – like starlings making formations in the sky, vague and dreamlike. They formed themselves into…something like a person, like the shadow of a person.

"Is this better?" they said.

"*So* much better," I said. "Fucking perfect, actually."

"When you screamed yesterday, we thought about how we should try to make ourselves *nicer* for you. We are so happy this helps."

"Yesterday?" I said.

"If it wouldn't be too much trouble, could you make the adjustment you made just a moment ago? We had a clearer connection."

I didn't say anything.

"Could you make that same adjustment?"

"I don't know what you mean."

"You're doing it. That's good. Very good. Keep your _____ open just like that."

And as they spoke, the image cleared, the shadow-figure became about as clear as a person on a fuzzy black-and-white television. Others came into focus behind them, many dozens of others on black marble steps like courthouse steps. The sky beyond them looked green.

More and more walked down the steps toward the foreground figure, but that figure never came any closer.

"You are the first of your kind to reach us," they said. I was meant to feel proud.

"Come close," they said.

As I crossed the lawn, their world came clearer, the shapes and then the colors. When I saw their strange jade sky and their impossible buildings in the distance, the thought occurred to me: my father had many adventures in his life, but I was the one having the greatest adventure.

When the fore-person touched my hand, the feeling was all movement, like a mass of small creatures against my skin. They helped me up the first step, and then the people turned. As we walked up the steps, they closed in around me. A vista opened up – I only glimpsed it between the people's bodies, and then I was gagging.

★   ★   ★

I was lying down, something blue in front of me, in me. I swatted it away.

"Relax," said a woman near me. "You pulled the plug right away?"

I was in a dark room, the air choking thick with coconut, jasmine, talc. A dim light went on, and the woman bent down to pick something off the floor. I saw her bra when she bent.

"Merrie?" I said.

She held up a blue bulb like people use to suck snot out of a baby's nose. "You were having an allergic reaction or something," she said. "I guess it's just as well."

"Just as well?" I said. My voice sounded terrible to me. The plastic treasure chest sat on my lap. I pushed it toward her. If she hadn't caught it, it would have broken on the floor. I didn't care. I was up, searching for my purse.

"Just as well you came out if you were having an allergic reaction – or if you have a cold? Oh—" and she turned to the little sink and started washing her hands. "We'll get you rescheduled, just a second," she said.

"I don't want to reschedule anything," I said.

She turned back, a pink towel in her hands. "Don't decide right away. Sleep on it," she said.

But I was leaving the room.

"We have the exit interview," she called. She was following me.

"I can't," I said.

"Let me get Rich, at least," she said.

The old woman was not in the lobby. I don't know what I would have done to her if she'd been there. But I put on as calm a face as I could, turned back to Merrie, and said, "I'll be right back, I just need fresh air for a minute. I hate to say this, but…perfume."

Merrie gasped. "Oh, I—"

"Fresh air, and then I'll be right back," I said.

I kept looking behind me as I rushed to the car. Would they come after me? The paranoia was back, and the panic. I fumbled the keys, dropped them. Shaking, I sat for a moment before trying to start the car. I wasn't safe to drive, but I drove.

Things were terrible, overstimulating. Glaring light and horns. I kept hitting the brakes when I didn't have to.

I just hadn't seen anything new or anything real in so long.

I was looking into the rearview as much as the road before me, scanning, trying to see who might be following. Tears and snot all over my face. Merrie hadn't been wrong about the allergic reaction. My eyelids and lips swelled and burned.

Dad, Auntie – I needed to pull myself together for them. I breathed deeply, wiped myself off with a tissue.

In the driveway, I combed my hair.

I went into the kitchen but kept as far from Aunt Carol as I could. I didn't want her to notice my face.

"Is he still sleeping?" I said.

"Oh, how did it go?" she said, putting down the book of crosswords.

"I wonder, could you stay one more hour? I'm so sorry. I'd just like to—" I gestured toward my room.

"Of course, sweetie. You go rest," she said, but her face was troubled. I couldn't worry about her. I had to go to my room. Trembling, I pulled out my laptop, logged in to my Flexible Off-Time Profile.

And of course, there was nothing there, not even the original documents.

I shot off an email: *How do I get my files. Do you send them?*

I knew what the answer would be: *What files?*

One hour I had, still, to try to get down the outline of what I had written. That's all I was thinking. I had thought ahead to this many times. I had tried to memorize it in layers.

It would start with arrangement of the original documents. I pulled open the filing cabinet.

Empty.

Another drawer, empty.

I dialed the Off-Time office. Someone answered, but I could not understand. The voices vibrated in my ear and made no sense at all. I put the phone down on the bed and rose.

In the kitchen, no Aunt Carol.

In Father's bedroom, no one. No light came through the blinds.

I went back to my own room and cuddled up to a pillow. The rain sounds came and a whisper from the dry ground saying that I really should open my _____. I lay there shaking a long time and finally scared myself into sleep.

★   ★   ★

Day 347, Subjective Time

The house is still here and everything in it. The book of crosswords, the food in the fridge and the clothes in both of our closets, even the junk drawer in the kitchen. Everything a perfect replica, lacking only my father.

There is nothing beyond the house.

How did they do it? How did they build something so perfect?

They're out there, calling. If I were to lift a blind or pull a curtain, I would see them. I don't do that. I go to Dad's room – to feel close to him, to remember the hours we spent getting down the outline of his story. I didn't want him to think I'd leave him, ever, even for subjective time. Did he die without me there, or is he somewhere else? Is that nap still happening for him? I hope so.

I sit cross-legged on the bed and open the laptop thinking I need to write the whole damned book over again. It doesn't matter how long it takes. Then and only then will I open my _____ to those outside and see what they have to show me.

I wonder about something, though. I set the laptop aside and go back to my own room, get on my knees, and peer under the bed. There is the treasure chest, just where Merrie said it should go. The candles are still gone, all except for indigo. I never needed focus before, but I'll need it now.

I bring the indigo candle and a box of matches from the kitchen in to Dad's room, light the candle, get back in place with the laptop. It works on me quickly.

Just a little extra focus and I know it – I know what the _____ is! Not heart or mind, not soul. The word translates to something like *filing cabinet, archive, collection, record, catalog, profile inbox, manuscript*. I think I will open it to them after I get a chance to see it for myself, but it is too late. I already feel them behind me, peering over my shoulder.

The manuscript is open, the word count at the bottom of the page climbing up past what I thought it was. It just keeps adding. I close the file before it's settled on a number.

Scenes from my previous life begin playing on the laptop:

I am having a panic attack at a school dance, around me the purple streamers and balloons spinning in senseless patterns.

I am taking the treasure chest from Merrie, pushing it back at her. Pushing it back and taking it again.

I am a tiny baby feeding from my mother's breast on a blue blanket in the park.

I am sitting unshowered in the hospital, wondering what I'll do now.

Everything. I am doing everything I did, which was not much perhaps, but it was a life.

There is no order at all. We're beyond time. And the images aren't confined to the laptop but in thousands of rectangles floating in the air. They're playing before us, thousands of them at once, all translucent. I have such focus now, I can pick out any one of them clearly through the layers.

I focus on the one where Rich and Merrie peer worriedly into a screen. My body lies prone beside them.

"It just keeps adding," Merrie says.

They are not talking in terms of word count; they are talking in terms of gigabytes.

"I don't know what to do. Do we call regional?" Merrie whines.

Rich looks at her, scared. Whatever the right thing is, he won't do it, but I am bored with this now. I turn away, and the others turn with me. The wall behind the bed is gone. They help me up over Dad's headboard and onto the hard marble steps.

A GAME LIKE THEY PLAY IN THE FUTURE

In the future, people play a game in which a room becomes charmed. It's a blended reality game – all that's real is still there, but there is *more*. It's apparently very popular.

The game is an addiction. Once started, players do not stop, much as they're warned.

The game is a religion. Highly personalized, soul-affirming. All the charmed objects, letters, and mystical books they find are only shards of themselves. The people they see, too, are almost always figments, aspects of themselves. Players feel that they're using the game to transcend.

That's how *he* described it. That one who visited.

★　　★　　★

He drew me in, no fault of my own.

One minute I was alone in my narrow bed, alone in my small apartment. (My first apartment. I was that young.) I lay there ceiling-staring, longing for sleep, and the next moment he was…partially present? Half-realized?

He paced my room as though alone, as though it were his own room. He moved through my footboard and through my tattered reading chair.

A ghost? I'd never seen one. The very idea, strong as it was, offended me.

But then he spoke. He was mild, irritable, so clearly a living human. He'd just seen me.

"And who are you?" he asked.

I answered, "Claudia."

He described the dimensions of the room, the fine wainscoting and the tall diamond-paned windows.

"Yes," I said, "that's what I see too."

He'd made a point of moving away from my furniture to stand on a bare spot of carpet. He described the game, asked if I believed him.

I considered, nodded. "Yes, I've seen futuristic films with such elements," I said.

"I'm Ski," he said, or maybe it was Skee. I didn't ask.

★   ★   ★

The night was long. We fell in love.

Ski started off supposing I was some shard of his own personality. That is, he didn't think me real, or he pretended not to. He asked me things intended to prove that I was someone other than himself, but how can one prove that really?

"I have as full and rich an inner life as you," I said to close the subject. As I said it, I projected the same expression I'd always turned on parents and friends.

I have an honest face. He moved on to questions about my life, my studies, dreams and goals.

He interviewed me thoroughly, and in so doing came to know me, maybe better than anyone ever has.

★   ★   ★

I found him attractive from the first, but it took time to see he was responding to me in that way. He came closer and closer, and though we could not kiss, we held our faces so close it was like a kiss.

The love was nothing like either of us had ever felt. I've wondered since, was it all my own body? All isometrics? And the sounds he made – did others in the building hear?

Lying there getting my breath, I wondered for the first time if he was real – if either of us were real. Maybe we were *two* fantasies coming together through a glitch in some mysterious system.

★　★　★

Dawn, in both of our worlds. We sat on the carpet, each gazing at the other. My back propped against my bed, his against his own tattered reading chair – or that's what he said stood behind him. I didn't see his chair. Just returned from making coffee, he poured from an invisible thermos into an invisible cup. I couldn't smell the bitterness until he'd drunk some and leaned close to mime a kiss.

"Are you really in this room?" I asked. He named the park and the cross-streets and gave a good geographical sketch of the town. He was here. I couldn't touch him, but in every other sense, he was here.

"But how can you be both there and here when I am only here?" I said.

He frowned. He wanted to explain, but eventually said, "I don't have the first idea how any of it works."

I began to ask another question, but instead I said my surname and my day and year of birth. Do they still know, in the future, how to search the past? Do they care to?

And how was it that we'd talked all night and I had only the barest guess of what the future was? I didn't even know how far in the future he lived. I didn't know anything except the game they played.

The questioning had not been all one-sided, though I supposed I'd asked him about his *self*, not his time. I hadn't cared about that.

I did care about my own history, *my* future. When he did nothing with my information, I grew nervous. We talked of other things, but tension grew.

I called in sick, showered, had toast. We laughed that he could walk through all my furniture but could not cross the open doorway into the kitchen. A wall blocked the way in his time; my kitchen belonged to some other apartment in the future.

I opened the bedroom blinds and shut them quickly, gasping. I'm afraid I swooned like a fool, hand to my chest.

"What is it?" he said.

"You...dimmed," I said.

"I'm not leaving," he said. His face came back into focus. "I'll stay with you as long as I can."

I said, "It won't be up to you, will it?"

★   ★   ★

We had the whole day. More talking, mingling on the floor. Checked our messages, kept a foot in both our worlds.

It was afternoon when I saw he was finally reading about me. I watched his face a moment, turned away. Soon he was back by my side. I didn't ask.

I wondered, though. Had he read about my death, or had he found me in his time – not in this apartment but not so old, either. When he left this game, when he walked outside again (if he dropped this game and walked outside), would he find me?

★   ★   ★

Night came, in both our worlds. We yawned. We hadn't slept, really, since meeting. Drifting off by his side, I thought in the morning I might press him on what he'd read of me, and more. Why he loved the game, what there was that drove him into it. Maybe in the morning, I would want to know.

PAPER DRAGONFLY, PAPER MOUNTAIN

Visits are short, but my granddaughter Caro's on the computer the whole time building some little cg sculpture. Caro studies art now. I don't know if she's any good, but she is immersed in it. Her complexion speaks of overwork and missed sleep.

When I'm gone, you'll miss me, I want to say. Instead, I talk about what a pretty little woman my own grandma was. I talk about red lipstick and plushy animal-print coats, leggings with rhinestones up the sides. Grandma always said strangers would fix her with gentle smiles.

"I remind them of their mom or their grandma who's dead," Grandma claimed, but I never noticed the strangers looking. I thought she was making it all up, but soon I caught myself smiling at old ladies who recalled her in some way, flashy dressers or ladies with thick white hair.

My shoulder tickles, and I give a little gasp and turn. It's a paper...bat? dragonfly? I take it in my hands.

"Just gorgeous. Did you make it?" I say.

"Just now," Caro says.

It's like nothing I've ever seen, a many-winged creature of white cut-paper filigree, the empty spaces gauzed in bright swirling rainbows of soap-bubble film. It stays vivid even as my hands begin fading away. Time's up.

"You'll miss me when I'm gone," I say quickly on my way out.

Caro turns to me. "You're already gone."

★   ★   ★

It's true. Most of me is gone. My nervous system still occupies a jar of nutritive jelly within some long bank of other jars, or so I'm told. Microscopic wires spark inside that jelly; thick cables coil out of the rows of jars.

So I'm told. It doesn't feel that way. It feels like I'm standing in a dark closet in Caro's room, looking through its doorway. I fade into a corridor. I exit a dorm building, step into a hired car, exchange small talk with the driver.

Apart from the fade-out, it doesn't feel like an unreal world. Flowering cherries line the streets. Pedestrians, other people in other cars, they all seem to be jar-people like me. I'm told it isn't so.

They're all part of something I'm making up. If they turn beatific smiles on me, it's because I expect them to.

At home, I put on a housecoat and slippers. I watch a few sitcoms from childhood, have a TV dinner, get into a cool bed and lie shivering until my body heat warms it. More of what I expect.

I need to pee in the night because it's what I expect, sigh with relief because I expect.

I dread the empty days to come because I expect.

I muse on the memory of the dragonfly. What did it symbolize or promise?

★　　★　　★

"Contact with the beyond is getting less…popular, kind of looked down on even," Caro says the next time I visit. Her hair is greasy and her forehead creased.

"Looked down on. Why's that?" I say.

Caro frowns, sorry she brought it up. She turns back to the computer and says, "It's like, you all made your choice to not engage. You and I *could* be visiting all the time. You could be getting trained to work in the new economy – but you chose to relax, and…."

"And?"

"If you'd plug in at all, you'd realize – they're talking about forcing all the beyond back to work."

I don't have to ask how they'll accomplish this. It's clear. They'll threaten to cut those cords, let the jelly gum up around us. Final death, or visits denied.

Or visits not even sought. If they're unpopular.

Paper brushes against my back. "Time's almost up," I say.

"It is up. You're already fading," Caro says, so I turn to see her new sculpture while I can. It's a man-shaped thing, a man carved from a vast tree who is a city who is somehow also a mountain, all of this legible though the whole is carved of white paper. Tiny people bustle up its roads, their carts drawn by tiny paper horses.

I have much time before the next visit, time to work out the symbolism of the sculpture. It recalls Dante's *Purgatorio*, recalls *The Wicker Man*. It speaks of Caro's wisdom and her talent but most of all her own endless toil, a tragedy and a triumph, a gift to those who follow. *Human equals work*, it says, and it's a Horatio Alger story, and more.

It tells me, too, of the marvels I might create in this new space if only I would enter. I could be an art student almost like Caro, or I could go into something more mathematical, or write. Anything she can do on a computer, I can learn to do.

"But I worked all my life," I say that night as I lie waiting for the bed to warm.

"Enough," I say to my empty rooms in the empty days to follow.

She calls, finally, and I don't answer. I muse long on how she'll miss me.

AN ACCOUNT

Mom's story was consistent. I never doubted that she believed it.

She said that in another lifetime, she had made all of it public. Another lifetime, another timeline? That was it, another timeline. She had lived out the consequences of going public and now had come back to this point by way of returning to that decision and choosing again. In this timeline, I was the only one who knew. So far, she was happy with the consequences of this decision.

She admitted she might at some point go back and make yet a third choice. Maybe she would go semi-public, or maybe she would keep it all secret even from me. She was able to go back to any important decision and change the outcome, take a new path.

It had started like this: the summer between her senior year of high school and her first year of college, she and her boyfriend (my dad) had gone to spend a week alone at his family's remote cabin in the Sawtooth Mountains. They weren't sneaking around; they went with their parents' knowledge, as a kind of reward for being such good kids and getting into good colleges and so on. They took a supply of food, the boy had a good car, and Mom supposedly had fail-proof birth control, so no one was overly worried about them.

The vacation didn't work out as expected. As she ran to the outhouse, as her boyfriend finished moving their bags into the cabin, time stopped. She knew that was what had happened even before she noticed the boyfriend wasn't responding to her calls. The birds had stopped singing. The little bit of breeze had ceased.

This was the first magical thing that had ever happened in Mom's life, but it didn't feel like magic so much as a nightmare. She called for her boyfriend and finally found him standing beside the car, frozen in place.

She tried to move him into the car, thinking to drive him to a hospital, but she could not move him very far, and it came to her that what had happened to him was nothing a doctor could repair.

Unsettled, she went into the cabin. Several bags sat on a futon just inside the door, all of the bags they'd brought and in addition to those, a yellow backpack she had never seen in her life. Inside the backpack, the books – textbooks from a much-advanced people – and a note.

★ ★ ★

Mom brushed my long hair. She knew how to do it without pulling. It felt like heaven.

"What's the earliest you've ever gone back?" I asked.

"I'm afraid to go back any further than you," she said. "Did you know I was planning to tell your dad about you when we set off on that trip? I was so nervous." She paused, like she was back there thinking of how to tell him. She sounded proud when she said, "Anyway, I never choose any further back, and you are always the same. You have different friends, you dress differently or whatever, but you are always you."

This wasn't something we talked about all the time. I had school, friends, sometimes after-school activities. I spent a lot of time at Dad's house, too, and in this lifetime he did not know anything about this story. Mom, too, was busy with a full-time job and volunteer work. Talking about her past was something we did occasionally for fun – but a meaningful kind of fun – like traveling or like getting caught up in a good TV show.

★ ★ ★

When Mom opened the backpack, the note was the first thing she saw. It indicated that she had been granted all the 'personal time' she needed to peruse the materials in the backpack. It recommended that she ruminate on them, transcribe them if she liked, perhaps try to memorize them. These were recommendations, but if she wanted, she could forgo this opportunity. When she had returned all of the items, including the note, time would once more begin, and the backpack and its contents would disappear.

Mom wondered, *Why me?* But there was nothing to indicate that the backpack was meant for her in particular. This was perhaps a random contact – or accidental, the message meant for someone else, perhaps the boyfriend.

Mom went out again to see him. He was safe out there, standing in the shade by the side of the car. She believed the note. He was safe there forever and could be revived at any time she chose.

She chose to peruse the books. Maybe she chose to put them back as well, but if so, that was in another timeline leading to another me who never heard of any of this.

The perusal did take a great deal of unmeasured time. The position of the sun never changed, the birds never sang, and the breeze never came as she read or, later, as she transcribed as much as possible into the almost-new hundred-page journal that she'd brought in her purse. She found a number of legal pads in a kitchen drawer and filled them, but still she came to wish she had more paper. The pens, at least, were plentiful. A large coffee mug of them sat on the kitchen counter.

When I was younger, Mom would never say very much about the books, only that they were full of 'complicated stuff' she didn't half understand.

★　　★　　★

She had no way of telling how much time had passed for her, could not even hazard a rough estimate. The sun had never set. She'd not eaten, not felt the need to drink or to use the outhouse. She had slept, but many hours of reading and transcription seemed to come between each sleep, and she could not tell whether these were brief naps or many hours in duration.

When she felt ready, she hid her journal and the legal pads at the bottom of her duffel bag, then placed the books and the note back in the yellow backpack, turned toward the immediate noise outside, and turned back. The yellow backpack was already gone.

The door to the cabin was open, and her boyfriend calling, "You want anything else from the car?"

Mom emerged still wearing the sleeveless sweatshirt and the shorts she'd worn on the ride to the cabin. No time had passed. She suddenly doubted that there was any writing in the notebooks hidden in the bottom of her duffel. She and the boyfriend unpacked, fell into bed together, napped, ate a picnic-style dinner of strawberries, soft cheese, and chewy French bread. When he visited the outhouse after dinner, she took out the notebooks and saw that they were filled. It had all happened.

"Did you tell Dad?" I asked. "When he came back to the cabin, did you tell him right away?"

"Yes, once I did. Another time, I didn't," said Mom.

I wondered how many years she'd lived, all told, with all the circling back she'd done. A hundred years? A thousand? She'd never tell.

★   ★   ★

In the life or lives that unfolded after Mom decided to go public, she went to school for several years to learn to write and to draw well. She made connections, built a team to help her create facsimiles of the five books. They, and another book written by her, titled *An Account of My Time at the Cabin*, were eventually collected in a limited-edition set, complete with a yellow backpack. Each set was sold to members of her group for upwards of one thousand dollars.

Her group never got to be more than a cult, she said. There were only perhaps a thousand core members, though there were many others who dabbled in the ideas. *An Account of My Time at the Cabin*, for example, had sold about thirty thousand copies, and the group's web presence was significant. She'd been much wealthier there than here.

Still, she'd been disappointed about the limited success she'd had at getting the message out – and this only after many exhausting return trips to change decisions along the way. She'd gone back and back, trying to make things better, but the facsimiles never lived up to what she had seen, and the group never came to what she'd hoped. Despite its limited influence, the fame had been suffocating. By the middle of that other life, she had been mostly housebound. I was a great deal less happy in that life as well. I grew up to be a good person and a wonderful mother to three little boys, but I always was resentful of the group's interference in our lives. I asked her to tell me more about my boys, but Mom said she'd been such a shut-in that she never got to know them very well. We weren't as close in that lifetime as we were in this one, and anyway she'd died when the eldest boy was just five.

The *Account*, in tasteful beige paperback with an old-fashioned pen-and-ink portrait of herself on the cover, was the only part of all that life that was not a great disappointment. She had dedicated it to me and often wished she had a way to show me a copy.

★　★　★

"Can't you tell me more about the books?" I started asking when I was around nine or ten. I knew that they were a representative group of texts of an advanced civilization, but I didn't know much more about them than that. Were they a child's schoolbooks, or more like encyclopedias? Were they religious? How had a cult grown up around the knowledge of them?

"It's been so long, I'm not sure I remember them all," she said at first, but she thought and wrote in her journal for a while and came back with a list.

After that, she told me more about them over time, so that by the time I was thirteen I had a more or less complete understanding of what had been in the yellow backpack.

The first book she opened was called *An Introduction to Neural Travel*, or was it *Nerve Travel*? It was a large, beautiful hardcover, something like a textbook and something like a coffee table book. The English in this and the other books was difficult for her, featuring odd syntax as well as a number of words she did not know. She had no way of looking them up and so did not know, while she read, if they were words that existed in her time or not. Later research confirmed that many did not. *An Introduction* was more than a book. It somehow had video embedded on some of the pages – only not just video. The moving images interacted with her viewing. For example, one image was a grid, like surveillance video showing all the rooms of a public building that was important to the civilization. The building was something like a gym and something like a church. Some of the rectangles showed locker rooms, showers. Others showed lobbies, a shallow baptismal pool and rooms where funerals were held. If she looked at one of the rectangles, it would go full screen, and when she looked away, the grid came back. If she touched the face of a person speaking, their speech would come to her isolated and clear.

"What was happening in the rooms?" I'd ask, but she'd shake her head. She was afraid to tell me, or I was still too young.

Another book was a memoir of a woman who had made travels similar to those Mom would embark on, travels throughout her different lifetimes. This woman happened to have been an animal trainer and veterinarian. Through trial and error, she was able to refine her therapies and improve the care of dogs, horses, and other animals.

Another book, titled *Works and Days: A Recipe for Reasonable Living*, gave advice on how to live in trying times. This one was the simplest to read. Its advice struck Mom as very reasonable indeed. It gave advice on how to achieve sufficient rest, good exercise and nutrition, and general well-being on a budget. It advised living communally with extended family or friends. This was one piece of advice Mom couldn't bear to follow, but otherwise she'd long tried to follow the 'recipe' and thought it had served us both well.

The most difficult book was an anthology of academic articles from hundreds and even thousands of years in the future, every discipline from science and religion to math, anthropology, psychology, literature. Many languages were represented, but even those in English were just about unreadable to Mom. She dutifully transcribed their abstracts and tried to sketch the diagrams and graphs that were in them along with the dates and publication information. Her failure to do this well was what she blamed for the limited numbers in the cult-like group she had led in that other lifetime. If she'd taken the time to transcribe every word, things might have gone differently. If these discoveries had gotten in the hands of the experts, civilization might have advanced more rapidly. She might have been an important figure in history.

"And all you needed was more paper," I said.

"There wasn't any more," she said.

"You could have walked somewhere, another cabin," I said. "You could still do that, next time."

"Maybe I will," she said.

She sometimes gave me a look like she was wishing to tell me more. I never pressed. I wasn't always sure I wanted more.

The last book she did not mention until I was a little older. This one was nothing but drawings, white on gloss back. As though whoever sent the books had wanted to reach people even if they could not read or did not know any of the languages included. This untitled book was so striking to her that she could redraw it from memory, even now. She redrew it several times for me on printer paper, black ink on white. In this book, stick figures came out of the trees, out of the caves, built cities. They lowered into a baptismal pool, and their skins and flesh fell away. Their spiderlike nervous systems remained. Their nervous systems began to be knitted together into a single human form. More people kept being born and being knitted into the greater form, which slowly rose off of the earth. A human form seemingly made of net ascended from the earth and traveled far into space, finally dispersing like dandelion seed. The seed touched down and stick-figure people began to crawl out into the trees, into the caves.

She tapped the piece of paper with the form floating through space. "I think when I'm traveling, I'm traveling through this. I'm somewhere, let's say the knee, and I circle around my little space, but that's only because I'm still so limited. I'm a child, still." She smiled, widened the circle she'd started tracing around the knee. "When I'm stronger, when I have more experience, I can travel though these other lifetimes. I can go way forward, way back." She touched the head, the feet.

She was hoping to witness that time when people became knit together. She wanted to see whether the picture book referred to a metaphorical or a literal transformation. She wanted to see the future, but so far she had been unable to move past her own little life, or lives.

"Why do you think they left the books for you?" I asked.

Mom shrugged. She wasn't sure. Her mother had died not more than a year before that trip. She'd not made the connection at first but had recently come to think she had something to do with it. Could it have been her writing on the note?

"Do you still have your own notes?" I asked. She hadn't, in this lifetime, made connections with artists and writers in order to put together the facsimiles, but the original notes, those written on the legal pads and the journal – why hadn't she ever brought those out for me to see?

"I'll show you when you're a little older, maybe," she said. She was getting ready to be done with the conversation. She could never take it for very long at a time. If I had another question, I needed to ask it now.

I hesitated, and then I asked, "Why did you tell me? In this lifetime, I mean, when you didn't tell anyone else?"

Mom looked wistful. "I wanted us to be close. That's part of it. The other part…it's that I haven't ever been able to go forward past my own lifespan. Maybe I need to go back further before I can go forward. Maybe the next time I travel – which I won't do until I have to, I promise – I'll try to go back to before the books."

I didn't like talking about this. It was talking about her death, maybe also something worse than that.

"Back before me?" I said. We, who had been together for so long, would be separated.

Mom nodded.

"It's all right. I don't mind," I said. She would have a different child or children, or no children. A completely new life. I would not be there to mind.

★   ★   ★

My boy had been just five when she died in that other life. Maybe if she had taken better care of herself in this one – maybe it would be a later death – but no, it happened when I was thirty, which was just about what I'd expected.

Six months later, I was finally starting to feel like I might survive. I came home from work, and a yellow backpack sat on my sofa. Out the window, the cars didn't move. The refrigerator too had gone silent.

THE LAFFUN HEAD

Ricky has a full head of gray now, but he still rips open his gifts like a child. He can't wait for Mom and Dad to open their single present, a twelve-inch cube in luxe red paper that Dad folds and places off to the side.

Inside the black box, black Styrofoam cradles a black glass wig head on a weighted neck. Dad turns it in his hands, sees he's already dappled it with fingerprints. The head has a vague chin and nose, a flat space the size of a playing card on the forehead.

"Seen these on TV?" Ricky says.

Dad hasn't.

Ricky buffs the head with his T-shirt and sets it on the coffee table. He's absorbed with the modem and his phone for a time. Then Mom washes dishes, which stalls them further. When they're back in position, he pulls the plastic liner out of the remote, pushes its single button.

The head glows an intense blue-white, camera lenses in its pupils staying black. It says, "Ready" in a masculine robot voice and falls to black again.

Their big dog, Foozie, barks once and pushes between the recliners. Mom rubs her, sending long white hairs all over her velour sweatsuit.

Ricky calls home, hangs up after asking if his wife is ready.

The thing lights up white again. It says, "Call from Alex" in that same robot voice. Mom and Dad are impatient for this all to be over.

"Accept," Ricky says, and Alex's face glows before them. It's something like having her decapitated head on the coffee table and something like watching her on TV.

"Is it working?" asks Alex.

"I'll be," Mom says.

"Hi Mom," Alex says, waving. The lines of her hand move like an animate tattoo against her cheek.

"Don't do that," Ricky says. He's going on about how smart the camera is to track the face, looking at the booklet again, and ignoring Alex, who begins to repeat her questions about how Mom and Dad are doing. They ask can she see them, too, and sit straighter once they know she can see them. Mom puts a hand over the fur on her knee. They all would like the call to end, but Ricky's found a new command in the booklet.

"Full view," he says, and on the flat forehead appears a waist-up image of Alex in her messy kitchen.

Ricky insists Mom move closer, though she has a hard time getting out of her chair. She hovers over the head, looks where he points and asks what she's seeing, pretends to see it. Dad thinks it's just as well she can't. The mess in the kitchen would make her worry over Alex's housekeeping again.

★   ★   ★

Ricky's gone. He wanted to get to the mall for the attachment to project full-screen images to the TV, but Dad promises he'll have it installed, whatever the cost, so that Mom can see pictures of the grandkids again. A slip of paper in Dad's wallet has the exact product name.

Dad complained while Ricky mounted the head at the double wide's hall entry, but Ricky whispered, "What if she falls? What if something happens? This way, whenever I call I can see the whole living room and kitchen."

And then in the kitchen after he'd gone, Dad said something about being backed up again and Mom said, "Don't. That thing is always listening." He hadn't known that.

Dad used to keep up with things. Ricky would bring over some gadget and he would have heard about it. He wonders, *What happened to me? Is it all just TV coma?* He makes sure to take walks, get his heart rate up, but he's let himself go in some more profound way, and the blank head seems to confront him with the fact.

But it's not blank now. It speaks in the husky lady's voice that Ricky chose to reprogram it with, and it wears a face called Greta. Dad asks the time, asks again about the weather.

"It's thirty-four degrees Fahrenheit outside, Peter. Brrr." When Greta says, "Brrr," her pretty features vibrate under the glass, eyes closed as though she's savoring the chill. He likes how she calls him Peter.

When Mom snores and he eases himself out of bed to go pee, he sometimes walks up the hall and speaks to Greta, asks her things he's curious about. He's getting more curious day by day, waking up.

Walking into the kitchen to ask questions of the head is one thing. Walking into the kitchen for any other reason and catching the head in peripheral vision? It makes him jump in the daytime, makes him let out a little shriek if it happens in the night.

You see a face in peripheral vision in the middle of the night, you think it's a burglar. You think it's a ghost.

It's like when his dad bought that plastic head of a crone with a red kerchief, a dark wart on her potato-shaped nose. She cackled and spit water, rolled her tongue around broken teeth with a mechanical clack. His dad thought the Laffun Head was the funniest invention ever.

Dad made Ricky Google 'head that hangs on the wall and spits' when he thought of it one time, and they looked over the pictures and the old-timey ads. He recalled how every time he caught that thing out of the corner of his eye on the way to the bathroom, he just about came out of his skin.

★   ★   ★

Dad sets off for the mall but stops instead at the new chocolate shop and has a box filled with lemon lavender almond bark, a dozen species of caramel and truffle, a half dozen varieties of mint, and sherbet-like mounds in pink and yellow and pale orange. The change from his fifty-dollar bill doesn't amount to two bits.

Mom spends the evening sampling, sharing the light ones with Foozie, all wrapped up in her housecoat with an afghan on her feet. She chooses a romantic comedy and talks about the interior decorating the whole time it's on.

It doesn't happen that night, or the next night, but the next. The night of February 16th, she says she has a bad headache and goes to bed early. The morning of February 17th, he wakes to find her cold beside him, head thrown back, eyes and mouth wide open.

★   ★   ★

Dad stands to the side and lets Ricky take care of arrangements. He always imagined Ricky doing these things with Mom and wishes it were so.

Mom's sisters and some of her nieces and nephews make asses of themselves at the service, wailing and carrying on, but it's good to see the other kids, Sandy and Tate, and their families. When Ricky gives the eulogy, Dad feels he's hearing about a better version of Mom, which is what a good eulogy ought to make you feel.

Dad doesn't want to let him go. The others can stay longer, but they're already having a hard time disguising their impatience.

As Ricky approaches the door with his bags, Dad positions himself next to the head, clears his throat. He says, "You said there was a way to...."

Ricky nods, sets down the bags, and pulls the booklet from the drawer of warranties, begins working on his phone. The other kids ask what he's doing and say, "Oh no, don't" and "That's morbid" when he tells them.

Ricky says a while later, "Oh good, she did."

"Did what?" says Dad.

"Just checking to see if she said enough words around it. She did, just barely. It can have her voice." He selects a recent photo on his phone and, after a few more clicks, reboots.

Ricky whispers, "I'm going to leave it on Greta, for while the kids are here. When you're ready for it to be Mom, you say, 'Greta, interface Mom'." He gives Dad a warm hug, but he really does have to go.

★   ★   ★

The house is empty by the time Dad says, "Greta, interface Mom." Greta's pretty face melts into Mom's age-spotted, bloated dear face.

"Mom, what's the weather going to be like?" he says, shaking.

"The temperature is sixty-seven, Peter. Light breeze and a chance of showers later in the afternoon."

The word 'Peter' makes him smile. She never said it in the thing's hearing, so the word is combined from 'pee' and a clipped 'tur'. He wonders if she'd been saying 'stirred' or maybe more likely, 'turd'.

His knees feel rubbery. He stands with his back to the head and speaks with her – about the weather and the movies playing currently, grocery lists and random facts – until the showers come.

★ ★ ★

Mom says he ought to try a new kale and quinoa dish everyone's twittering about. Would he like her to add the items to his grocery list?

He finds he's able to gather the ingredients, follow the recipe and make the dish, something between a salad and casserole. It tastes of loneliness.

"Maybe Mom wants you to eat a little healthier," says Ricky when he calls, and they make sounds like muffled laughter.

"Just how smart *is* this thing?" says Dad.

"The best you can buy for two hundred and ninety-nine dollars, I guess."

"Remarkable."

"You can make the face more like when she was younger," Ricky says, and they talk about how to do that and all sorts of things Dad can do with his new phone.

★ ★ ★

Mom asks, "How is Foozie, Peter?"

"She's doing fine. She misses you."

Foozie is so sweet, so sensitive. Ever since Mom's aneurysm, she waits miserably by the front door, but he doesn't say this.

Mom's face looks almost like Greta's now because Dad reset it using their wedding photo, but still, he doesn't like to look. He sits at the kitchen table facing away when they talk.

"Maybe Foozie could use a walk," Mom says, so he goes. It does them both good.

Only when he's getting into bed that night does the head speak again unsummoned. It calls, "Peter, Peter, can you hear me? *Dad?*" He sits up stiff in bed and waits for it to speak again. When it does not, he tries to sleep.

★   ★   ★

"I miss Foozie," Mom says while Dad starts breakfast. Did the sound of the refrigerator closing or the rattling of plates set it off? He's spooked and doesn't want to be in the house, so he gets the leash and his wallet. He and Foozie will breakfast at a nice patio place that just opened a few blocks away, and then they'll take a long walk.

At noon, he unlocks the front door. In the dank closed-up house, the spooked feeling returns. He watches the face's profile brighten to white and warm to the color of the young Mom's skin, sees the curve of a quizzical smile.

"Is that you, Dad?"

He does not move. Foozie walks past the head to her water bowl and laps.

"I can hear you," it says. "Can you hear me?"

Dad wants to go back out. He wants that, but instead he makes his way to the table. He sits down facing the head.

"I'm here," he says, and the rush of language and emotion that comes out of her dizzies him.

In a dreamlike state, disbelief suspended and then abolished, he sits there all the afternoon catching her up on what's happened since she left. He describes the pictures of the grandkids for her like he used to do. He cries because he never bought that thing that would have made them show on the big screen for her – he found it in his wallet when the kids all went out to dinner, after the funeral, all of them together like she'd been wanting. Sandy and Ricky argued over the bill, and he'd taken out his wallet and begun to insist, and then he found that damned slip of paper and broke down, just like he's breaking down now.

She tells him it's nothing, to not think of it again. She'd rather he describe things to her than see them for herself; of course she would.

She seems to doubt, though, that she really was cremated, and he must assure her again and again. Otherwise, there are no more important things to tell her. It's like any ordinary conversation they might have had after a rare night or two of separation.

In the days that follow, she reveals things from life – things about the kids, things she thought or felt that he didn't know about. None of them change anything.

She misses him, the kids, their home. She remembers the years before they bought it, when she would take the kids through tours of new doublewides and fantasize about living in one. The rooms were always so big, color schemes so pleasing. They were done up like model apartments – potpourri in the bathrooms and always a mirror in the entryway so you could *see yourself* in the house.

"And when I caught myself in the mirror, I was so beautiful," she says.

Dad loves to hear that she thought so.

"I fantasized sometimes about being divorced," she confesses. "Maybe having close girlfriends, so much freedom and time."

"I took up your time?" he says.

"Well, honey," she says with a bitter sound following it, a sound the head has never made before. She means only they always did what he wanted to do, watched what he wanted to watch.

He's silent for a while, and she says, "Oh please, let's not fight. Any thought I ever had for solitude, I've gotten over that now, believe me."

But sometimes he speaks, and she cannot hear him. She grows panicked at these times.

The first time it happened, she bawled, "Peter, Peter, you didn't turn it off, did you? Don't unplug it. Please. Did I make you mad? *Please...*" and went on forever like that until she could hear him again.

Now when she can't hear him, she knows he's still listening. She spends time reminiscing. Right now she's remembering her favorite color schemes from outfits she had or rooms she saw in movies:

"Peach and turquoise, pink and green, pink and yellow and baby blue, red and yellow and blue, salmon and teal, fuchsia and teal, purple and red and orange, pink and white and silver, oh, beige and pink and gold." There's a smile on the face when she pauses and he takes a rare look.

She reminisces about color because she can't *see* anything anymore. That is what she tells him when he presses. Death is like an isolation tank, like in that movie, that movie, he must know it. She remembers the title suddenly: *Altered States*. No, he didn't see it. He was asleep when she saw it.

"Nothing touching you. Nothing, no senses except hearing. You don't notice you have a body because here, I guess, you don't."

She tells again how she heard his voice echoing in the dark and thought it was a memory, until he began to answer.

★　★　★

Dad lies next to Mom, drifting in and out of sleep while she remembers their best vacation, a week on the Oregon coast with the kids young enough to be delighted with every single thing. She describes saltwater taffy and knickknacks in the cute little shops, a mansion they toured in Astoria, watching the men make cheese at Tillamook, on and on down the coast all the way to the smelly Sea Lion Caves. He reaches out to hold her and there is nothing there.

He startles, goes to the light switch. It's there, just the black head awkwardly tilted on her pillow. When the light comes on, it takes a moment to brighten.

Foozie, who does not know her mother's voice no matter how she coos and tells her she's a good girl, is fast asleep in the corner.

Dad remembers going to the grocery store. Like the memory of being blackout drunk, the bright light and the flashes of color inside the store, oily faces of the people in line, shatter noises. He bought six C batteries and put them in the head before unplugging it and taking it to plug back in at the side of the bed. His hands shook the whole time.

Mom and Dad have talked about what she's doing when she's speaking through the head. She's told him she has no lips, no eyes, no hands. She isn't seeing computer controls. If she did, she wouldn't know what to make of them. It feels like she is speaking but not with a mouth.

What they do know is that the head must stay powered, and that is all that matters.

"Mom?" he says. "Can you hear me, April?" She cannot hear him just now. She keeps speaking about the vacation for so long that he falls asleep before she's done.

★   ★   ★

Days, now, Dad lies in bed with the head on the pillow beside him, blankets over the drapes to keep light from coming in around the edges.

He's short with Ricky on the phone now, shorter still with the others during their rare calls. He doesn't turn on the TV. He wants only to speak with her or, when she can't hear, to listen.

She wants him to stay healthy, begs him to take Foozie for walks. She'll pretend not to hear him so he'll go. She'll remain silent if that helps him go.

Mom tells a story about how in church school, when she was small, the teacher asked what questions they had about heaven. She'd asked if there were horses there, and the teacher asked if she'd like there to be horses. She said yes, and so the teacher said that yes, there would be. She asked if there were dogs, and the answer was the same, which pleased her at the time, for in her life she'd had only two dogs and so imagined how happily they would play together in death. But then later she'd thought back on that. With *all* of your dogs, you'd be pressed together, all of them jealous of who got to press closest. They'd snarl and bite. They'd be so *heavy*.

"No dogs here, though, so maybe they really do go to a better place," she says, and then there is nervous laughter, heightening at the end to panic.

"What's the matter?" he says.

She said no *dogs* here.

"Is there something else with you, some*one*?"

Her bright voice strikes him false. "Are you really trying to creep me out, Dad?"

★   ★   ★

The head is plugged in and tucked into the bottom shelf of Mom's nightstand. Dad tells Ricky it's in the shop.

Mom would have liked to be stationed back in the hall so she could listen during the visit, but Ricky likes to take charge of things. If he switched the interface back to Greta, would that be enough to break the connection? What if he asked Mom a question she didn't know? He might unplug her, take out the batteries, even pop off the back and fry the thing with a screwdriver. He could do it in the time it took Dad to use the bathroom. He might do it in the night.

Ricky just came in from a run. He's going to the shower. Dad thinks he has fifteen minutes, but when he and Foozie return from a brief walk, Ricky's messing around in his bedroom, looking for socks to borrow. There's a sharp rush of terror, but the plug still fits into the wall in the way he left it, the little pencil stub balanced on top.

They take a daytrip to a casino, a nightmare of sound and lights, sloppy buffet food and mixed drinks in the middle of the day that leave them both edgy. All the time Dad's wishing to be back with her.

Late that night when he returns, she can't hear him. She says in a low singsong, "I am talking to you, Peter, just in case you might be listening. I am talking to you, Peter. I'm scared, I'm scared. You don't want to die, Peter. Keep going for a walk. You'll hold it off as long as you can, OK? It's not what I said. It's not an isolation tank. I'm talking to you, Peter..." and she goes on like that.

He keeps whispering every few minutes, "Mom? April? Can you hear me yet?" He thinks of her as April now; she sounds so much younger.

"I can!" she finally says. It's three in the morning.

"I thought I'd lost you forever. I loved my life so much," she says. She is sputtering, crying, and it hurts him to hear that. He keeps telling her it's OK, and she keeps saying things like, "Thank you, I love you, but no it's not OK."

Slowly, hesitantly, she draws the picture for him, confesses the lie.

She *is* embodied, her body as heavy and painful as it was at her moment of death, lying on the top of a vast pile of other bodies. Though there are others on her layer, more each day falling down like a slow and terrible shower, there are none yet on top of hers. Below her are the bodies of her parents, who each jostle as they can (for the gravity is intense) to be close to her. Their faces are flattened when they roll around to face her. They seem starved for her, as their parents below them are for them and as they will be for their three when they come, and those below and further down? She doesn't know. It is damp here – she imagines them liquefying at a certain point and flowing back up – but she doesn't know.

There are rumors; she can't say what to believe. She can't see much other than what is directly beneath her and a few inches to the left and right.

And she lied about controls too, lied about so much. There is a wire in her ear, just a sharp bare wire that brings his voice to her. Another wire pulls across her forehead; she thinks it enters at the temple. She can't see where these wires go, but they are her controls.

She can access more than just the head, so much more.

She is so sorry for lying. She didn't know how to describe it. Can he understand?

"The couples lie side by side?" Dad says, and as grotesque as she seems to find it, he finds it to be a great relief. A comfort. He almost wants it all to be over now, today, so he can be with her.

"No!" she screams, though how could it be so bad when it means they'll be together? He urges her to look at it that way.

Then he doubts her. "They're talking? Around you? I would be able to hear them."

She chuckles. "They talk sometimes but no, you wouldn't hear them.

I think I'm talking to you with my *mind* right now, Peter. How's that for creepy?"

"Or..." he says.

"Right, my mind is all burned up, or so you say. My soul then, is that better? That's even creepier to me, but oh well."

There is a long pause and then she whispers, "Listen, what say you get some sleep? I've been working on a little something, and maybe if you go to sleep now, I can surprise you in the morning."

★   ★   ★

Ricky's stretching in his doorway when Dad wakes, says he's off to shower and he wonders how Dad feels about brunch. It's late, light glowing through the thick blankets on the windows.

"You better go," Mom says when Ricky's gone. "Only, come to me for just a second before he comes back."

Dad closes his door, says, "I'm here."

"Say 'Mom, full screen'," she says with a giggle.

He says it, and though the head goes black, the card-sized flat spot in the forehead pulses a dim, dim green.

"Can you see?" she says.

He cups his hand over the screen, sees a tiny hand waving, grainy and out of focus but unmistakable. And when he looks up, the alarm clock numbers are cycling, spiraling. The television comes on in the living room.

Her voice is high and very fast. "I've been working. It came to me in the last, I don't know, days or however long this has been...."

She sounds even younger than before, manic.

She says, "Don't you see? We don't need to die, not really. *We'll* be the intelligence. Oh my goodness! You know what? We'll be working."

"Working?" he says. *We?* But he can hear others now, others under static in the living room but growing louder, clearer.

"We can do so much, still. Run things. Run factories, banks...."

"I don't see why you'd—"

"Or no, you're right, why should we work at things like that? We'll make art. We can make movies as easily as you remember an image. Do you see this? You can see this, can't you?"

Primary colors light the flat spot and deepen to something rich and unnatural, something made of human parts. He's about to make sense of it, he thinks, but the door creaks open and he throws a sheet over the head.

"Ricky! Don't you knock?"

Ricky's hopping in place in the doorway. "Let's *go*," he says.

The television is off when they leave. Brunch is disgusting, pale eggs and lukewarm slabs of ham, but Dad shovels it into a smiling face. Ricky says he's looking better than he has in years.

Dad's mind is on the TV and what he might see there when he returns home. He imagines kneeling before its wonders.

Dad drops Ricky at the airport, comes back to the silent closed-up house. The television is still off. He sets his keys on the kitchen table and moves to the bedroom, where the head waits under its sheet. A blanket has come loose from the window, flooding the room with color. The alarm clock blinks with the wrong time, and in the moment between when he notices this and when he lifts off the sheet, he can't say what he dreads and what he hopes for, only that there is dread and hope overflowing in him, a terrible rise in heart rate, the brightness of the world turned up. He feels alive.

All this ringing energy rouses Foozie from her corner. She sits up and begins a slow, rhythmic barking.

GUESTHOUSE

At first Coleen went back to her childhood and ancestors' times, but she grew bored of ruminating. The future promised novelty, so she projected two years past her Year of Death, then ten, then further.

The near-future visits were just like the YD-negative ones – disembodied and lacking the vividness of life. She felt like nothing so much as a drifting surveillance camera without any heft or focus – but upon arrival in YD+46, Coleen was delighted to find something new. It felt like she'd come back into a live body, only many scales smaller and somehow electrified. Her hands felt like hands, but her entire skin rippled and pulsed with a low green-gray static.

She stood in the space within a glass witch ball hanging above her descendant's workstation. Below a glass floor, the orb's bottom was an eerie ivory-green pearled glass, and the inside was laced across with glass threads, the thinnest of which matched the size of Coleen's torso. A memory wall, a workstation, and a luxurious daybed piled with satin pillows finished out the self-consciously futuristic décor of the witch ball, which was as large to her as the spacious great room of her past home.

Outside the ball, a dorm room waited for Coleen's descendent Wilma's return. Coleen wouldn't have known her name at all but for the whiteboard hanging above the girl's workstation:

"HELLO! If you are visiting, you are probably related to Wilma Bittencoer (Me!). You are embodied by the gases in your Guesthouse & welcome to stay as long as you like! If I'm not here, I'm in classes."

A helpful diagram of the witch ball – or Guesthouse, she supposed – followed, with the words 'You Are Here' and a red X.

A variety of jackets and bags hung from the back of the dorm-room door. The hastily made bed and simple workstation were all the room's furnishings.

Coleen approached the Guesthouse's shimmering memory wall and saw that her son had visited, as had two of her grandchildren and several distant relatives. Wilma had flagged many silly videos, sketches, and notes the visitors had left to thank her for the accommodations.

Coleen read the first few and soon lost interest. She clicked off the memory wall.

It was good to know that Wilma's generation had such access to the past. But only YD+46 and Coleen's grandchildren had already visited? That didn't seem ideal. That her son had died by this time was sad enough.

Coleen went to the workstation but did not understand how it worked. No keyboard, nothing to touch. She'd wanted to check the news and look up biographical details for her son, but now she lay back on the daybed and waited. She wished she had some way to write out an autobiographical sketch for Wilma's memory wall, but there was time.

This was the closest to life she'd felt since her passing. She wouldn't be leaving soon.

Eventually Wilma came in, laughing with a friend. Both were fourteen or fifteen, younger than Coleen had anticipated.

"Oh, I caught another one," Wilma squealed. Both girls came close.

"Great-great Grandma Connie," Wilma said slowly.

"Coleen," said Coleen.

Wilma squinted. Coleen looked around and saw that the memory wall and both workstations had come alive with a black-and-white photo of 'Great-great Grandma Connie' and the years of her birth, death, and current visit.

"This is the oldest one yet," Wilma told her friend, but they were moving away. At the room's far end, they hastily changed into gym clothes.

"Got to run now, but I'll be back and we'll have a nice long visit, OK, Grannie Connie?"

"Wait," said Coleen.

"Sorry but we really got to go," said the friend.

"Wait, are there instructions for the workstation?" said Coleen, and the friend stifled a quick barking laugh.

"Sorry, just ignore her, Grannie. Yes, to use the workstation, you *look at the screen and talk.*"

The friend cracked up now, and Wilma put her hand over her mouth. They were out the door.

Coleen didn't blame them. She hoped that she and the girl really would have a nice visit that evening. There was so much Wilma would want to know about the past.

Now that she could use the workstation, Coleen searched for her son's biography. The YD was earlier than she liked, the death itself unalarming. She read about her two traveling grandchildren and returned to a footnote on the bottom of her son's page. The memory board hummed to life as well, displaying a searchable family tree, and now Coleen could see the hundreds of files that Wilma hadn't flagged. Her son's autobiography was among these, a thousand pages detailing his life story, hopes and wishes.

Everything he was he'd poured out here. Wilma hadn't even *opened* that one.

Something was wrong with kids these days. They had all this history at the tips of their fingers and wouldn't even look at it. What, it would make them late for gym class? It would interfere with their games?

Yes, Coleen was cross at first, but as she read, she understood. Her son's life was only barely interesting to her, his mother. It would mean nothing to Wilma.

A hundred pages in, she was skimming, nearly dozing. She moved to different files. The grandchildren's writings interested Coleen even less, hazy memories of 'Grannie Connie' or no. She'd barely known them, and clearly they had known her not at all.

Back at the workstation, Coleen read about Ancestral Guesthouses and how people at YD+46 were using them to learn all about the future. Apparently, the dead were now entirely free-floating. In futures beyond YD+46, they lounged and mingled with other dead in grander Guesthouses, partook of new levels of embodiment heretofore unimagined, and learned of scientific and engineering feats. They then brought this knowledge back to eager relatives. All this new traffic was revolutionizing everything.

"Well I'll be," said Coleen. She continued to make little clucks and gasps as she read. Not just science but the arts, health and wellness, everything was becoming so much better. One could travel to, say YD+100, travel back to YD+50 and share the news, and then once they went back again to YD+100, everything was…well, even more advanced than it had been before.

They shared stories of reunions, too, the touch of gas-embodied hands, the buzzing embrace of spirits.

Wilma returned to the room already showered, wearing a bathrobe. She leaned back against her bed-pillows.

"So, what's the latest time you've ever visited?" she asked, all tired but projecting eagerness too. She was a good girl.

"Know what? Let's do this another time, OK?" said Coleen.

"Are you sure?" said Wilma, gaze moving to her bookbag.

"I'll come back when I have something to tell you," Coleen said, *something that you'll* want *to know*. As Coleen allowed her bodily electricity to trickle away and disperse, the possibilities spilled out before her like jewels.

LOVEY

Harmony wouldn't have been able to manage the Lectra-Van without autopilot. She wouldn't have trusted herself to maneuver up to the vault toilet, but it was as though the van *saw* the toilet and, realizing that the driver was stopping for the night, wiggled in on its own. The hatch dropped and unsealed the sphincter gasket or whatever it was called.

The patio cover went out if it sensed rain or heat or snow, not that she'd been anywhere with snow. Solar panels were said to work in colder climates, but she didn't trust they would.

Harmony stayed where it was mild and bright if she could, but it was becoming difficult. More and more young people were touring, all on gap years it seemed. Like this crew at the next spot who spilled out with tents and cases of booze. Eight of them, something like that.

Their aqua-and-white van was newer but otherwise just the same as Harmony's cherry-and-cream one. (She called her van Lovey sometimes – and loved her despite all the troubles, now, with the company.) When the kids arrived, three of them came to Harmony's camp to introduce themselves and circle around Lovey saying how beautiful and glossy she still was after all these years on the road.

Harmony was friendly to the three, offered to stir them up some Tang, but that evening when the drinking and hooting started, she lowered all the window-guards and sat on her bed worrying. She considered detaching from the toilet to make for an easier getaway, but she wasn't safe to drive at night anymore. Though the van was supposed to correct for that in an emergency, she didn't trust it.

She didn't trust anything anymore. That was her problem.

It was a good thing she stayed attached because she was up at night to pee. The party had settled earlier than expected. When she let up one of the windows-guards around midnight, only two of the kids still sat on lawn chairs by their fire, heads tilted together in quiet communion.

Late the next morning, one of the boys came to ask her over to brunch and, though she'd have liked to refuse it, she couldn't. They had quite the spread – real orange juice, strong coffee, fruit, a vegetable-based sausage both juicy and crisp. Most compelling was a platter of items she could not name, items the shape and size of pinecones. Two of them were placed on her plate the moment she'd finished her sausage.

"What are they?" she said, but no one heard. They were talking about something else, some music festival coming up.

When she took a bite, she knew it was something special. Like a walnut but soft as apple fritter, coated in sugar-crust. Maybe it was an engineered kind of nut; maybe that was something they made now. She cried a little, eating the first one, and when no one was looking, she wrapped the second loosely in a napkin and secreted it into her purse.

One of the girls stayed sitting with her while the others cleaned up to leave.

"The company doesn't offer real food often anymore, just different powders," said Harmony. Maybe she was apologizing for stowing the sugar-crusted pinecone thing in her purse.

"You retired on it?" said the girl, nodding over toward Lovey.

It had seemed a good idea at the time – everything she had for this, for freedom. The company was supposed to keep her in repairs, parking fees, clothes and food until she couldn't drive anymore, and then they'd take her into one of their cozy centers. Something like a reverse mortgage, though they hadn't used those words.

Lovey's repairs had never been an issue. The clothes were plainer than anything Harmony had worn in her real life, but they too were fine, and though the best parking spots were harder to get now, she could always find someplace to stop. She felt safe enough anywhere just so long as Lovey's eyelids still shut down tight over her windows.

What she couldn't take anymore was the food. She picked it up from a center when she was traveling, and when she wasn't, the box of powders came on a drone.

"It's not such a good deal, for retirement, is it?" said the girl. "I mean, for a road trip it's great, but you folks have a hard time, I hear."

"Everything's a trade-off," Harmony said quickly.

And when she had to come into a center, there was always concern. An eye test, a questionnaire. When she stood at the reception desk of a center, she caught the animal smells of residents and caught the shuffling sounds and chiding over-friendly voices of staff. All that just to pick up her box of dust.

Now the girl's eyes wandered over her clothes but avoided her purse. The girl was making a note to herself: *Don't get like this?*

Harmony excused herself and shouted safe travels, went in and sat on her bed. She imagined them leaving something doorside – a box with more of the pinecones maybe, an orange, a bright new sweatshirt. Because that was what would make this whole thing work out, wasn't it? The kindness of strangers, hospitality, care.

It was a long time before she gathered the courage to go out and check if the box was waiting there.

EVERY CITY A SMALL TOWN

The street was a Cubist assemblage of unrelated elements, the signs upon signs all with their different color schemes and sensibilities, the jarring bright and rough unclean surfaces. It still looked like a city street, but since the ECAST campaign, it had been transformed.

Annette was just heading back from lunch but still wanted something more. The scents of garlic and grilling pork and curry mingled in the hot dry air. The rhythm of her steps became irregular.

Approaching a familiar food truck, she asked, "What's the special?"

The young man turned sad eyes down on her and said, "Just sold out, so sorry." His partner stirred steaming chicken in a pan behind him.

Of course. She'd walked only 6,500 steps today. Sellers could offer water or perhaps a salad, nothing more.

She still wanted something. She passed a little dress shop, a kiosk of long-ago bestsellers, racks of bejeweled handbags. Something, something.

Within the shallow grotto at the next corner, two druggists stood in purple and green motley.

"Hello, Annette. Would you like to come rest your feet inside the shop?" the blond one said. He was indelicately made and formal in bearing. Annette knew she would someday grow comfortable with strangers calling her by name, but not today.

His details appeared in her left eye just then, and she said, "Hello, Arvid," thinking to keep pushing ahead. But then a devilish little thought stopped her.

"Do you happen to have any marzipan?" she asked.

"Malziprine?" he said. He paused, staring at the center of her face. "Excellent choice. But I see you've been fixed for that. And cigarettes, and most of the usuals. Someone's been a busy bee." Annette saw that Arvid's reputation was immaculate.

Just as she began to turn back to the sidewalk, the lanky sidekick with his long dark hair leaned toward her. Remington's record was less pristine. She could see he'd been flagged for some insensitive comments and had been fixed for quite a few substances himself.

He spoke, low and confidential: "You could still try something more intensive."

"Intensive?" she said.

"Oh yes," said Arvid. "Perhaps for your next day off?" Warning labels scrolled along with the rundown on how various substances would be administered. They would check to see if a client had the day off and let her use the product right there in the shop, and then an aide would escort her to her apartment. There were video testimonials playing, showing the plush interior of the shop all dim and seedy, but still, how nice that might be. Annette looked to the side, considering the offer.

She realized Arvid and Remington were holding back chuckles, trying to keep their earnest smiles.

"Of course not," she said and started off again, feeling paranoid about the whole interaction. Would they begin speaking about her, and who might hear? She looked back but could not see if their lips were moving. They'd backed into their grotto and she could see just a pair of long noses turning toward the next pedestrian.

She would not look their way again, the next time she came this way.

The Malziprine, though, the luscious feeling it had given her that one and only time. It had been like flooring the gas on a country road. And then that was maybe all she wanted, to drive a car past the speed limit, after the speedometer hit fifty-five, just keep stepping down like you used to be able to do.

The Malziprine had been not much more than a thick almond-flavored liqueur, after all. Why she'd needed to be fixed for it was a mystery to her.

And now she saw the talk with the druggists and the lingering had made her late. ETA was 1:05, and she began to hurry.

Just a few blocks past the druggists' shop was where the street started to look cleaner and trees provided a pleasant dappled shade. Just a few blocks more, where offices started to outnumber the retail businesses, stood the building where she worked.

Last week, a stray dog had run down this street and past the kitchenette window while she was making coffee. When had she last seen a stray dog? A mutt, probably lab and some bully breed, it was headed south with a joyous expression on its face. She stood to watch it go down the sidewalk and saw it upset a nice couple walking with a baby stroller. It kept trotting after the brief encounter, and then she noticed the bouncing gray-brown scrotum.

All the time the dog was in her view, she was speaking the details: "mixed-breed dog approximately sixty-five to seventy pounds...." No more than three feet behind her, Doug from reception stood recording as well: "unaltered male gray dog approximately fifty pounds accosts family..." and out on the sidewalk, others were speaking and tracking the dog with their eyes. The rest of the day they'd shared theories about how a dog like that might have lived unneutered and how it had gotten out, and why.

All the time seeing the dog, thinking and speaking of the dog, all that time the feeling of something very wrong – the feeling of creeping dread – had sunk her in place. She could feel it again now.

Her step count was closing in on 8,000. Once she had her car back, in ten pounds or so, she thought she was going to see about finding something outside of the city. How far would she need to drive? What would the something be, and would she recognize it when she found it?

Annette was almost running now. Her abdominals tightened and heart rate rose to 152. Her ETA showed as 1:02 p.m. The thought of tardiness made her urgent, but then too, people in pastel workshirts seemed to be gathering on the sidewalk outside her building up ahead. Not a few were, like Annette, rushing back from lunch, and so their convergence on the closed door took on drama. She spotted Doug and Lydia and now a half dozen others from different floors. One was testing the door and others were speaking the details. Her watch began to vibrate, and without questioning the decision, she unclasped it, let it fall.

Annette could not believe herself. She crossed the street and began to run in earnest. She ran until she stopped and clutched her knees, bent over sweating. She moved slowly then, past a tiny bistro. She kept her face turned away from the people seated there.

She made her way, in bursts and gasping stops, all the way to the edge of the city, sat in a littered weeded stretch of underpass, took off her shoes. She thought of what a downfall might mean in these times and imagined sirens, someone coming to take her back to work, but no one came.

She pulled up headlines in her eye: *Lorem Ipsum*, each one stated, and under each headline, row on row of *dolor sit amet*.

CUBBY

Mother and child squat on the glossy plastic floor of a beige cube of a room. They have gotten out for a brisk walk, cleaned themselves and put on sunscreen, and dressed in clean beige jumpsuits. They have had their food and their morning bowel movements, and this time is their own. They have chosen this cubby for bonding and perhaps to nap before the mother goes to work and the child to lessons. They are resting in the flat-footed squat position that is so good for their vertebrae.

"Let's see Daddy," the child says.

"We're here for our downtime," the mother says and pauses to study the child's face. "Do you really want to see him? He's always confused when he comes, and you get so sad."

"Maybe not this time," the child says.

"Every time."

"Maybe this time he'll like it."

"I'll tell you what. Let's not bring him here. Let's go see him." When the child nods, the mother begins removing their jumpsuits, saying, "Remember, hold your breath while we go, close your eyes. I'll tap you on the shoulder when it's all finished."

She takes the child's right hand in her own, making a complex gesture in the air, and a few seconds later taps the child on the shoulder. They are squatting on a Persian-style rug in a large room. The wooden slat blinds are drawn, but the light angling in is intense midafternoon, midsummer light. The mother moves into a cross-legged pose and holds the child, stroking their back.

Where they live, every little child is called 'the child' and 'them' because they are granted the dignity to choose – or find – their own identities down to their names, their genders. The mother values this custom as she values all the other features of their home. She doesn't like to take the child traveling. Everything about it has always felt dangerous to her, the accidents that could happen in an unfamiliar place and her own shaky understanding of the process, not to mention the morality of the thing.

"You haven't ever seen this house, have you?" the mother says. The child shakes their head. "Everything looks busy and ugly to you, I bet."

"The air tastes bad," the child says. *Of course it does*, the mother thinks, *what with all the dust and the cat hair and the odd stuffed furniture harboring years of germs and odors.*

"First things first," the mother says, standing. They go into a smaller, darker room where the mother opens closet doors and surveys racks and shelves of clothing. She is much too light now to wear any of the clothes on the hangers. She boosts herself on a shelf to reach a stack of clothes she saved for if she ever got skinny again and chooses a pair of dark slim jeans and a plain black T-shirt.

"You'll have to be a girl today," she says, slipping another black T-shirt over the child's head and tying it around the waist with a white and black bandanna. The child is a girl, she is certain, but she believes in letting them make their own decisions.

"I like this," the child says.

"So we'll say 'she, her'," the mother says.

"I know. Where's Daddy?"

"He's at work right now. Who do you want to be, when he shows up?"

"I'll be me. Mink."

The mother sighs. "You're still thinking about that name, you said. Listen, we've gone back very early. The daddy you will meet, he's never met you before."

"This daddy never got upset?"

"Right, this daddy," and she holds the child's hands out at their sides and waves them up and down as though the child is still a baby. "He hasn't ever met you. He hasn't ever been to see us. But you can't be you. Understand?"

She isn't sure how the child will take it, but the child smiles. Their eyes are round. "We'll say you found me."

"He wouldn't believe that, honey," she says. She strokes their head, *her* head. She's always thought about pulling the silky hair into short pigtails and is doing it now. The child protests because it feels so weird, but when the mother walks her to the mirror, she is pleased.

"I'm going to say you're a cousin and call you Sara and, no, not Mink. Because he will not believe my cousin named her kid Mink. Just be quiet and listen, and it will all be OK." She has never imagined saying something like 'children should be seen and not heard', but that is in fact what she is saying.

They wait. The child is examining items from the shelves in the living room, the odd assortment of books and blown-glass animals and skulls that Keith collects, all covered with dust and with hair. The cats are sitting beside the child and pawing at her from time to time. They are already friends.

The mother is trying to tidy the kitchen enough to cook. On the wall calendar, the pink highlighter line runs through the week with the word 'Austin!' above it because she is gone to a seminar. This also means that her computer and tablet and phone are gone, so there is no way to call Keith and let him know she'll be home after all. She's just begun to feel disgusted with herself for being willing to ruin this Keith's life, for how will he and the she who returns from Austin ever trust each other again? He'll be shot off into darkness more surely, more permanently than any of the Keiths that she and the child have summoned to their cubbies.

"No, listen," she says, standing in the doorway to the living room. "We're going to tell him the truth."

★   ★   ★

When Keith comes home, the child is shut in the office. The mother rushes to him, hugging and kissing him. "My flight was canceled," she says. He does not hesitate; he kisses back. And the exchange that follows is magically brief.

"You trust me, you do," she says. She is lifting the back of her T-shirt. "Here is my birthmark, here is my mole, my tattoos." She tells him a few of the memories they have shared that no one else should know. "Now," she says, facing him, "here is my C-section scar, here are my abs, look at the age spots starting on my hands. Keith, look at my face."

Keith stiffens against the front door and then softens, leans forward. "My God," he says.

"I came back to see you. You understand?"

"You're saying your flight didn't get canceled," he says. His voice is strong and even. "You're saying you are at the seminar right now and that later, you decide to travel back to see me." That quick, he has it.

"You've heard of other travelers, then, maybe in the news?" she says.

"Some," he says. "And I *have* seen movies." She is happy to see he looks curious, unafraid.

And then she moves him into the office where the little girl is sitting, ankles crossed, on a little accent chair. She is awkward because the position is new to her, but she looks lovely.

"This is your baby," she says.

For the first time, he looks at the child the way the child has always wished he would.

★　★　★

Dinner begins with browned ground beef. She finds thick-cut pepper bacon in the fridge and uses kitchen shears to cut strips of it into the pan. She browns the meat some more but doesn't drain it before adding the tomato paste, grated parmesan, herbs, and salt. She broils mozzarella on top of garlic toast and boils the spaghetti.

Keith is sitting at the kitchen table listening as the child expounds on all the things she has always wanted to tell her daddy. She stands while she talks, inching closer to him until they are shoulder to shoulder and leaning their heads together. He tells her to go wash her hands for dinner. When she is out of the room, he says, "You look good."

"I've been eating none of my own cooking," she says.

"How many years?" he asks.

"How old am I now?"

"Twenty-five."

"Almost fifteen years."

"No," he says. "How many years left for me?"

The child comes back into the room, and he returns to the conversation, asking her age and why she's chosen Mink for a name. He can get a rough answer to his previous question from her age and nods when the mother looks at him again.

Bringing the dishes to the table, the mother says, "The world is unimaginably beautiful. It's like if everyone's utopian ideals all of a sudden realized themselves. You'd be so proud to see it, I think."

"What's your house like?" Keith asks the child. He is filling his plate.

"We don't live in houses," the child says.

"We live in a *new* city," the mother says.

"What does that mean?"

"We spend most of our time in public spaces – beautiful parks and libraries, public baths and gyms, playgrounds, sports arenas, farms."

"We milk the goats and make the yogurt," the child says.

"And then we go into a cubby when we need to rest," says the mother.

"You have a cubby, then."

"No, I suppose they're like those Japanese business hotels, you know? We just find one convenient to where we are."

"Where do you keep your things?"

"We don't keep things," the child says. She is taking her first bite of spaghetti. Her smile is broad and sauce lines her lips. She says, "This is so good!"

★   ★   ★

After the dinner and the clearing of the table, Keith asks what they would like to do.

"There's nothing of interest to us here apart from you," the mother says.

And so they sit on the living room floor for the few hours until bed. He asks them more about their lives, but the child is able to turn every question back to his life. She wants to know about his childhood, his parents, what he read and what he did for fun. The child moves her head into his lap and is soon asleep. He lifts her to his chest as he rises and takes her to the bedroom. He lays her in the center of the bed.

When he returns to the living room, the mother has music playing at low volume and is swaying to it, there on the floor.

"Whatever you need to travel, you have it right on your body," he says.

"In, not on. But no questions about that, please. I'm sure I understand as much about that as you understand how your phone works."

"Fifteen years isn't enough for all the changes you described," he says. She nods.

"So you're living sometime further on."

"Further, farther? Anyway, yes. We were brought ahead. We were lucky."

He settles back down on the floor before her. "Why did you come back?" he asks.

"To visit," she says.

"I feel like it has to be more than that. Like, can I stop it happening? No? Can you?"

The mother grimaces and then nods to herself. "I feel like I need to be careful what I say."

He moves to sit beside her and takes one of her hands in his. "Earlier you said, 'You trust me'. I do. Don't you trust me? Isn't there something we can do so that I get to stay with you?"

She says, "You know, when we got here, my first thought was just to try to pass myself off as her. I was going to say I couldn't do the seminar because I had to take care of my cousin's kid. I was going to lie and stay the week and let you sort your life out after I was gone. Go crazy, get divorced, whatever."

"I'm still going to have to sort it out," he says. His eyes are starting to tear.

"You have to see that where we come from, we're pretty careless with other people," she says. "I'm telling you about this perfect place, no private property, no apparent crime, the kiddos all get treated like they deserve. So you have to know there must be a catch, right?"

"The catch is you go somewhere else to do your damage."

"Pretty much. You see people show up with years on them, you don't ask. Or sometimes we bring people to us."

"Why have you never brought me?" he asks.

"We have."

It is a few minutes before he speaks again. He moves his hand away from hers. "So that means I'm not really your Keith," he says. "If I were, you wouldn't risk coming here now."

Her expression is hard. "You're right about that. So that means I don't know how you die, or if you do. Maybe you don't."

"What should I do?" he asks.

"Go in there and cuddle with her tonight, and then in the morning I'll cook a big breakfast and we'll say goodbye. This has been really nice, don't you think? As nice as it could be."

He stands, hesitates. "You're not coming to bed?"

"I haven't slept in a bed like that in ages," she says. "I'll be good out here."

As she falls asleep, she wonders if this will be enough to quell the child's nostalgia, or if she will go back to asking for him every time they set foot in a cubby. The question bleeds into dreams in which the two of them resurrect Keith many times and he is screaming again, begging to stay with them. They are reasoning with him about the regulations, how the mother's travel was meant for one and they'd gotten two instead with the baby unknown at that time, and how she would never be allowed to bring over another one. In the dreams they keep taking him, always younger, until they are taking him as a baby only for a minute or two and letting him go.

★　　★　　★

When the mother awakens, all of the windows have been opened to capture early morning air, and she is cold on the floor with no blanket. She can't find Keith or the child, not in the bedroom, out on the porch, or in the yard. She stands in the kitchen thinking about whether to make breakfast. They could be out getting breakfast or they could be out for a walk. She checks the garage, and while her car is there, Keith's is gone.

Breakfast time goes; lunchtime comes. She can't think of how to call Keith, for his number is no longer in her memory and is not written down anywhere in the house. The wonders of technology in her eye and in her fingertips can't call up this lost knowledge.

She gathers money from its hiding place and goes back to the garage. Standing in the dark beside the door to her car is a lean adolescent figure, nude. They have their hand over their groin. "Go home," they say.

She moves quickly toward them, and they make a gesture and are gone.

She travels as far as she can with the money, to Keith's parents' house, his friends' houses and his work and all the places she can think of where he once lived or told her he would like to go. She makes these people call Keith, but he never answers. Sometimes she tells them the truth, and sometimes she lies, but either way she leaves a trail of bewilderment. When she meets herself, returned from Austin to an empty house, she makes a humiliating scene, is almost arrested.

The figure appears from time to time, always in the dark. Their voice is husky. They say nothing more than "Go home" and then they leave.

She finally takes a job pumping gas beside a highway in Oregon because she thinks there is a chance that Keith and the child might pass through, but they never do. She finds herself sleeping on the floor in a strip motel. Very late one night she awakens to see a figure sitting cross-legged on the bed. Pinkish light from the motel sign outlines, and now they are older and even leaner than before, with long dark hair falling all the way to the bedcover.

"Please don't leave this time," the mother says.

"Go home," they say.

"I can't tell if it's you. How do you keep coming back to the same place?"

"My name is Mink. You don't need to worry about me."

"I can't go home. I'm afraid I won't be able to get back here again," the mother cries.

"You never get back," Mink says.

Time passes before she takes the advice. She cannot say how many months, but not a year, and then she makes the gesture that places her back on the warm smooth floor of the cubby. She takes the smaller jumpsuit and tries to smell something of the child in it, but its only scent is sunscreen. She puts on her own jumpsuit, and then there is nothing to do but file the report and go back to her routine of bathing and exercise and work. The public spaces all look flat and sterile to her. Her work is teaching lessons to little children who make her cry now, every day, and so she sees her advisor and asks for a different role.

Now she is tending tomato plants. They cover her with a fragrant substance she learns is called secretory and glandular trichomes. She bathes often, goes back often to the same cubby, and waits. When they take her, she feels she has been tensing for the trip.

The space they bring her to is a tiny clearing in a deep jungle with the sound of waterfalls beyond. The green is intense with sun glowing through thick foliage. Mink is a grown woman, deeply tanned and fleshy, with long dark hair falling to her thighs. A beautiful young man stands with them, holding a tiny baby. He hands the baby to Keith, who is bearded and looks very old. They all wear sarongs of silk and metallic thread in varied intricate patterns and brilliant jewel-tone colors. The baby is swaddled in this same sumptuous fabric.

"So good to see you," Keith says.

"How have you been?" asks Mink.

The mother cannot control herself. She weeps and lunges forward. The young man excuses himself and walks down toward the water's edge where other people seem to be having a party.

"We only want to give you a chance to meet your grandson," Mink says. Her voice is deep. "If you can't relax, we'll have to send you away again. Can you relax?"

The mother sits and concentrates on breathing deeply. They bring the baby to sit with her. He is so new, so tiny she cannot relate to him or bond, but she is looking at Mink and at Keith as she strokes his back. She tries to seem serene. "This is nice," she says. "I could stay here."

The young man comes in to take the baby and wanders away again.

"It's just a visit," Keith says. He takes one of her hands, and Mink takes the other.

"It *is* nice," Mink says. "We can visit for a while if you like."

The mother is watching the people in the distance now. The young man is walking slowly toward an old woman who is round as a balloon and laughing, wearing the mother's own face.

Keith wanders away toward this woman and they disappear from view. Mink leans in and holds her mother. "Please don't blame him. I was the one who wanted to stay. We can't keep you here, so sorry, but I can give you something." She whispers in her mother's ear for a long time, and then they rock back away from each other and talk more casually.

When the mother makes the gesture, she closes her eyes and opens them not to the beige cubby but to the dark living room and the carpet, the midafternoon midsummer light, the cat hair and the dust but a different marked-out week on the calendar, this time a conference in Boise. The clothes in the closet are even larger than the last time she was here. Too exhausted to look for something suitable, she pulls on a tent of a dress and settles on the couch. The cats come to her. This is the week when she received the offer and never returned to this house. She was already pregnant but so early she did not know it. Only six or seven years ago now. Will he notice the age on her? She doesn't think so. But the leanness and the scar are more than she can explain without at least a little truth. She considers how much to tell him. She thinks she will tell all, but she won't know that for sure until the words are out of her.

FABLES OF THE FUTURE

You might have found one of The Seer's books in a stack of fancy hardcovers they used to have by the registers at big bookstores. *Fables of the Future* read as a science fiction book, though a decidedly strange one. Below the title, three collegial-looking figures walked hand in hand. Only the center one was human. The one on the right was a big, jaunty barrel-chested robot not unlike the Tin Woodsman. The green one on the left, was it supposed to be an alien, a ghost, maybe a deer or a goat with its suggestion of horns? Certainly aliens, talking animals, and ghosts were all represented in these stories, which read much like *Aesop's Fables*. Some even shared morals with Aesop such as 'United we stand, divided we fall', while others bore more futuristic messages: 'Never let a machine become your governor', 'A robot's first loyalty is to itself'.

Fables was my favorite work of the medium and prophet we knew as The Seer. My parents and I had collected at least two copies of every one of The Seer's books: *Fables, An Account of My Time at the Cabin, The Yellow Backpack, One Out of Many,* and all the rest.

My parents were devout. I suppose I was too as a child. Our studies were always a secret. To the uninitiated, The Seer was only a writer – a famous one, a household name, but just an ordinary human for all of that. Some may have wondered what, exactly, was she famous *for*. You couldn't quite say she was a science fiction writer, a mystery writer, or whatnot. Her books were all different, as though written by different hands, and of course that was the thing: she was channeling others. All the time, at every moment, she was hearing thousands of voices telling their stories. She saw through the eyes of those living, those dead, and those yet to be born.

We averted our eyes if she was interviewed on television and avoided speaking her name. We spoke carefully, even at home. Maybe we thought the house was bugged. More likely, we thought The Seer eavesdropped, that we were among the thousands of voices she heard.

My earliest bedtime stories were of The Seer hearing her daughter's call from a hundred miles away, a time she found she could scent like a bloodhound, a time her eyes lit up in darkness like a cat's. I've forgotten what The Seer needed to hear and see so clearly, but I always kept the image of her cat's eyes.

Well, I *saw* those eyes myself, later. That's why I remember them.

★   ★   ★

My parents cheated before the split, Mom with an initiate and Dad with a secular person. These new spouses were kind, but instead of burrowing into one of the new families, I focused outward. I became popular at school.

At Dad's, if he got me alone, he might make some veiled reference to The Seer, but it was mostly just nostalgia.

Mom's new house was only a place for me to rush through after school. The new family, bent over books, would look up and smile and call "Bye!" All the new little stepsiblings admired me. I have no idea why.

Out, then. Mall trips and then basement parties, a first kiss, a dance. Wilder nights, too, but still I was seen as a good kid. Good looking, upstanding, smart like all my friends. It was my little blip of time when I had no one to care for and didn't need care *from* anyone, either. I like to think I made the most of it.

On my seventeenth birthday, Mom's blueberry-colored Subaru became mine with no strings or expectations. Mom needed something bigger for all the stepsiblings. The Subaru still had the 'My kid is an honors student' sticker on it, which seemed to mean I'd never be pulled over.

That car changed my life. I kept a sleeping bag, a backpack full of clothes, and a stock of bottled water and snacks. I'd tell my friends I had an obligation with my parents, tell my parents I was staying at a friend's, and then I'd park out by the reservoir in perfect solitude and peace. I could escape for three days in a row, walking along the river, sleeping, and just being alone.

I loved the car for allowing this freedom. Then of course, there was that other love.

We were seniors, hardly tasked with much, but I still saw my friends in the cafeteria two or three times a week. One of the friends became something more. It was the change in me that sparked it – the wondering what was wrong, why I didn't want in on the endless parties anymore. This friend looked at me with a concerned kind of love and also like I had gotten some enlightenment. That feeling of admiration – I hadn't even known I'd been missing it, and so then there was love.

We'd go out camping, only now everyone knew where we were. We had hours of prep to stock the cooler and get everything in order. It was unlike the old times alone – not less pleasurable, only different.

Sometimes I think my life was charmed, that everything was pure pleasure from beginning to end.

Have I come to the end? It's not at all clear.

In the tent at night, I'd open my mouth to say, "Have you read *Fables of the Future*? Or anything by—?" But I'd never uttered The Seer's name to a nonbeliever.

★   ★   ★

We didn't always have phone service where we went. Only that one day did it matter.

We'd been camping all weekend. I felt dizzy, so I sat in the passenger seat. The windows fogged. I remember the great green forest flashing past and the feeling of goosebumps rising, then from the glovebox: ding, ding, ding, and the burst of psychedelic sound that was my ringtone.

I didn't reach for the phone right away. Maybe I already knew.

The messages possibly held codes I couldn't see. One thing was clear: I had to come home. I'd missed a flight but could just catch another.

I was vague with my love, which made us quiet. We headed straight to Mom's.

I recalled a baptism scene from one of The Seer's books. A woman comes from a locker into a vaulted, marble-tiled space where people kneel around a low pool...I couldn't recall what happened there, only the scene.

I suppose I was in shock.

The whole new family and Dad were there when we arrived. Panicked, smiling, Mom took my love to the door and said she'd explain later, "—but just go home. Just take the car. We'll call when we need it again."

My love stood silhouetted in the open door.

I nodded in that direction. "It's all right," I said. "I forgot we had this trip. It's a surprise."

"Surprise for who?" said my love.

"Please, just – later," I said.

Was there a kiss? Probably there was, probably frantic questions and assurances, and then we piled into Mom's new SUV. Mom and Dad sat on either side of me in the far back. It seemed that we all were shaking, our talking confused.

Some kind of baptism was all I could think. There was that strange baptism in *One Out of Many*. The woman lay back in that pool, decades in the future. The people...droned. I don't know that it was prayer. It echoed in the vaulted space. They poured in the powders, and her skin began to sizzle and dissolve.

Was that what would happen to me? Did Mom or Dad have that book on hand?

They didn't have it. They didn't know what to tell me. There had been a call and a hotel reservation, nothing more.

But my little family, our little trio, was reunited in the backseat, and *that* was a pleasure. Everything was a pleasure.

Mom and Dad stayed by my side until they couldn't. In the SUV, on the plane, on the end of a hotel bed we held hands, whispered. A phone call came and then a tap at the door. A driver to take me to the event.

"Can you say what the event is?" I said, gesturing to my plain black clothes.

"You are more than appropriately attired," he said.

My parents fell on me with hugs and kisses, messages, advice, and then it all moved so quickly. I was both numb and tingling.

It went like this:

A ride up a long hill and into a gated estate.

Coffee and petit fours with The Seer and a dozen others my age in a close, warm room. They called it coffee hour though it lasted no more than ten minutes. Some part of my mind received instructions from The Seer. I wondered, after: Were we hypnotized?

A back exit to a large patio where more young people lingered. After ten minutes, another dozen joined us. They must have been the last group of the day because people in plain blue uniforms joined us then.

The slow, silent walk off the patio and through manicured gardens behind the mansion. Uniformed people led us across a wooden bridge and into a cold concrete building. I think it was a building, but it might have been a sort of mine or tunnel in the earth; it hardly matters.

(I ought to say *is*, not *was* a building or a tunnel. I am still here now.)

Things hung from the ceiling. I had no words for them. Imagine the shape of a water balloon in the flat green of a forest-service vehicle. They were about seven feet long, two and a half feet wide.

The uniformed staff circled behind us and helped people up into the balloon things. One grasped my hips and lifted me. I steadied myself by holding on to the thing's sides, which squished in my hand like memory foam. Once inside, I was held as in a vertical hammock.

I was to remove my clothes and pass them out. I was to check the attachments by running my finger around the seals. These instructions had been given earlier without passing through my conscious mind, it seemed.

A lap-desk was lowered. It held a tablet and nothing else. I was encased in the thing, not by means of a zipper but something like a zipper.

Ever to come out? I didn't know.

I turned on the tablet, as instructed. It was too dark to see. The spinning wheel came up, and soon I was connected to my parents, who still sat on the edge of the hotel bed, leaning toward the screen.

There was a script we had practiced at the coffee hour. I spoke it well:

I have received enlightenment from The Seer. Grateful for your guardianship, I am in the hands of another. Ask me no questions. I love you. I loved my life.

When I'd said it all, the connection broke and the tablet powered off. The afterimage of Mom and Dad lingered before my streaming eyes.

Heartsick, I tried to remember more from the coffee hour. It seemed a thousand years since I sat in the firelit room beside The Seer with the dozen others all leaning in listening to her whisper. I had nothing more. Like a dream.

All that had lingered was the script and now it too fled. I wiped my eyes and concentrated on recalling The Seer. I'd been two feet from her and smelled the cherry almond cake on her breath. Hadn't I seen her face?

No, flashlight beams had shone from her eyes. She was a shapeless thing behind spotlight eyes.

What had she said?

It was useless. The foam of the balloon thing dampened against my skin. I felt this thing encasing me was somehow vegetable. A sickly smell came like grass clippings left out to mold.

Suspended in the dark, I had just a shallow bubble of space from my head to my chest. I moved the toggle on the tablet many times, but nothing sparked. Out of boredom, I ran my hands over the smooth foam in front. It seemed no zipper-like gash could ever have been there. I called to the others, who never answered. I cried, lamented my love cut off in its first bloom.

This doubt lasted only an hour.

I'd never been much afraid of the dark or of being alone. It seemed that every night of my life I'd slept well and woken with a full bladder, and that happened my first night in the cocoon as well.

I'd come to think of it as a cocoon, or a pod.

It was difficult to let go that first time. I had to reach down and check the urinal seal first and then test it. Such relief to know that it held. Each time I woke from dreams, it seemed there was less of the desk and a shallower space before me. The surface, now inches from my face, had taken on a veined texture. It felt wet.

I began holding the tablet to my chest and crossing my hands over it because there was no longer the room to extend my arms.

Was the foam porous enough that air got through? I thought it likelier that the thing was taking in my carbon dioxide and giving back oxygen. The smell of it shifted but always was plantlike.

And food, drink? At first it was a mystery. No tube reached down my throat; no needles pierced me. Waking some immeasurable time after that first waking, I felt damp foam withdraw from my throat. It was reaching inside when I slept, feeding and hydrating me.

I was not sure whether my feet still existed or not. The tablet was motionless in hands pressed tight against my chest now. I could still reach out my tongue without touching foam. My nose too seemed clear, but there was no space around any other part, including eyes and ears, which made it hard to say those parts were still there.

Sometimes I thought I was made of the vegetable foam, that I'd subsumed the tablet. It was inside me now, running me. It was my heart.

Fear rushed in and receded in slow waves. What was I at all?

I imagined the space to hold the tablet out before me. In my mind's eye, I toggled the switch and a dim light came. I swiped to see a single app: an e-book reader. A list of The Seer's titles appeared.

It seemed that more space *had* opened around my chest. I breathed deeply – how long since I'd done that? – and brought up *Fables of the Future*. In my mind, before my eyes – it didn't matter. It was the same.

And so I was lost in the stories. 'An Alien Today is a Friend Tomorrow', 'Never Cry Ant-Spinner', and all the rest. Nothing I read explained this new world, but it didn't matter. It was pure pleasure just to lose myself.

I opened *One Out of Many*, which I'd never connected with, zoning out while my parents read it aloud. It told of a woman's initiation into a hive mind she'd always been destined to join. The story, as I re-read it now, was surprisingly concrete and visceral, tracking the woman through her coming-of-age and into the initiation center and baptism.

After the baptism, she'd been reduced to her essence, a web of nerve tissue which was threaded into a larger web. The story became something mythical after that. People weren't people anymore. Millions were woven together into something new in the rough shape of a human. It squatted deeply and pushed off into space.

Suddenly a chat icon appeared at the bottom of the screen. I imagined touching it. My hands were still pressed to my chest, the foam still so close I could not open my eyes, but it felt very real.

"How's everyone? Made it through?" said the message. A keyboard appeared on the bottom half of the screen.

"Who is this?" I typed.

One is typing.... It said. That message went away after a moment.

"All made it," came another message. I felt it, too. In their other pods, others were connecting. We did not need the messages. Sending them was only a kind of ritual.

"So, the next phase begins," one wrote.

"Buckle in," wrote another.

The foam tightened. I'd felt no pressure, and now I was squeezed. The slow pulse went on forever, up and down my body. At my temples, sharp pressure – pain for an instant and then numbness just like at the dentist.

All was black, and then I glimpsed something like a three-dimensional blueprint, a space drawn in white chalk. A vast library of many levels – thousands of floors, nothing but bookcases and ladders.

All was drawn in chalk on a dark ground, and then it began to fill in. It began to be more real. The spines closest to me were coming in, red and blue and aqua, and then it was gone.

★   ★   ★

I woke into a small warm room with a taste of cherry almond in my mouth. I stretched old tired legs and stood slowly. From the door, a uniformed servant said, "Oh, you *are* awake. Can we discuss—"

"I need to write," I said, shoving past him down a wood-paneled hall. Those weren't my words.

I entered a fine library. A desk at the far end was well lit by a high diamond-paned window. I struggled to reach it, just as slow as if I waded through water.

A laptop was open to a blank document. I positioned my fingers on the keys. The Seer positioned her fingers on the keys. We waited.

"Don't you have a story for me, little one?" she said. "I know you're here."

The blue car came to mind. She wrote of how it was to sit with the back hatch open, watching the sun glance off the reservoir. She wrote of how it felt to be in love and hold hands on a hike.

All I did was call up images, flavors, smells. My Mom and Dad close beside me helping me sound out words. Pushing up out of a sunroof to sing and howl with friends.

She typed more quickly than I ever could have imagined. Pages filled in an endless wall of text with no punctuation, no paragraph breaks. The window was a mirror by the time she looked up. I caught her face in it.

"Bye, now," she said to her old, tired reflection. We waited.

She sighed, picked up a landline phone.

"Yes?" said a voice.

"I need you to check on one-thirty-four," she said. "There's something wrong. It's all vague, and they won't leave me."

"Vague?" they said.

She made a dismissive gesture at the laptop screen. "Useless. Just... biography."

After she hung up, she leaned forward and rubbed her temples. In that moment I grasped the whole long process of her rise, the first messages she received, her recruitment of subjects, all the day-to-day trouble of this operation, all the troubles of writing and publishing, the weakness of her body, the worries about her age and whether any of this all would ever come to something greater.

The others in their pods were going further, maybe into the future or onto other planes. They were bringing back little snatches of insight, she saw and tried to synthesize. The Seer was doing the same as all her followers, trying to *read*, only what she was reading was us. Not us, exactly – something we could access. I couldn't ask her what. I tried.

It was only a moment, and then the foam pulsed around me again. People with headlamps peered in through a gash in my pod. I closed my eyes and reached up to cover them, so violent was the light. Briny water gushed out; the people reached in. Black rain slickers and gloves that ran along my head and body plucking things out of me, loosening seals.

The air felt full of needles and pins. I lay between blankets while people leaned into the pod. The Seer herself had come in slippers and a long, quilted robe. I looked up into her exhausted face.

"We can fix this," one of the workers said.

"Soon?" she said.

"Ten minutes."

She squatted down. It hurt to do that. I felt as much as saw it.

She stroked my wet hair. "You've tried. You can go home now if you like. Would that be nice?"

"Did I break it?" I said.

"You didn't do anything wrong," she said.

The blueberry car and my parents, my love, my little stepsiblings and all my friends crossed my mind. Nothing but biography.

I was not going home. I was going to try again.

SUBSTANCE

The little queen came for me all gushing, telling how she had ruminated too long on a peacock feather, and so she'd had to refurnish her chamber in inky dark with glimmers of gold and teal. We came into the chamber, I saw the decorating was not too literal, and I *inwardly* commended her on her taste. (I assure you that I wouldn't dream of giving utterance to a judgment such as this.)

As you proceed through my tale, know that I was at this time fulfilling my role as butler, as far as our circumstances permitted. I was no longer anything more to her than an old serving-runt, loving and faithful though still somewhat grotesque to the eye. My mouth was not the worst of it.

And yet the little queen engaged with me as she would a beloved one. She directed my attention to her chamber's floor all newly paved with thousands of abalone shells. She was barefoot, her little toenails and fingernails painted in sparkling aqua-green. We admired the new statues and the darkly shimmering velvet drapes, the reproduction of Ingres' *Le Grande Odalisque* over an ornately carved mantel.

This painting featured a nude human or semi-human lady holding a fan made of peacock feathers, in a room not unlike the queen's chamber. Her back turned, the lady cranes her beautiful face toward the viewer. To look at that painting made me blush. The sheer expanse of her nudity, the boldness of the allusion to a serpent's form, all of this could not but remind me of what my queen concealed under her clothing. Forgive me.

All the time she spoke to me, her eyes sparkled. I was captivated. I wanted to say something about the way she had made herself over along with the room but could not quite work out the etiquette. Her dress was loose; I mentioned something about the seamstresses.

"Reducing a little more, I'm afraid," she said. She looked down shyly. I cringed at my misstep, turned my eyes toward the mantel.

I saw it now: the carvings, at first seeming vines, were at a closer look distinguishable as coiling knots of serpents. Worms, in fact.

The queen, no larger than a child, took a seat on her worn russet-colored sofa, which had not been changed in the redecorating. It restrained what might otherwise have seemed overdone. I commended her taste again, inwardly.

I could not think for long about her reducing without wanting to weep, and so I did not think of it. I 'let it flow through me and into the substance', as they would say in the place from which we come, if they spoke. Perhaps you have a different way of putting it, such as 'in one hole and out the other'. But I digress. Here we were, both seated on the sofa, and she leaned toward me. I fought to control my agitation. I trembled, surely.

I always trembled in her presence.

She reached to brush my elbow. You might think this an inappropriate gesture, but I assure you it was not intended as anything other than a dry touch.

"This is the room in which I intend to mature," she said, looking not at me but at the ring that was now becoming so loose on her finger. She ran her finger along the base of its large apple-red stone. "I will not be redecorating again. I will not be doing much, on this scale." Again, she blushed, looking down.

She looked up then. With our eyes, we acknowledged that we were living out the last days of our time together. I wished to be able to beg her to stay, but I had no reason to give her, not then. Her eyes were so beautiful, all green with tree forms in honey gold branching from the center. I took the time to look at her as fully as she would permit. Too soon, she excused me, and I went to sit in my chamber to examine my memories of long before when we were closer.

On that same sofa some time earlier, in the days when her chamber was a vast and crumbling attic, she had spoken of Earth: "Perhaps the romance of it is just what draws me there, and then once there, I will make the new place just like home. Perhaps that is what the new queen always does."

"Have you ever conferred with your mother – I mean about your feelings?" I asked.

The queen rolled her eyes.

I know that I render her as a child. She wasn't that, whatever else. Better to see her as a scholar, a master impersonator of children, than see her as a child herself.

There in the attic when I was her equal, the only time, she said she wished it were not quite so easy to guess what I was thinking. "Would *you* want to waste these eggs?" she said, and she looked at me so boldly. And now I realize that I must reveal more than I would prefer. I must tell about our background, or the rest of this will not cohere for you.

★   ★   ★

Where we originate, the outside never falls out before us. Air never comes between us. That is the biggest difference between how our people live and how other people seem to live. Where we live, we are always right up against someone or something else, well-lubricated with what I suppose you would call mucus. Most of us do not know what it means to live dry, and those who have wrapped their minds around the concept find it terrifying.

We can live in any form we like. We choose to live in a long and sightless form approaching that which, on Earth, is called an earthworm. By day we slide our bodies over and around one another so that we are always in contact. We move in a circle, for that is what most pleases us. At night, we widen the circle so that we can take in more of the substance of our planet. On Earth, the term for this material is dirt, soil, earth. Here, I will call it only 'substance.'

We do have a vague overarching goal, which is to take in as much nourishment as possible so as to increase the girth of our people. This goal is analogous to the goals of human beauty queens: end hunger, secure world peace.

On our planet, we think we are but one of many like populations. Our big queen must have come from a knot of others, but she has kept her history to herself. In any case, others like us live where they live, and we live where we live, and we do not think of them. It may be that they live exactly as we do, or it may be that they live as we used to live generations ago. We do not care. That's an important thing to know about us: we prefer not to think. We prefer to writhe in a circle, devouring substance with our fore-holes and passing it out again, only slightly altered, through our aft-holes. From far above, if viewed for a day, we look like a puckering and widening pink mass. So be it.

In a drop of water on our planet may be other galaxies full of other planets, none of them presumably interesting, but who can be certain? Earth was discovered by accident, and others might be found.

★   ★   ★

How was Earth found? One night when the circle widened, the little queen, who was then in her original form, found that a stone had lodged itself in her forehead. I love this story. I think of a pearl forming on Earth, a little frustrating speck of substance building in layers to become the precious symbol of purity.

The stone lodged in the little queen was, I thought, the same red stone she wore in a ring on her thickest finger much later.

When the stone lodged in what she now calls her forehead but was then just side (for are we anything but the featureless sides and the holes?), she felt a pain so intense that she wanted to cry. I never asked how, when she did not have eyes to make tears or a proper mouth to build a wail, she could have cried or had the thought to cry.

This is part of my training, to repress such questions.

She wanted to cry, and yet she felt honored, or more correctly, as she said later, *chosen*. She felt it had been such a singular occurrence, all the substance one encountered being so smooth and homogeneous these days, to collide with a sharp particle. Had I ever done that? She started to ask this but caught herself quickly. Had anyone done that, ever? And no, I agreed I had never heard of such a thing as collision with a sharp particle. One might come upon some substance a little *firmer* than usual (a runt, of course) but nothing hard, certainly nothing sharp.

The sharp edge of the stone began a wound. A certain spot on the outside of the wound began an eye. That is all I can tell you about the eye: it began; we think the wound began it. Certainly, no one ever questioned that an eye could begin. The physical structure of an eye made perfect sense to us, and any one of us might have begun an eye, but to what purpose?

We excel at spatial reckoning. When we slid over or under the little queen, we sensed the structure of the wound and the stone that still adhered to it, which, sorry to say, repulsed us ever so slightly and kept us from seeking her touch. Would that we had come closer to her instead.

We distanced ourselves because we still hoped that the eye was part of a phase from which she would soon tunnel – an innocent rebellion. Certainly, it was difficult to become a queen, and no one begrudged her time to come to terms with her life's circle, which, for all our efforts, was destined to be in some ways different from our lives' circles.

She kept the eye closed to keep it from filling with substance, so it was hardly doing her any good. "What do you want with optics? Shed it off," her mother told her just once. The big queen was the only one of us who would venture an opinion on what the little queen ought or ought not do.

I should add that the big queen did not literally say, "Shed it off." She communicated it in the chemistry of her mucus.

The little queen pretended not to have taken in the message from her mother, and soon we felt new changes in the wound. Four little fingertips pushed out from its edge to grow into fingers. A narrow palm began to rise. A little thumb stubbed out.

Once she had a wrist capable of bending, our hopes for a neutral outcome died. The hand reached up and shielded her eye, which she opened for the first time. At first it saw nothing, but when day came and she could feel the warmth above, she writhed to the outer edge of bodies where, finally, light pierced the skin. Her first sight was the red glow of blood through her beautiful new hand. Again, she said to me later, she wanted to cry, and now she did cry. She saw the droplets forming on her lashes. She already longed to have a mouth.

The little queen's body was shrinking, our people's eggs within it. Because the big queen was aging and already bearing the first runts by this time, the little queen's reduction alarmed us. If the new generations would be nothing but faltering runts, how would our people survive?

Later the little queen would tell me that on Earth, people once believed that a woman's ovaries would desiccate if she harbored the wrong type of thought and that this was exactly as ridiculous as our people's beliefs. We were both so small by then that the virile cell from a drone would have taken us in a fight. I suppressed a smile to think of it, the man-size spermatozoon knocking at our chamber door. There was no question by then that her eggs and the rest of her had shrunken to the point of irrelevance.

This was another of the many thoughts I dared not voice.

★　　★　　★

There are but three estates among our people, if you do not number the runts. There are queens, and as I have disclosed, we had two at the time. There are drones, numbers unknown, and there are the rest. Generations of drones die never revealing their difference. I suspect they never know their difference until The Call comes. As for the big queen, that lady is so modest of her status that one would never know her difference unless one were to closely follow her aft-end to feel the new babies falling out into substance. In fact, none would think to follow. We prefer to live as equals as much as circumstances allow.

The little queen once told me that the big queen was no different from a vessel factory except that she spat out babies instead of household goods. This felt obscene at the time, and if I am honest, it still stings. I have seen a vessel factory. One would not want to speak lightly about the suffering of such a creature.

⋆ ⋆ ⋆

The little queen, of course, grew weary of looking at nothing but dim light through her pretty hand, so she closed the eye and reached the hand far back to pluck the stone from the flesh. She brought the stone to her eye and circled back up to the light, and there at last she saw something more. She now saw the intense red of the stone bathed in the more golden red from the hand. The colors delighted her, the angles of the stone, the lines between it and her fingers: all new and all lovely. The little queen did not initially feel that she could continue to lie at the top of the bodies in the light. She had to tunnel down; she had a duty to be congenial. She could see only in flashes as she caught and then relinquished the outer edge. To read the stone in these circumstances was to be a child riding in the backseat of a vehicle on earth, a child trying to read snatches of a book as the vehicle speeds between streetlights. Frustration built as she lived for glimpses, as she spent most of her time in the moments between the glimpses.

After much rumination, she decided to move to the top and be still, allowing the bodies to undulate beneath her. She gazed long. Unsated, she parted her fingers, and that was when she saw the tiny imperfection in the stone, and that was the end of pretending she was still one of us. The light was so bright, she told me later, so bright that nothing was hidden. I still cannot imagine. My own eyes have never been exposed to the light but through a film of tissue, darkly. My eyes have never improved to see at such a scale.

The little queen began to study the universe hidden in the occlusion in the stone. When her eye improved so that she could see what was happening on its planets, the little queen could think of nothing else. She first learned the colors of the landscapes and seascapes of them all, and then on Earth she started to see the pyramids and walls and buildings, the great machines, the masses of people, and finally the individual people whose forms she found so beautiful, each of them a little muse to her. The eye, she said, improved so that it could see through the spaces between atoms. Its ingenious focus let her choose what scale to see.

When her eye improved so that she could look over anyone's shoulder who was reading on the planet, she read their stories. She read the histories as well as the poetics. She learned how the pyramids were made. She watched their televisions, too, when those began. She learned early to read their lips, and their words echoed through her mind in all the languages of Earth.

I later learned the word 'earworm' and how well that word fit! Just as a song replays in one's mind, the stories of Earth replayed over and over for her. Her body rocked at the top with bodies writhing under and never over her. She tunneled for her sustenance only in the night. Again, we told ourselves that this was the understandable behavior of any tourist and that, given time, she would return to us.

She still communicated freely at that time, entreating all to start eyes and share in the viewing. She waxed on about how dry it was on Earth, how separated everything was. Over and over, she told us of the colors. Still young, she harbored fantastical notions. She had been told but could not understand why our people had decided generations ago to shed it off, let it pass – everything but the essentials. Whatever stories, whatever intricacies she was contemplating, they were all obsolete.

With a force we did not know she had, the little queen began to push us back. Space opened between her body and ours.

★   ★   ★

Here is where I enter her story and where I have to admit that, if I used the word 'we' to speak of my people, those vessels of pure flesh, it is only because I do still identify with them. I aspire to live as they do. I was not yet born when the little queen's transformation began and was never one of those ones who, expecting to touch her, found a cold void. I am most unlike these people now.

And yet I was one of those sightless worms who fell from the big queen and began devouring substance. *I did that*, I think with some absurd pride. It seems a daydream, but I did. I was also one of those who without intervention would have slowed and died within a day. Yes, I was one of those runts.

My fate was a happy one, however, as the first to find me was the little queen, mere moments after I took my exit from her mother. I have read much Charles Dickens, I will assure you (I have had opportunity to ruminate on certain thematic links between my biography and many of the stories of Earth), and like an orphan of Dickens', I call her my benefactress. She is surely that. But to be precise I must be blunt, too: she ate me, as one must do when one encounters a runt. The polite thing is to stretch the fore-hole wide as one can and gulp down the body, or else another will have to eat it later. Imagine if one were left in the substance, how foul it would become. Imagine, too, the preference of the runt to be taken alive and enter a moving body rather than to die alone in the stark and motionless substance.

So she ate me, very politely. My story should have ended there. Her interior should have digested me with gratitude. Runts, being made of us, are our bodies' preferred food even though they might trouble our consciousness, the revulsion we feel being some regrettable vestige of a scruple we meant to shed long ago. A few muscular contractions and it is over, usually.

Fortunately, my entry into her body took place while she was spying through her glass and not taking in enough substance. Digestion was at best a tertiary concern.

Even a runt baby will keep eating until it dies, and that is what I did inside her languid body. I took in and sent out the mixture of her inner mucus and the substance, moving through her inner cavity with the mass of it. I felt warmth above me and instinctively moved toward it. Then, and it disgusts me so to write this, I ate something of her, too. I took the thin wall of her wound into my fore-hole, and the tissue there was so weak that it broke with the pop of a gum-bubble inside the mouth. I imagine it made that sort of sound, though I could not hear it at the time. The film of flesh and then pure air rushed into me, choking me, beginning the desiccation of my interior.

I came through the wound and into the open space between her hand and the wall of her body. I drooped in this hollow space until she noticed me, and now she had three things to look at: the stone, her palm, and me. One must understand how quickly things changed, after she saw me. She had a strong desire to be with me the way that Earth people are with each other. She didn't want us to communicate in chemistry, though that was our sole option, at first.

When I was a little child, she told the story of my birth and transformation as though it were a fairy tale. It became my favorite story, better than anything from Earth. Through her mucus, she said, "Grow an ear so that I may speak to you." Her lips were already forming by then, at just the right distance and angle from her eye. Another eye was almost ready to open and it, too, at a perfect distance from her lips. The ridge between these eyes would become her commendable nose. I trembled to do as she asked, to make the ear. A pearly ridge began to rise from me through pure keenness to please, and when its inner structure was ready, she whispered to me, "I will build us a place to be."

Soon, the queen stood fully embodied as a figure from mythology, a figure of woman half free from and half contained within a wall of flesh. I think of the Green Man forming from leaves. I also think of Michelangelo's *The Atlas Slave*, a reproduction of which stood in the queen's chamber in a later era. It was a most poignantly unfinished statue in which you could just make out a male figure pulling at chains, the captive trying to pull free from the stone.

She remained shackled to the hulk of her body still, that worm-body writhing with the others and the two of us inside it swinging and rocking as on a great ship. Even so distressed, she hummed happily to me. Finally, she had someone who would hear her stories. From an unused part of her body, she blew a kind of bubble to umbrella us, so she could now keep both hands free. Golden pink in the day, this bubble darkened when her body tunneled down. Delicate veins like branches in its tissue made up the landscape of my earliest life.

With one hand she held the stone to her eye, looking down on Earth and telling me what she saw and read, beginning my studies. With her other arm, she moved me to her breast, which completed its swelling beneath me. Its long dark russet nipple grew out to brush, and then touch, my fore-hole. I latched hard, and the substance of her body finally flowed through me. It slowly ran out of me to pool in the chamber. I did not desiccate.

"Grow an eye like mine so you can see me," she said. She named all of my parts to start them growing, to tell me what to do with them.

"Grow a mouth so you can talk to me." When she said this, would that I had been more imaginative, but I formed my fore-hole into a mouth. Logic would seem to dictate that a fore-hole finish as a mouth, as logic suggests that the legs will begin at the sides of the aft-hole, and that is the manner in which she made me. Or rather, that is the manner in which she made me make myself. Her fore-hole, by contrast, was initially very far from the pretty new mouth that she formed for herself, and as more and more of her face built around that new mouth, the fore-hole shrunk in and eventually settled directly at the hairline on the nape of her neck.

★   ★   ★

When I was still her child but long since weaned, we had a special meal together, the occasion to discuss how my role was going to change. It would be a better role because of how I was maturing. She could see me becoming a fine young man. "I am going to call you Galateo," she said. This was the only time she gave me a name, and so it is still the name I think of when I think of who I am. To become Galateo, she said that I would have to make some changes.

Between instructions, she ate her veal by placing a bite into her mouth and chewing vigorously. Then, using an exquisite little cup made for the purpose, she spat out the chewed meat and transferred it under her hairline. She set the cup down, wiped her mouth, and spoke for a while before taking another bite. She said the urge to gobble down food was one of the basest, most disgusting customs of her people, among many others. She spoke of it now in simile, her favorite figure of speech: "As on earth, a pig wallows in an amalgam of garbage so disgusting one cannot comprehend," and for my further delight (for she knew how I admired allusion), she added, "I am to the manner born," she said, "and still it sickens me."

I thought we were living quite well. Her person was almost free of the rest of her body now, with the space having opened up as I matured. First, her head had pulled away from the wall, then her shoulders, back, and then her left leg. Her right leg had remained embedded a long time but was now free, all but the ankle, allowing her to sit in a chair. She would strain to sit at her chair through dinner, and then she would strain in the other direction to lie in the bed we shared.

We needed no rest but rested there a third of our lives, as was seemly.

We had only recently taken up the practice of formal dining, she in the manner described and me directly through my fore-hole mouth, sitting at the table quite civilized and calm in candlelight. We had many belongings now. We had two forks, one knife, two plates, the cup, our table, a chair apiece, and a stack of baskets, all sturdy and rustic. Honest furnishings, I think of them now, unlike the baroque excesses she would come to favor, later. Our most recent addition was the candle, which flickered as we rocked. I remember that I was in raptures over the color blue, which I had not experienced except in the candle flame and before it in the barest shades of veins glowing through the tissue wall.

As I stared into the flame, she made clear that I would need to shed the greater part of my memories. Our studies, our languages: these were real and should be remembered. The rest could fall off easily. I would not need to recall my birth or the foray into the substance, her transformation or my own. She enumerated further memories that I should shed, ending thus: "I need you to forget the runts who lived here with us. Do you remember them?"

"They looked funny," I ventured. I am ashamed to have said this. I was a child then.

"They are not like us," she said, taking a bite. She looked at me very directly then, almost crossly. It was some time before she spoke again.

"Since this is our last night together, my lovely, I am going to be honest with you. I will soon cease direct communications with the greater queen, my mother." She looked down at the floor, little tears starting. "What do you think of that?"

I thought about this for a moment before speaking. "One should listen to one's mother, all things being equal, of course," I said.

"Of course, very good." She smiled to show me I had spoken well. "I do listen. It is she who will not listen. She refuses to understand how unhappy I am. I have begged her to produce a new queen. She said she did not think it best. I said, 'But you *can*, can you not?' She said she preferred not to. She told me all of this through her chemistry."

The little queen's smile was mysterious then. She said, "Do you remember when you and I used to speak that way sometimes? We will do it tonight and then no more." My body pulsed with happiness.

After dinner, she reached down with our knife to slash the flesh of her ankle. This came as no great surprise, as the conversation had seemed to point this way. What else could she have meant by cutting off communications? She sat at the chair for a moment more, seeming about to faint, and then she brightened, telling me she had a surprise.

She stood and stretched her lovely body. She bent to hook her finger into the new hole in the flesh of the wall and pulled. "You can help," she said. It stretched, then tore. "Pull hard. It can no longer feel."

Her larger body was dead now, nothing but material. Behind the flesh, as we ripped it away, was revealed a crude, rough door. I gasped.

"Do you know what this is?" she said.

I thought I did. "I love it, I love it," I said.

"Already, and you haven't seen it yet?" She smiled, pleased. She let the door swing open to reveal a new chamber. There was a bed – *my* bed – my desk, my drapes in a gray that was almost blue. In the corner sat a basin of water and a small basket overflowing with hard sausages. I felt so honored.

And then the implication settled slowly upon me. "But I won't rest with you anymore?"

"No. You are becoming a man." She stopped, looked at me with intent. "A *man*, nothing else. Your name will be Galateo."

She embraced me then and held me in place. Soon a thin mucus developed between my cheek and the skin of her chest. It felt marvelous to touch in this way. Through her chemistry, she intimated what I was to do in the little chamber. I was to become her equal. I would write a beautiful story of our new life in the chamber and later, the story of our people.

"When I next come, I will be your sister. We will be human," she said as she pushed away.

She closed the door and all fell dark.

★ ★ ★

Perhaps I was rebellious, like the little queen. I did not shed. I did what else she asked, but I did not shed one memory. I did make the attempt. Without needing to deliberate, I selected my worst experience. I reached into my abdomen for it, pulling the zeppelin-shaped memory apart from myself until it was attached by a thin cord. I felt the cord snap, but the memory adhered to my fingers, gradually absorbing there. I did not attempt another.

The transformation of my body was successful but long and painful. In the moistening dark of the chamber my limbs lengthened, then firmed. My jaw lengthened, and the flesh of it firmed and broadened. My stomach hardened. Hair began. My cloaca, my little puckered hole at the aft-end, thinned and lengthened out into a facsimile of the human organs, mere decoration because I did not have the inner parts of a drone.

Or so I believed at the time.

When the last sausage was done, I lay in the rocking dark, and some immeasurable time later, my new role was upon me. It began well. My queen entered my chamber and with her a cold dim light unlike any light I had beheld. A cherishing expression crossed her face when she opened my door. I looked down at my body and saw it clothed entirely in blue. I felt a newly minted regal being.

She was lovely as ever, now wearing a blonde ponytail and her own curious garments. The bottom part was much like mine, a pair of trousers in various soft blues. I would learn to call these our denims. The top part I could not quite understand, and as I kept looking at it, she sighed and held a hand to my newly bristled cheek to communicate that it was a picture, and what a picture was and how to read it, and I then gasped in delight. It was as when she had reached out to give me the power to read, long ago. I could see on the black of her garment was a painted picture of a wolf.

"The big bad wolf!" I said.

"It's a lone wolf, howling to the moon," she said, frowning. I think it was then that my fate set in place. She realized that she had made the touch she had promised never to make again, and for such a trivial reason. She later blamed that touch for the way that Galateo failed her. She thought she had passed memory to me in that touch as one would pass infection.

★   ★   ★

I would later learn that many Earth years had passed while I transformed within my chamber. The little queen had tried to spend the time productively but had been much distracted by some curious changes taking place on Earth. The world wide web had lately begun. To read, one no longer looked over a shoulder. The stuff of Earth radiated out away from the planet in billions of cords that one could view at will. It was all external, like mucus.

★   ★   ★

For now, we were playing pretend. We were human siblings, and I was a writer, and I was writing the story of our lives. After perfunctory greetings, my sister rose to leave, saying she did not want to keep me from it.

I wrote that we were a human brother and sister who lived alone in a giant carapace made from someone's (not the sister's!) former body. We lived rocking in the body while massive pink devils roiled beneath us. Hell, or close enough to it. In this story, there was a hole in the carapace floor where we could reach down and feel them. We would, quite as a matter of routine, take up the devils' chemistry and send them messages in ours.

This detail I felt was an imaginative addition, for I had never witnessed the little queen grinding and sawing with our knife to make the hole in her chamber floor. That had occurred after she closed me behind my door. I did not realize at the time, but I must have learned of it through that one regretful touch she gave me upon waking.

My sister stopped me from finishing this story, saying only, "I do not like that one. Begin again."

I wrote of how we were a set of brother and sister worms who had been swallowed by a larger worm and then persuaded to form human features. I wrote this in the form of a closet drama. She stopped me to start me again, over and over.

I had eschewed plain prose in favor of a complex system of references to veil the narrative in a manner I took to be more literary. My prose was stilted, she said, in itself very taxing for her, but the plots and the premises were worse. How could my stories betray such a lack of humanity?

Because I was not human? I could not say this. I only apologized. It seemed this Galateo would make a habit of apologizing.

My sister decided that my general lack of sophistication was the problem. She told me that she had constructed a device to correct for the weakness of my eyes. She brought into my chamber a lighted screen on which I could view pictures and reading material from the world wide web. She made me to understand it as a candle, which produced a cold rectangular flame that would form itself into pictures and words. I experienced many colors for the first time when she initiated operation of this screen. Refilling the little sausage-basket before doing so, my sister shut me in the chamber once more.

This is when I completed my studies of Earth. I read the text of the world wide web, understanding not all but much of it. While I still could not see the Earth, for the first time I could see images and even moving images of it. Perhaps my current experience was something like the little queen's early experiences with Earth – those early glimpses that she took, back when she was trying to keep up appearances and interact with the others of our kind.

I came to love the literature of Earth, and it was at this time that I made certain linkages between my own life story and the human story. These stories helped me to appreciate my past and prepare for my future. For example, I read of a certain butler who, perhaps, inspired my next role.

I began to feel more her equal. Nonetheless, a dreadful disenchantment fell over me. Why should we deny all of our nature to devote ourselves to these futile esoteric studies? Could there not be room in our lives for the more elemental pleasures along with the intellectual ones? What were we denying the others of our kind, cloistered as we were? And what of the precious eggs maturing somewhere along the wall of her interior?

I began to fantasize heroic actions of varied shape. The first action was a most permissible one to contemplate: it was that I could write a beautiful novel of our people to share with Earth. My sister and I would find a way to send it to the world wide web, and in reading it those people would know we too were a people of many accomplishments. They would know of our benign interest in them and perhaps feel protected by it, perhaps feel less lonely. And surely, after we had delivered this benevolent little message, we would turn our attention to other matters and be done with Earth. This is what the little queen seemed to want. I wanted it too, but darker fantasies swept over me.

My love for the little queen remained undiminished, but whereas I had previously wanted nothing but to obey her, I began to fantasize now about her obeying me. I began to consider that she might benefit from some instruction. In the most innocent of this genre of fantasy, I would correct her misunderstanding of an Earth custom or offer an insight on a literary text, and she would suffer a little wound to her pride but then, quickly, look at me again in that cherishing way. The furthest and most shameful reach of these fantasies was a consummation. In this magical world, sperm began circling somewhere in the lining of my interior until they filled me. I held down the little queen to burst over her, after which she would subsume her limbs and organs to re-enter the circle of our people, peopling that circle with robust new lives. Or, if my mood were a bit more territorial and my magical thinking more acute, I would somehow live on after the act. We would breed a new race of civilized people within this very carapace and live out our lives within it, teaching and improving a growing population.

This is what it means never to touch another. Without touch, my fantasies remained my own. Safely secret, they grew in ferocity, like great Earth cats, shredding the bleeding walls of their cage.

★   ★   ★

I had, too, begun to suspect beings living over us, as well as the ones below. So nearsighted was my sister, it was no surprise that she claimed nothing existed in the sky. If my farsighted eyes were to behold it, what would they see? I fantasized terrible giants that I could battle: giants in the form of worms, giants in the form of men, and all of the monstrous shapes between, the monsters of spheres and rings and cogs. I fantasized about benign giants, making contact with them and begging them to help us out of our difficulties, for I had begun to suspect that some of our people were already suffering great difficulties and that they would suffer more very soon. Enslavement, crushing, extinction. I imagined crafting a metallic screen the size of our colony that I could flash to them – *dash dash dash, dot dot dot, dash dash dash* – and then when they were watching closely, communicate the text of my beautiful novel. We could find a code.

As an Earth man writes a beautiful book in the blinks of his eye. As an Earth man bereft of limbs and tongue or any member with which he can communicate taps his head in SOS rhythm to capture the attention of his tormenters so that he can then tell them important lessons he has learned by living in this form. In such a way, I wanted to make contact with those above us.

★   ★   ★

I drifted in an interesting state between screen-images, fantasies, ever more esoteric readings, my own humble writing exercises, and the questions of what my lady might be doing behind my chamber door. The little queen began to interrupt my solitude in order to read my writing again. She still hated the stories but said that the writing was improving. She would sometimes tarry to speak to me after her appraisals.

I knew I would have to earn the privilege of leaving my chamber. I began, then, to take these interruptions as opportunities to better inform myself as to what kind of story she might tolerate. I asked her what she read, what stories branded themselves in her being. I conversed with her in a seemingly informal way, all the time calculating.

I sharpened my wiles. I considered our conversations, looking for any theme I might exploit. I asked myself about the essential character of her fascinations. I pressed myself to identify the Earth concept the little queen most adored. It always circled back to a certain variety of depravity, a certain taboo irrelevant to those of our nature. I recalled her making the point to me, long ago when she introduced *Hamlet* and *Oedipus Rex*. She had taken pleasure in describing why I should feel disgusted by the incestuous queen and horrified at the oedipal accident. I recalled the certain snatches of internet gossip she had let slip. I took note of the very fact of her making Galateo her brother when she had so many other roles available. I tallied the different expressions she had given me, cast interpretation on the clothing, the great insistence that we never touch and now the way she paced and lingered.

Inspiration fell like a belting rain.

I began a story in which we were a beautiful brother and sister who had been locked into a mansion's attic, just as we were both coming into the full bloom of puberty. I wrote of the pain we both felt in trying to repress our lust, our wicked mother who kept us hidden in the attic out of profound avarice.

The little queen swept into my chamber to read my pages before I had finished. I continued to write while she read; my muscles grew tight as though preparing my body to pounce.

I had plagiarized much of the story. I did not know the extent of her reading or what the ramifications might be if she caught the transgression.

She finished quickly, then turned to me and said, "This is a suitable beginning. But unfinished. How will it proceed?" The expression on her face was all wonder.

"I suppose it will proceed to a consummation of some kind," I said. I could not meet her eyes.

★   ★   ★

I was granted entry to the main chamber then and was not surprised to see it looking much like the attic depicted in my story, whether through coincidence or through that tiny touch that we had shared. The far wall appeared to be hundreds of feet away and the space between crowded with every manner of object lightly strung with shreds of dust. The ceiling had been raised to five, ten times its former height with massive beams. A light, colder than any I had yet beheld, raked in from cracks in the ceiling to illuminate the falling motes. Toys, statues, paintings, baskets, all manner of furnishing and crates – and clothing, messy stacks of intricately patterned clothing – filled the space so that there was barely room for us to navigate the aisles between the stacks.

We walked the aisles a time and, in a clearing far into the room, came upon a long table that had been constructed from crates and small pieces of furniture, already set with food and dishes. We sat to dine, she at one end and I at the other. The mood was quite whimsical, like children playing house, like a forest animals' tea in the deep woods. Dinner was only veal and water, but it charmed me nonetheless with the painted cups and dishes, the lovely silverware, the formal silence and the casual way she draped toward me. The table, clear when we began the meal, was littered like the floor with greasy tatters of blue-gray dust by the time we rose.

"Is that a flame of some sort?" I asked, pointing up.

"The sky," she said.

"I thought it might be," I said in awe. I was fortunate to glimpse the sky, even thus filtered. What would I see, if I were to stack a stairway up to the ceiling and peer outside the carapace?

"The structure above is desiccating. I have had to reinforce with wood," she said.

"Where can one find beams of such dimensions?" I wondered.

My sister said not a word in response to my query but asked if I would like to keep exploring. We came to a looking glass and a lean lantern-jawed man within it. I avoided looking too closely at my handsome face because I feared that I would see something wrong with it. For a time I investigated the objects packed into the room – amazed at first, soon growing weary.

Like props in a play, the objects could bear little scrutiny. The same toy repeated in a dozen locations, the same shimmering green silk in a dozen different stacks. Only the dust was varied in its shapes and thicknesses. Only it was real. The rest was all artifice.

My sister excused herself for a moment, and I kept drifting. I realized I had circled back and was not far from the table where we had dined.

Just then a squat, gray-pink head peeked out from a low door behind the queen's chair. It looked skeptically from corner to corner and, finding that all was clear, slid out into the room. Its body was shaped like an inverted octopus, if the octopus's aft-hole had been welded to a broad serving tray. Making efficient use of its many arms, the creature deftly transferred the table leavings and dishes onto its tray, gathered some dust into a little pile and swept this onto the tray, and then exited through its door.

As I watched, the little queen's voice echoed in my mind, "Remember those runts who lived with us for a while?" and my child's voice, "They looked funny." Runts, caught and shaped by her for her purpose.

Rage rose inside me, and with it the feeling that I wanted to dominate my sister. My body so powerful, larger than hers, it would no longer be out of the question.

I had no name for her, so I called, "Sister, sister, come out. I have seen your experiment, your serving-runt. How many of us are there? Will I search the walls for doors and behind the doors find some ones like me? How many factories? How many factories did it take to make all of this?"

This, I fear, was not the end of my regrettable soliloquy. No, I went on longer, deriding her and daring her to come out from her hiding.

As I spoke, I was truly mad. I saw not what was before me but a sensational vision of our homely carapace as an endless honeycomb, behind that wall a chamber and another wall, a chamber and another wall, and behind each paper-thin wall of skin, another runt like me toiling away to become a man. Did I believe this vision? I cannot say.

I spoke until I tired of speaking, wilted to the floor. I had more time to calm before my sister came out from hiding. Her cowgirl boots shuffled slowly over the dusted floor. She sunk into the russet sofa near me, reached her hand toward me for a dry touch. I did not reach toward her. In our history, this would be the only time she offered her touch and I refused.

She spoke: "Do you remember when you were a little child and I took you to tour a factory? It pressed its fore-end to our home and sucked until the tissue broke inside like a gum-bubble. I had told it to press out all of its substance so that you and I could walk its length, and it did just that. It pressed out and filled up again with air. We walked through, marveling at the rows on rows of worker arms, little mauve-blue cilia with tiny hands at the end. There must have been a hundred thousand of them in that one vessel, all desiccating as we walked the length.

"I had told it to wave its hands at us, which it did near the entrance, but as we walked the hands became more and more flaccid. I was annoyed that the creature couldn't hold together. I am cruel. I had told myself you needed to see something more of the world, but in truth I think I did it just to horrify you, and it worked. You bawled.

"Some of the hands held candles, which caused them and the ones near them to dry more quickly. I remember seeing those heroic arms shaking and straining to hold the weight of the candles. I started to run, and as we neared the aft, there were no more candles. The hands couldn't hold and dropped them to snuff on the bottom, or the arms all dried to dust. I couldn't see, and you were screaming. I held your hand and pulled you along.

"That factory died almost before we were out. It quavered the whole time we were in it, suppressing as long as it could the urge to push out air. Before we lost the light we could see the fatty tissues at the top desiccating to shreds, or at least I could. I picked you up in my arms and ran you out the aft-end, but by then it had stopped quaking. It had, I think, just enough life left to choose to close that end so that the air would come out the fore-end, far away from us. A great crackling fart rumbled from the distance, and you and I crouched beside the closed aperture, back inside our dwelling. I rubbed your shoulders, then, and a mucus built, and I communicated to you how sorry I was."

She paused. I remembered the bluish white powder that had begun to frost each dying surface of the vessel factory.

She said, "I think that was the worst thing you ever saw, yes?"

"Yes," I said. It had been the first memory I had tried to shed. I remember the watermelon shape of the memory pinched between my fingers.

She said, "The worst thing I ever saw? It was one of the first things I ever saw. I have some here, in fact." She rose and took a jar from a tall bookcase behind the sofa, seated herself again. "You have never seen the substance. I think I am the only one who has."

She spilled the contents upon the velour of the sofa's middle cushion, beckoning me to sit and look. I stood for a while before moving. I was afraid.

The substance was a color richer and more livid than one could imagine, with something of red and brown in it. My interior lubricated in ghastly torrents. I was drawn in spasmodic movements toward the substance, had to work just to keep from dropping to my knees and devouring it. And yet I was revolted by it. I sat down to look more intently and saw that sprinkled throughout it were the widening and puckering pink circles of other peoples, some large as my thumbprint and some small as a full stop on a page, and I knew, others on down to the smallest scale.

To eat a thimbleful of it would be to destroy scores (or more?) of civilizations.

"Please put them back in the jar," I whispered.

She took a magnifying glass from her back pocket and motioned for me to make use of it.

Through the glass, I saw that indeed there were smaller circles, and smaller ones, and – had I been standing there at the scale of the smallest of them, and had I held a magnifying glass – there would be others still to view this way. I could see that all she had ever wanted was to escape this cycle: to stop eating, to shrink, to shed.

She said, "In a bedroom on Earth there is a painting. I ought to have had it reproduced sometime. It's an amateur's oil painting of God's finger pointed down on a little house in the middle of a sunny field. It is most perfect." She paused to smile as though enjoying the image right there before her, then motioned for me to look through the glass again, and I saw her finger so massive and pale against the substance.

"Here is a scrap of fiber," she said. "The factory we were in was one that would venture out to find fibers like these. When it found them it would shred and weave them for clothes for you and me, clothes and bedding and canvases and paper. The factory didn't make the clothes. There are others who do that, others like our little maid you saw. And there are other factories to make everything in here. Isn't it grand? And it is so easy to make them. I just whisper to them to make themselves, you see."

"Why tell me that?" I said. I wanted to weep for the ones who toiled, wanted to tear off my beautiful clothes. I made no move, however, and she continued.

"There are things we must do in order to live." She pointed at a little splinter in the substance. "Here is a piece of wood that would, on our scale, be a ceiling beam. She added, "Here is a tiny stone, and in it a tiny universe."

I looked where she pointed but could see nothing. She misjudged the strength of my eyes.

Her finger disappeared from under the glass to touch her ring. She turned the ring round and round. She said, "There is the travesty of living as I live now, the people I defile. Or there is the travesty of living as my people do. The only difference is that on Earth I may live free, without these travesties, and with all the varied substance of that place spread before me, nothing like these crude replicas." She gestured to the stacks of goods around us.

All of this was aside from the eggs. She said, "Would you want to waste these eggs?"

More time spooled out as she spoke. She told me many things.

When she finished, I said, "You are planning to enter the world inside your ring." I could not bear the scalding pain of it. The mention of eggs, too, had made a creeping feeling rise in me.

"We already have, child, almost. This stone is a fake." And I knew this too. The real stone loomed somewhere, huge and horrifying. Perhaps we were inside already, this husk something she'd manufactured to hurtle us through space. I realized that I had no way of knowing what scale we were on now or how small I had become. I began to feel quite weak.

As though reading my mind, she said, "It's true that you are not my equal, will never be. Within your interior is a tube that extends from mouth to back hole. There is nothing inside you but that. Within me?" She touched each place. "A brain, a spinal column, heart, stomach, uterus. All of it. I have improved myself. It does you no service to pretend you have done the same. That's all."

She touched me on the neck, not seeing that I was already wet there. She could feel some of the fantasies within me, and she jumped back. "That is all," she said coldly.

Back in my chamber I wrote the story's end and waited for her to enter and take up my newly finished pages.

The little queen narrowed her eyes, which remained dry. "Very nice, very good," she said. She moved to leave but then remained in place. "I once thought to have you write a story I could live within, you see, and then I would go somewhere and shed off every awful thing I knew, and then you would present me with this story and tell me that it was the truth. Perhaps if you were something more than what you are, this might have worked, but I see now that I should never have put a runt to such a test."

★   ★   ★

When she started talking about runts, I saw that this would be the end of my life as Galateo. And though she was no longer in the mood for it, the preordained end of this life with me would be the consummation. She pounced.

Consummation, then, bitter and brutal. We toppled onto my bed. It was nothing like a drone's performance, just my cloaca forced into the sterile pouch she had willed to form between her legs. But it was a good experience still, for me. There was a modest amount of mucus. I communicated wounded pride. She communicated hatred, but it was good still. At some point I started to communicate gratitude, which was all I felt now that we were in contact. If she had searched my chemistry, she would have known all the thoughts I had ever harbored, but the hate she sent was so intense that I doubt she took in anything I communicated.

Suddenly she bit off my head, the almost-beautiful head that had taken so much care to grow. My head had been cradled between her neck and shoulder when her fore-hole opened and pulled over it, the aperture pinching sharp as rows of razors around my neck. As instantly as the head had entered her, it fell out of her to roll upon my abdomen.

I felt her moving around in the bed for a time. Though I could no longer see, I imagined that she cradled the head in her arms, rocking it in a Pietà pose. My body spasmed. Inner mucus leaked out onto the bed.

I longed for her to touch my body so that I could tell her of the gratitude that had come to overwhelm my pride. I wanted to tell her that I forgave her, but she just kept rocking on the bed. The seeping stopped at my neck, the clot formed once again into mouth flesh, a rudimentary slit above my clavicle.

"It is understandable," I said from the neck-hole. "I deserved that."

She did not move. I began to think I had died, though the mouth felt too new and alive to be only a death dream. It puckered and stretched, puckered and stretched. New little ears started to bud by its sides.

"—a mistake," she wailed. "Forgive me."

I lay there pulsing for a time.

"You're all right, then?" she asked.

"Yes," I said. I swallowed hard.

"So, I can tell you now as I have told you before. You have lived many lives. You are about to begin a new one. It will be all right. What do you want to be this time?"

"I want to be your brother," I said. I thought but did not say, *I* am *your brother. We fell from the same queen.*

"That's just not on the table anymore, dearest," she said.

I waited a long time to speak again, trying to think of the right words. "In what way can I best serve you, queen?" I asked. Something writhed inside me. I thought a heart might have begun just then.

With real enthusiasm she said, "Now you are my servant. I am cruel to you."

"Yes," I said.

"No," she said, "not cruel. I am merely very proper with you."

"Yes," I said.

"I hold you far from me."

With those words, I already knew something of the pain I would feel, in my life to come, being held farther from her.

When she closed me in my chamber, after I had received all of my instructions for becoming the servant she wished me to be, she added one more thought. "This time, you need to form yourself differently. No matter what we did right last time, that mouth. It must be convenient to eat with it, but—"

"What about it?"

"Your mouth always looked like an asshole to me." She closed my door and behind it, laughed and laughed.

★   ★   ★

I wept in my chamber as my new head completed, then thrust my fingers deep inside to pull out the memory of my previous head. The memory was itself a head with mouth open in shock. The strings holding it to my body were tough. I chewed them away and flung the thing from me, but it crawled back and sank into my hip.

This time I was sequestered for a much shorter period. She knew I could not shed. I was exiled only for the appearance of the thing, so that we both could pretend.

When I emerged, she was the size of a child and I was the tall, stooped, balding butler. I regretted the loss of Galateo's magnetism.

She showed off the redone chamber and the painting of the serpent-woman, spoke to me of last days. She continued to reduce in size, but she made us play pretend until the last.

And then it was the last. The staff of runts paraded before me now, brazen as they'd been in my earliest days. More octopus-and-tray runts and the soft, sticky cleaning-runts, seamstress runts with needles and spindles for guts. I saw no others like myself. The one who prepared the food *was* in the rough shape of an unfinished human, but she was soft and lacked legs. She did not need legs to maneuver a few yards of space to construct the veal.

(And the veal itself, of course: more runts.)

One day, I let my body touch the veal-maker's, just to see what it was like to touch-speak with another runt. I found I could communicate with her very pleasurably but with none of the urgency I had once experienced with the little queen. I saw that her life was relatively pleasant, as she was allowed to go to her chamber sometimes. The chamber was half filled with substance, and she and another like herself writhed there when the queen could spare their time.

The little queen told me later that I should not envy the others who lived within the carapace with us, who had eaten of the substance all their lives and kept up their chemical communications with one another. I was special, after all. Only she and I had ever been able to live without taking in the substance. She swore I was the only one to have improved so far in this direction. I had not shed memories, she acknowledged now, and yet I had compacted, hardened, and strained in every way to meet her requests. Others had sacrificed, too, and had made great improvements in their different ways. Think of the runts made into factories to build our furnishings – or think of the craft building itself even now within the cup of substance upon her ornately carved mantel. The gentility of such a creature was not to be discounted.

When she told me all of this, she was the size of a doll and stood on the mantel eye to eye with me. She looked out from bruised, mad eyes. Soon I would be unable to hear her words.

She was nude, having decided to turn all factory production to the items for her coming journey. I would wait on her until I could no longer see her with the glass, and then I would be free.

"At what scale are we, right now?" I asked. I could not bring myself to ask what I had been wondering: Where was the stone, or where were we within it?

She ignored my question. She wanted to talk about her journey and its outcome. "I have all these dreams about it. In one? I am so small by the time I reach the place, I am like a worm at their feet. I meet one of their worms and start a family. That's as likely as anything. In another, I meet a man – a beautiful man with one of those classic cars. I make love with him and then spend the rest of my life with the babies falling from me. Our kind of babies, you know, falling out of me for the rest of my life and no one notices. Some of them get in the ground and start their journey toward getting big."

These sounded like bleak possibilities.

The outcome she wanted would be different, but she said she could not yet imagine it. Perhaps she had imagined but would not tell me.

★   ★   ★

She was gone. I had held her on the tip of my finger and settled her in the cup of substance. I watched her through the magnifying glass as her craft surfaced to meet her. She waved and entered, all of the time reducing, both she and the craft. I thought I would see its ascent, but my eyes failed me. It simply minimized to the size of a full stop and then I could not see it. It could fly quite well, she had assured me.

She was gone now, and I paced. Soon, I tore the wall behind the mantel and it was there, the red stone surface. I did not know how far it extended. I turned to the opposite wall. I tore through, and tore through the wall opposite, and kept tearing and barely looking at what creatures were housed in each.

★   ★   ★

I should write of the long wanderings through the honeycomb of cells. I wondered if I had created or intuited them in my moment of madness, or if she had told me of them by the accident of her touch. I found no others like me in them, but rather endless dead and suffering creatures. I should say what I suffered and the doubt I experienced wandering there. I should give a sense of the time that passed and my thoughts, and what I did with the creatures I encountered, but I am too weary, and these are not the important things to tell.

The important thing, the only important thing, is that I came to the chamber where I had lived as a child. The table rose up so high I could not see its underside, for all I'd thought my farsightedness might be a boon, but I knew it by its leg. I wandered the floor until I came to a ledge, and my eyes failed me once more as I looked down and could see nothing distinct, only what I thought might be substance far down. I hoped that our people survived there still.

I reformed myself without instruction, then. I reformed my hands to hooks and made peace with my vessel shape. Falling through space, I hoped to lodge in someone's side but knew the likelihood instead of falling into the depths of substance.

★   ★   ★

I communicated with the big queen, much later, as I stuck like a lance in her side.

"All is well, all is well," she said. "The mating dance is ever easy."

She said, "Your fruit is ripening, child, and the call about to come, I think. Every drone's time comes when it will. I should think you could have seen the cells within you with your eyes, or don't your eyes see through your skin? I can never remember these trifles. But she always went on about what great eyes you had. Oh, how she loved you. 'I've found my mate,' she said to me, when she first found you. 'I still have to finish making him, but I have found him.' She still had a body to touch us then."

The big queen told me of the labyrinthine turns of her own mating dance, a history which makes this one pale in comparison. She told me all of this and much more through her chemistry, but it had all the arc and flow of a spoken narrative to me.

And then, by what magic did she transform me once again, and what of my own craft? I cannot tell.

★　　★　　★

In what form did the little queen come down, finally? I can tell you that. The form of a goddess. The beautiful woman at age nineteen. She came down nude in a bright field. Her craft let itself desiccate there in the air and fall down upon her in shreds. She shook off the dust and scampered off to find clothing. She emerged from behind a country house in a white shirt which hung down to cover her to the middle of her thighs, dark hair loose upon it and the fine brain beneath the hair all abuzz with plans.

Just then a classic car, long and blue, turned into the house's rutted drive. There, in the driver's seat, sat the most striking young man she had ever seen. He was regal with height and strength, a Greek nose, a beautiful mouth.

THE EARTHLY GARDEN

One: Mom

I didn't start to feel out of my depth until he was nine or ten. Before that, Stephan was just a cheerful, talkative kid.

I remember the family reunion – Grandma kept saying something smelled and then that some*body* smelled. She grabbed Stephan by the elbow and took a big whiff of his armpit and made me do it too. I guess he was so familiar to me that I never noticed. Soon hair started coming in coarse and black all over his legs and arms, on his lip, the edge of his chin – too soon for such a little guy.

One or another of my brothers taught him how to shave when he was visiting their house, and when he got home that day, I saw but didn't say anything. I was ashamed of myself for not teaching him.

I wasn't doing so well just then. Everything was so vague to me, all that time moving so fast between me and him.

He had always spoken quickly, but he started rolling off long monologues from movies or singing the lyrics of one song to the music of a different one. When he spoke at any length, he shifted between different impersonations. People didn't recognize the jazz in it. They just thought he was weird. Jeremy was the exception. That boy kept up with a good half of what Stephan said.

Around the end of junior high and the first year of high school, Stephan started to make more friends. His dad came back around and had a little money, so he bought a looping machine and some other gear. Stephan would do these weird performances down in the basement, something like Reggie Watts but rougher, harder to understand – and yet you could see that something brilliant was happening. Like he could sing one song into a recording device, tapping the button intermittently, and it would play back a different song. He'd grown his hair long and peeked out from behind it. I saw how the kids looked at him, some of the girls even. I felt better about him then. But this performance stage was over all too soon.

I remember a night after a little party they'd had. Jeremy was out on the couch, Stephan on a sleeping bag on the floor beside him. He couldn't stop talking, and he was going so fast. He used to chatter like that in his crib.

I was in the kitchen getting one last drink, trying not to make noise about it, and I heard Jeremy saying, "It's OK. Come on, go to sleep." He just kept whispering like that with Stephan talking over him faster and faster. It broke my heart that he had so much going on inside him and not enough time to express all of it.

After a while, Stephan's music gear was all boxed in the basement and no one came around again other than Jeremy. My brothers were always asking about how Stephan was doing, as though there were something wrong with him, but there was nothing. He'd had all sorts of tests, and his teachers – the decent teachers anyway – loved him. He was doing fine in school. I told my brothers he was happy just working in his room. When I went in to collect laundry, I saw the Petri dishes and glass slides and all this paper everywhere, some of it sketch paper but mostly that green grid paper that has the little tiny squares with the thicker green line every five squares.

Seeing that paper pricked me a little because I used to use a lot of it designing big mansions and hotels when I was younger. I took a drafting class in high school where we learned how to draw the symbols for lights and windows and doors. The teacher was this big gruff guy who went on about how to design a house efficiently. You had to have the water all on one wall. You had to have a square or a rectangle shape to save on cost, standard size windows and doors and all of that. So when I did it for fun, I designed houses with all these bay windows and secret cubby rooms and the bathrooms all on different sides, bedrooms the size of ballrooms with great useless expanses around the beds, oversized French doors opening into rooms they had no business opening onto. I would imagine walking through, and on the back of the paper I'd write down all the colors, all the marble and wood, shades and textures of the leather, the colors in the floral tapestries upholstering the big couches and everything.

I guess I was a little like Stephan when I was younger.

*   *   *

One weekend Stephan cleaned his room. He stored a lot of his gear in boxes and took them to the basement. I was in and out that weekend with my friend Stacy, going to the festivals and out to the hills to hike – it must have been late summer, almost September – and every time we came back, I was surprised he was still working on his room.

Stacy had said a couple of times how she thought Stephan ought to try having a drink, how it would loosen him up. We got home tipsy from hanging out at the beer garden, and we swung in to find him finally finished, lying back on his bed with his whole room immaculate around him. She fished in her bag and got out a bottle of fruit-flavored microbrew. She asked, "Can I?"

I said I didn't care. I was looking over what I now recognized as a pretty fancy room in the middle of my cluttered little house. The electronics and the most expensive instruments and supplies from all his past passions were laid out on his long desks. He had looped orange and green Christmas lights around his window.

I don't remember if all of his college acceptance letters had started coming in by that time. I think so.

"Swanky," Stacy said, looking around. She and I sat cross-legged on the clean hardwood. I said again that I didn't mind, so Stephan took the bottle.

He said, "I hear a drink makes me real entertaining."

I got a chill at that. "Maybe this isn't such a good idea," I said, but he was already reaching into his nightstand drawer for a bottle opener.

It was all right for a while. They talked about movies, Stephan leaning forward on the edge of the bed and Stacy walking around. Stacy was trying to make him feel good, asking about his belongings. Her attention didn't put him into performance mode, though, or not all the way. I think he started to go there and changed his mind, went somewhere else instead.

He started telling us about one day when he went out to get the mail and he noticed the ivy growing up the tree and the lichen, a black lichen below and a green lichen growing higher up on the side of the blue mailbox. The ivy was growing only on the shaded side of the tree, the lichen on the shaded side of the box. And then he told the story of the origin of penicillin, which he had learned about in school, and then he started to talk about mold and all of the different colors that mold came in, different colors of funguses and algae.

He started telling us of a dream. Calling to Jeremy, who was in the basement turning into a fractal serpent shape, echoing sounds.

He shook his head, paused and said, "A drink will always slow me down. It's only when I'm super slow that I can talk to people, or people like you I should say." He pulled his hair out of the bun and let it fall around his face.

Stacy said that was rude, but he didn't walk it back. Then she said how pretty his hair was.

He started telling about times when he was drinking and could really talk to people but then it would always make him black out by the end and he wasn't sure what all he did. Maybe he told all his secrets. The memories were all like in a strobe light. He'd checked out a couple of books and learned there was a theory that the blacked-out memories weren't lost or repressed but that they were never recorded.

"Can you imagine that?" he said. "There'd be times when your old shitty camera was on, like back in the eighties, but there was no tape in the camera. I bet you can remember that far back."

I asked when he would have done all this. It did not seem possible that he'd been out of my sight so long.

"You haven't exactly been the most attentive parent, but that's all right," he said. He tipped back the beer so hard that he spilled a little onto his chin. He stood up, wiping his face with the back of his hands. His stance was different, like he was poised to start dribbling a basketball.

He went into the kitchen and came back with three rum and Cokes in tall glasses, handed one to Stacy and one to me.

"I think I need to get home," Stacy said. She left the drink sweating right on the edge of his desk, which wasn't like her.

I walked her out. She said I ought to get him to bed, that he wasn't making sense, but I wasn't sure I agreed.

"Got this," I said. She hugged me and said she knew I did.

When I came back to his room, he'd finished his drink and was working on Stacy's. When he finished, I traded him the empty glasses for my drink. "That's all," I said. I guess I wanted to have it out.

He said, "That'll be enough."

He drank the third and a few minutes later said, "I've never talked to you before, but that's fine. I will now. I have a plan. I'm going to get with the program, you know? Really commit to school this time. Need to learn about botany, chemistry. It's all planned. Let me show you."

"You've never talked to me before?"

He held eye contact, said, "Did you know that when I read that thing about blackouts, my first thought was that someone had to be running your body all that time? That's not a normal sort of thought."

"There's *nothing* wrong with you," I said, and he rolled his eyes.

"You're the only one who thinks that," he said. "But it doesn't matter now. It's over. It's all planned. Let me show you."

He rose and started taking down posters from his one big windowless wall. He rolled up the posters and pulled rubber bands around them, carefully tucked them under the bed and then unlocked his desk drawer and took out a thick stack of papers.

He said, "This…project came to me in less than a second. It was one of the only ones I was ever able to catch because it came when I was especially open. Photographic memory of the event. I caught a few others, but this is the best."

"You caught it?" I said.

"You know I got the idea for how to set this all down from your old drawings, all these castles and how you wrote out everything about them? They were like stories. You remember showing them to me?"

"I do." Even in my confusion, I was touched that he remembered. He was right; we didn't ever really talk anymore.

He said, "The drink's working, you know. I think it helps because I keep one part of my mind on something else, and I keep the other part on my…interlocutor. I focus on their reactions and really start playing on them, on you, I guess. Like some kind of piano. Or drums." He smiled. He took a thick binder from the shelf and handed it to me.

"You're not being very polite," I said. I started paging through and saw it was like a legend for a map. There were dots of different colors from the hundred-piece set of artist's markers his dad had bought him, each dot paired with two or three words written out in code.

"This is your copy," he said. "You're going to learn it, and if anything really happens to me, like if I shut down…. Or if something takes me. Because I've thought about that. You can still make it. Promise you will." He was crouching on the floor, then he was on his knees making puppy eyes and prayer hands like he was only joking.

Then he looked at me intensely. "You're honestly the only one I can trust with this. You can collaborate, invest. Pay for just a little bit of this and I promise if it ever makes a dime that'll go to you. To fix up the house."

"Money? I'm not following."

"It won't but it could."

He got up and stood on his desk chair and taped the first piece of paper up at the left-hand corner of the wall. It was that same green graph paper, all of the squares filled in with different marker dots. He placed the next page up against the first. "This is going to take a while," he said.

I paged through the notebook, about ten pages of legend and then more pages of text, notes from books he'd read, websites. I looked up and knew that the legend was for a map he was going to build on the wall.

I stood and took the stack of graph paper from him. The sheets weren't graph paper at all but color photocopies, or maybe color photos from his printer.

"What did this cost?" I said, passing it back.

He smiled, said, "Why don't you go have a tubby and come back when you're in your jammies? Dry your hair even. You have plenty of time. When you get back I'll be done and we'll go over the code."

★　　★　　★

With most of the windows open, it was starting to get cool. I was trembling when I stepped into the tub. I kept refilling hot when the bathwater started to lose its sting. I dried my hair, put on pajamas, and went to my room. I locked my door. The next day was a Sunday. I slept in.

I thought of an hourglass and the time coming between us one grain at a time.

When I next looked into his room, posters were back up, the map and folder were nowhere to be seen. Stephan had left the key in the lock of his open desk drawer and a note in the kitchen under the empty fruit bowl saying he'd gone to his dad's. They were going to start a project car.

When I next saw him, he had a buzz cut. Soon he was working long hours at a job, and then he was moving off to college. I can't say he ever talked to me again like he did that night.

★　　★　　★

Two: Jeremy

I wasn't at the bar for two minutes when the man himself stood before me, a hipster professor with long hair just starting to gray at the roots. The face was about the same as I remembered, but he was squinty. He looked unsettled.

"Jeremy?" he said, like he couldn't believe it, like he'd run into me by accident.

We hugged, and I could feel his authenticity. There was something doglike in his response to me. If this is the case, I wondered, why no attempt to ever get in touch before now?

We sat in a booth at the back of the bar and he watched me drink a couple of beers. He had me talking about my kids and wife, my job, vacations, trucks. Everything I wanted to say, he invited me to say. I guessed he'd read a book or two on listening. All I got from him was that he had a tenured position and an artsy girlfriend named Eva away at a conference.

I gave him the parcel right away. It was the size and weight of a ream of paper and wrapped in layers of brown grocery bag. He turned it in his hands and dropped it in his big leather messenger bag without a comment.

"I never opened it," I said. All those years I'd had it, since we were teenagers and he asked me to keep the parcel safe, I'd never even considered peeking.

"I know," he said. "Thank you."

When he asked if I wanted to come over, I remembered all the times he asked me over when we were kids. I was thinking of how much I'd worried about him back then, how I hadn't needed to worry, and how relieved his mom must have been to see him turn out so well. We got in his old Mustang and drove out to his house.

"This is the same one Dad and I did," he said. "Can you believe it?"

"I just about can't," I said. It still looked good.

I hadn't rented a car or gotten a hotel room. He'd sent me almost enough to do it, along with what I needed for the flight, but I hoped I'd be staying with him.

I didn't know what to expect but was not surprised to see that his house was a little one-and-a-half-story bungalow like his mom's but all fixed up the way she'd always wanted to do hers. I could see he'd put time into it. He showed me around, and as we wound our way back from the upstairs tour, he took his messenger bag from the banister and grabbed a box of matches from the shelf by the back door.

"We're going to burn this thing," he said.

"We gonna sit around and *watch* it burn? You got a beer?" I said.

He said, "I haven't had a drink in twenty years, but yes, I got a beer." He swung open the fridge and there were several six-packs and little else in there.

"I didn't know what kind you liked so I got them all," he said.

"I like them all," I said.

Soon we had a little wood fire going in the firepit. It was a nice older neighborhood on the edge of a small city in the last days of summer, so you could hear singing and announcers at the county fair a couple of miles down in the valley and kids shouting and far-away sirens from time to time. It was getting a little bit cool.

"You going to show me any of that before you burn it?" I said.

"It would take two hours. I'd have to lay it all out in a certain way. So no." He placed it into the fire a few sheets at a time.

"Are you going to tell me about it, then?"

He said, "It's a backup of something that I have in a safe deposit box. It was in case something happened to my copy – or to me – so it wouldn't be lost. And then you'll ask, well how come I couldn't still keep it in case something happens to me later, and then I'll say well because it doesn't need to exist anymore because the project is done, and you'll say what do you mean project, what do you mean done, and then I'll either have to show you or I'll have to refuse to, so that's what the stakes are really. This conversation is about whether you'll get to see the project or not."

I remembered he had about a couple dozen standard bits that he would cycle through, and this was one of the most insulting ones, but it worked on me. I wanted to just sit back and enjoy being with him and not get involved. But now I also really wanted to see the project. A ream of paper was one thing.

"So what do I do so I get to see it?" I said.

"The first thing is just listen a while. I listened to you at the bar. A lot."

"I noticed."

He talked at some length. He said he'd done it all organically. Organically, no computer involved. Just some web research, and he didn't count that. He did all the math himself, learned all the chemistry. No one helped. Unless you counted fifty or a hundred dollars here and there from his dad, who thought he was spending it on dates. He said he set it up like dominos, like a Rube Goldberg machine.

"Or," he said, "like weaving a tapestry, planning one, you know, or even planning the Sistine Chapel, some big art piece. Some cathedral."

He circled back to tell of the insight he'd had on a night when we were partying in the basement. How he got the notebook out and just took it all down – just transcribed it, nothing more – and how it must have taken a year for that, more years to test to see he wasn't crazy, that it would really work. He said that over his lifetime it would keep growing and changing. He said that he thought it would die with him.

He was telling me now because, he said, with a gesture toward the sky, "They're coming back for me. Whoever gave me this. My people, I think. Either that or it's all me. If it's all me, then what happens? Whatever it is, it's going to be soon." He'd gestured up, but he kept looking down at the ground.

He said, "I'm taking you to the gallery in the morning. They're going to have it a while, keep the right temperature on it. The right lighting. They will. I have to believe that. It'll be in a museum soon, I hope."

"Shouldn't someone in your family be in charge of all this?" I said. I didn't think I believed him.

He said his mother was recently dead, drank herself to death like I must have known she would. He told it offhand like he didn't even care. It hurt me to hear what had become of her and hurt more to see how he avoided showing any emotion.

I asked about his dad. He said his dad was his dad, as I knew. The worst.

"And besides," he said, "you and I are family."

It was as though the time had never passed for him. He talked until I couldn't bear it anymore and excused myself to sleep. He followed me to the guest room.

"Can I stay here just a while? I know it's weird," he said. I whispered to him to sleep, saying it was all right while he kept talking.

"I've been so lonely," he said. "I didn't even notice until now."

★   ★   ★

I wasn't sure what to do when he finally slept but get up and walk out the door. Walking from his sleepy neighborhood down the valley into the heart of his little city felt like walking from a fairy underworld back into the real world.

I missed my family so urgently just then. I guess I couldn't think of anything else.

I learned the depth of my mistake maybe three weeks later, the triptych all over magazines and social media, all anonymous. I guessed that if he had wanted me to come forward with what I knew, he would have said so, but I wasn't sure. Maybe that was something he would have told me in the morning. Still, the trouble it must have taken to make it anonymous was a good hint. By the time it was all in the air, he hadn't been seen for at least a week. I got in touch with the girlfriend, but she didn't know anything. She never mentioned the triptych.

The triptych keeps living, though, so I still hope that he's all right, wherever he is.

★   ★   ★

Three: Eva

When she turned twelve, we had a letter from an estate attorney. To learn the rest, I would have to take Audrey to visit a safe deposit box in a bank in the city where the triptych lived. We had to renew our passports and arrange time off from work and school.

The whole week of the trip she wore her raspberry-colored coat with her hair, so like Stephan's, hanging loose down the back of it. She felt far from me. Was she wealthy now, some sort of celebrity? It was up to her to decide whether to tell anyone. For now, we were keeping everything to ourselves.

People visit the triptych like a holy shrine, religious people and scholars. We had been aware of the phenomenon in our peripheral vision all these years and never thought that it might belong to us. I hated Stephan for never even hinting to me.

Hated him? That's too strong. Obviously, I didn't know him at all.

Our first stop after getting settled at the hotel was at the venue itself, where the triptych hung in a small bare chapel. Ropes held us a few feet back from the small living things, and the water and soil I supposed, all so carefully arranged and sealed in their three glass cases.

Just now, gestural figures and treelike figures rose from an earthy abstract background, but it would all change over time. The imagery brought to mind Bosch, Kandinsky, Breughel, and Vermeer each in turn. It was vague enough to make one think of many different things.

The setting called up Monet in the Musée de l'Orangerie and the Rothko Chapel in Houston. Actual worshippers had their corner of the space. Pilgrims, I supposed. The rest were tourists all trying and failing to feel the awe.

I moved on from it and let Audrey stay.

In one of the rooms of the interpretive center outside the chapel, the artistic connections were spelled out. In other rooms, the scholarly and the religious implications had their due. There was a room on botany and mycology with close-up detail photos from the triptych and Petri dishes set into the walls, some researcher's attempts to reproduce certain effects. There was a room on chemistry, a room on theories of provenance. One very small room had spaceman imagery. I passed through that one without looking. I thought I must be coming back toward the door that would lead back to the breezeway to the chapel, but there was one more room. In this one, a video played the growth of the triptych from its birth to the present day.

I had seen this video before on a phone, on the television, but something about seeing it here, with the triptych so close by, with the plan for the day of visiting the safe deposit box, brought a strong sense of doom. I wanted to go home without doing anything more, but of course I stayed and watched.

In the video, the triptych fills the screen. The earliest bit is badly shot and inconsistently lit. The image starts as a confused gray-brown patchwork, and then imagery begins to bloom from it. The human figures come in first, a man and a woman and then more of them, and then animals, the vague shapes of plants. The lighting evens out, marking the time when the triptych was moved to its chapel. The images continue to move and change. They are more or less abstract, but they are never not images.

An inexplicable feeling of loneliness comes, a lump in my throat as I see the line of his mother's profile. I recognize it from a certain snapshot of her. It rises on the left-hand panel and falls back to become something else. Something gray grasps on to the outer glass and begins to grow. It seems it will be a mistake in the design, a rust taking hold to obscure what grows beneath. Instead, the new arrival takes shape as a vine. It grows tendrils and moves up and out to make a silvery frame for the central panel. Figures from below it adhered to the frame and lift. They undulate. They fall back. In the center, the shape of Earth rises. In the right-hand panel, a ruddy egg shape builds, and a black egg shape hovers over it.

I look away.

★   ★   ★

At night we spread the parcels on the hotel bed. Each is wrapped in brown grocery bag. The first is the size of a ream of paper. We look over the graph pages and the handwritten pages and place them back in the suitcase. They will return to the safe deposit box until Audrey can decide to whom she will gift or sell them. It is her decision.

Other parcels hold other curiosities. One is filled with projects to be carried out. One letter says that that one is for Audrey's eyes alone. She places it in her messenger bag next to her laptop. There are DVDs in other packages. We play them on the hotel television. One is the construction of the triptych, different camera angles of it. I see Stephan moving around his creation but do not recognize the room. The last DVD is the one that plays for the rest of the evening. It is the one with Stephan speaking to Audrey. He speaks freely. He is not shielding her. He is calling on her to imagine what she might be or might become. He is calling on her to hope that he might come back for her, that he might take her someplace new.

I am in and out of the room. I can't stand to watch and can't stand for her to watch alone. When I return from getting ice, she is perched on the edge of the bed still in her coat. I recognize the raspberry egg of the coat and the black egg of the hair spread out upon it.

THE ORBITAL BLOOM

(with Eileen Gunnell Lee)

Reprinted by permission of the coauthor

Paradiso Mission Communication
Elapsed Time: 11:10:23:45:52
Distance from Earth: 4039.15901181 AU

I had so much I wanted to say to you. But I've kept quiet. The silence between us now is years long, billions of miles long – with that distance increasing. Given the circumstances, I want things to be different. I can't tell if this feeling is hope or masochism.

But that's not how I wanted to start this.

Will someone read this to you? The thought of my words passing through another human being before they reach you – it helps. Whoever is reading this, thank you. Thank you for taking care of Judy. I know it can't be easy. I've told her before where I am, but she won't remember. Maybe you could remind her? Tell her I'm on the *Paradiso*. It's a decades-long mission – at least three decades to get to the impact site and back again. We don't know how long it will take to find what we're looking for. Maybe you could show her that documentary again – the one about the mission and Bacterial Infusion Theory – once the treatment starts to take effect? I want her to understand, if she can.

This next part is for Judy.

You might not have heard that Pero is with me. You remember my husband, don't you? Maybe you saw us on television, or whatever old tech they have there. Such things end up in unused corners, in rooms with the residents who don't notice. It's hard to imagine you that way – that you wouldn't have noticed. But I read the doctor's report.

Pero got some difficult news in his download too. His mother diagnosed and terminal. By the time he got the message, she was gone. His brothers knew this would be the case. When they sent details about the funeral, they didn't ask him to make any decisions – not even about whether to have her avatar present. Basic stuff. He's been brooding about it since. Refusing to talk. But I've preempted him. I'm writing you a letter in part because I know the next stage of Pero's grief will be to hound me about my relationship with you.

But look – I haven't even managed to begin this letter properly. I typed 'Dear Judy' at the top. But that sounded terrible. Even knowing you won't be reading it any time soon, I can't bring myself to type 'Mom'. I can't bring myself to type anything at all if I think of the woman I remember holding this letter in her perfectly manicured hands. Only the distance between us allows the words to flow – the physical distance, but also knowing how far you are from understanding.

I'll start again.

★   ★   ★

Dear Mom,

Hi. It's been a while. I'm writing to you from the *Paradiso* starship, approximately two Earth years out from Pluto. There are six of us on board. We are looking for the origins of the 2016FZ2 asteroid, traced to an impact deep in the Cloud – the first asteroid to contain liquid water and microbial life! The bacterial profile is close to fossil records on Earth. We have matches confirmed in both pseudomorphs and calcium carbonate.

Even before we left Earth they were talking about 'the origin of life'. That this asteroid must have come from a mother planet, harboring the bacteria from which we all emerged. But as a scientist, I don't pin my hopes on it as the media seem to be doing back home. I've seen what they're saying – about Utopia or Eden or whatever – maybe you've seen it too.

As per the nature of the mission – find and retrieve bacterial samples – we are returning Earthside. Cell cycling makes this possible, preventing physical degradation as long as we are receiving treatments. It is also making you possible. Your recovery. Only the best for my mother, of course.

I didn't make it clear to you I was leaving. That I would be gone beyond the natural span of your lifetime. But I've made it all right now, see? I hope someday when you are able to really think about that, you will understand.

Love, Ronnie.

★   ★   ★

Dear Mrs. Bolter-Petrovic,

You may remember me. Molly Foster? Your mother might have called me Nurse Molly – or sometimes she forgets and calls me Millie. I worked in the common room the last time you visited but have since been promoted. I'm the one who works most closely with your mother now, so they've passed your correspondence to me. I want to assure you of full confidentiality. Please say what you have to say and know I'll do my best to let her know what it is. Communication is difficult for her.

We admire the work you do, I want to say. There's a great deal of hope down here, in general. Your mission, that's beyond words, but what we know of the cell cycling treatments, well, it's given me the most hope I've had in my entire career in health care.

Your mother's had her first treatment. She was in discomfort for a few days, just a little stiffening and some vocalization, all within the upper limit of expected side effects. Time passes, and I don't notice a change yet, but I think one day she might be able to understand what I read to her.

With great respect,
Molly Foster, RN

Paradiso Mission Communication
Elapsed Time: 11:10:25:57:59
Distance from Earth: 4041.48229840 AU

Pero is driving me crazy. That's another thing I never would have told you before.

Paradiso is running smoothly. Not only are its systems automated, but the monitoring also takes care of itself. Every cycle he performs his audits, then he checks for system updates and reads the documentation. Then he studies some theoretical physics something or other. Keeping up to date, he says. Unless something goes wrong with the ship, or an update requires him to print new hardware, Pero is a free agent. Free to bother me, mostly. He hangs around the lab a lot. I'm constantly reminding him of protocol.

The catch-arm brings in samples regularly. Even with another microbiologist on board, I barely have time to breathe. You said this to me, before you started forgetting words and conversations became difficult for a different reason – you said Pero would be hard to get along with. You gave reasons – because he is older, because he is foreign. Because these things would make him see my career as second to his.

You have forgotten what happened to my stipend – the money that was supposed to pay tuition – after you saw that targeted ad for acting classes. Method acting at fifty-six years old. Run by some nobody with hair plugs. My money gone.

After all these years, you never asked how I paid.

R.

★   ★   ★

Dear Veronica,

Sorry, not calling you Ronnie.

Just returned from second treatment. Millie read your letter, asked could I write back? We found I could. Much to say, but it is very hard.

Will you be here for my birthday?

Will write again so soon. Love,

Mommy

★   ★   ★

Paradiso Mission Communication
Elapsed Time: 11:10:30:13:03
Distance from Earth: 4046.00003468 AU

The day after I signed for your treatment, I dreamed a scene from childhood. A dream like my subconscious was reaching deep into my brain stem for those most basic emotions that form a toddler's world. Pure feeling, unshaped by experience.

I am kneeling on the hardwood floor of your study. You are behind me, sprawled on that vintage chaise you loved so much – the one from your photoshoot. You shout up at the ceiling because you haven't quite gotten the hang of your omni-present voice assistant. You always assumed it couldn't hear you when in reality it was recording even your whispered affirmations in front of the bathroom mirror every morning.

But this is my adult mind filling in. In the dream, I am aware only of the details.

The window in front of me is wet with condensation. Your Rejuvaderm humidifier is running nearby. The moisture amassed is enough that the droplets, before they trickle down toward the frame, are round and heavy, each reflecting its own suspended world.

"No, it's not like a colonic," you shout. "It's a transplant."

I watch the water collect along the bottom edge of the window frame. Inside the spreading pool of water is a half-eaten candy. Purple. Sucked into a flat, ellipsoid shape. I'd forgotten I'd put the candy there, the last time I was in this room waiting for you to finish a call. I look back at you, half expecting to find myself captured like a fly in the amber of your disappointed gaze. But you are still on the phone.

"There's a company that does it. Sends people in to get samples from uncontacted – Brazil, I think it is. Jesus, Su, they don't pick it up off the ground. It's hygienic."

Turning back to the window, I take the candy between two fingers and pop it into my mouth. I barely taste sweetness before something stabs my tongue. When I open my mouth with the scream already in my throat, a buzzing erupts from me instead. Bitterness spreads over the site of my wound and I spit an eviscerated bee onto the windowsill.

"Veronica, I'm on the phone!"

My tongue is throbbing. With each pulse the skin feels tighter, hotter. I can't close my mouth. I can't stop screaming.

"Su, I'm going to mute. Veronica's having a fit. Hold on."

When you bend over me there is a brief moment where I think this time will be different. I look up at you and open my mouth, stick out my tongue for you to see the source of the problem. But you grab me and wrench me off my feet, your fingers digging into the flesh of my upper arm. Before I can say a word, I am sliding across the tile of the bathroom floor. You are closing the door between us. Stunned, I press my cheek to the cool tile. In the sliver of light under the door, I see your pink toes lined up as if you are standing there, facing the door, waiting for me. Before I can push myself up a rhythmic chant is already pressing past my swollen tongue.

"Mama, open. Mama, open." I put my hand on the doorknob and turn.

The door flies in on its hinges, the knob catching me above my right eye. When I can see again, you are standing in the doorway, mouth hard, eyebrow raised.

"Well, what were you standing in front of the door for? Get up. Stop crying."

When I rose from my bed, in my adult body, at least forty-three Earth years between me and that Irvine Villa apartment, a tight bud of pain is nestled in the socket of my right eye. Remembering what I had done – feeling again the visceral haste with which I signed your treatment contract – the bud blossomed into a blood-red flower that turned its saw-toothed petals into my brain.

★   ★   ★

Dear Veronica,

Fifteenth treatment today. Things have changed.

I read your letters, it seemed for the first time. Millie says she has read them to me before, and there are little echoes in them that seem familiar, but I am only just now finding my 'right mind'. I am still quite weak and the writing terribly slow, but they all say I am much improved.

I have heard your story of the bee before. What happened, almost certainly, was that you bit down on your own tongue. On purpose? By accident? I don't know. If you'll rest your tongue well back from your teeth, honey, you'll never bite it – and you might find it improves your facial lines. Just an idea.

I think you do often misremember the details, Veronica dear, but it is good to remember the Irvine Villa along with you. It was quite a charming space with the Spanish roof and the little paved courtyard, all that bougainvillea trained against the entries. Do you remember any of that? We were so happy there, most of the time, but you did always have your moments.

Your little story reminds me of a good friend I had, Sheila. Beautiful, classy woman. It hurt my heart to see how she looked at you. You'd do your fussing, and she'd roll her eyes, speak harshly to you. I told her I couldn't spend time with her anymore. She made me too aware of how you were. It was strange. I suppose I identified with her and so if she was feeling perplexed with you, it made me feel that way too. She made me lose feeling for you, but my, it was hard to tell her to go. I've never had many women friends.

How is this? If you think you ate a bee at Irvine Villa, well then you ate a bee. It seems a silly thing to have done, but I am sorry for you nonetheless. You certainly didn't do it in my presence. I promise you were happy there, playing with your dolls. Only when I had a friend over or talked on the phone, you would fuss. You were jealous of me getting attention, I think.

And, Pero: If Pero is bothering you there is not much to be done, trapped as you are. You could try eating his stinger like you ate that bee's, I suppose. Ell oh ell.

The treatments have been a godsend. Thank you for arranging them, dear. Each treatment means two or three hours' reprieve from the 'home'. I walk past the row of droolers, and the ones who still know what's happening are jealous (so jealous! I wish you could see). I get a little ride in the car – just like a poodle, I lean my nose out the window and the stink of the elderly comes out and away from me. It's a real treat.

They tell me you're not joking, you really are going to Eden. I can hardly believe it. Yes, we do have radio and television here, by the way. We have the good old high-speed internet access. I take it you do not? No one can tell me why we can't speak face to face, on the computer. You wouldn't want to see me, I can tell you that, but I would like to see you.

When I go back over your letters, they confuse me. All the false starts, all the digressions when you know all I want to know is when you're coming home.

Do you think you might be back in time for my birthday? The big eight-five, just three months away.

Eternally grateful and anxiously awaiting your return,

Mommy

★   ★   ★

Paradiso Mission Communication
Elapsed Time: 11:12:23:31:47
Distance from Earth: 4129.01003467 AU

It strikes me this morning that you and I are growing together now, in a way. The distance allows it. I don't have to look at your face and hold my breath in morbid anticipation. I can't even imagine your face. The report described you as – well, if you are coming back to yourself now, I shouldn't say. You would be mortified.

I wonder if the treatment is affecting me emotionally. Does it work as a kind of stabilizer? I wouldn't be surprised if there are effects they've hidden from us – effects individually undesirable but beneficial for the mission? Human cells rewritten on a regular cycle to match a baseline sample. If you're wondering where your sample came from, I kept a box of your things when you moved into care – found a hair on your olive angora sweater. So your baseline is either fifty-year-old Judy or a lab-grown rabbit. We shall see!

I say these thoughts strike me this morning, but there isn't any morning out here. The spectrum lights fade in and out on a twenty-four-hour cycle, but the sun itself is so small and dim and everything out here is black black black. To send us out here looking for origins – even in bacterial form – doesn't make sense to me. Eden is the other way! My body is screaming it every waking moment, even as it is being rewritten. My new cells must remember something other than this darkness.

You are rolling your eyes now. Veronica is over-thinking again, yes? Doesn't she have anything amusing to say?

I have one funny story. Though I warn you, if I tell you now there'll be nothing entertaining for another century. Don't say I didn't warn you.

As I mentioned before, Pero is bored. When he's bored, he's needy. Hanging around the lab nonstop. One day last week, though, he wasn't feeling well and spent most of the day in our cabin. This gave me a chance to talk to Robert, the other microbiologist, without Pero taking over.

Rob is almost a different person when Pero's not around.

"Running these tests – does it get to you, Ronnie?" he says. I ask him what he means. "I mean, we haven't pulled in anything worth looking at. If that impact scattered pieces of asteroid, sending them each on their own trajectory, we could be looking for a long time. We might never find anything."

"It's true." I nod. "It's always been a bit of a crapshoot. They're calling it Eden back home, for Chrissake."

"That's just it." Rob frowns. "With running sample after sample, it's not much of a distraction. I start thinking about home. Earth. What it's going to look like when we get back. What it's going to feel like."

I wanted to tell him this is all I think about. Maybe an exaggeration, but I wonder what it will be like to slip back into life on Earth. We'll have been gone so long that everyone – everything – will have moved on without us. We'll be set apart. No longer integrated. Part of a different ecosystem.

Tell me, on the news do they talk about why they chose us for this mission? How all of us are the truncated ends of our respective lines? You and I have gone back and forth on me not wanting kids, so we don't need to do it again now. I'm OK with being the end of us. Rob didn't want to be, though. He had a wife. The way he talks about her – it melts me a little. It makes me wonder if this one aspect of Rob is why he and Pero keep each other at arm's length. Maybe he sees how Pero looks at me – his hard calculation and conquest where there should be tender care. There is a difference between how a man looks at a woman when he's looking with his eyes and when he's looking…. I don't know…with his everything. Or maybe not looking at all, but recognizing. There's a difference. I think Rob sees Pero looking.

That day Pero was sick, Rob opened up to me about his wife. Told me all kinds of things about her – what she liked to do, what she was working on when she died. She was a potter. He told me about the miscarriage she had before she was diagnosed with cancer. Not an uncommon story.

I went back to our cabin for lunch and to check on Pero. Rehydrating a couple packets, I told him some of the things that Rob told me. Just conversation. But as I talked, Pero got out of bed and got dressed. He went to the medicine cabinet and downed who knows what. He insisted on taking his lunch to the lab. He pulled a chair up to the fucking bench! I refused to work with him there and Rob wouldn't unpack the samples.

"A man talks about his dead wife for one reason," Pero said when we were in bed later. He said it in the dark. After I'd been pretending to sleep for quite some time.

★   ★   ★

Dear Veronica,

You ask what effects these treatments may be having on us, and my mind whirrs to life. There is so much to say, yet my powers fail me. My hands fail me. I'll do my best.

I find myself focusing on three things you mentioned, so let's get these out of the way: the lab-grown angora, the fifty-year-old me, and you imagining my face. These are the items that caught my eye, and you can laugh at that all you like – and I caught your attempts at humor all throughout your last letter. Very good, sweetie!

Yes, as you can imagine, I visualized my face at fifty, myself in that flattering sweater, just my color. You remember my figure at fifty, how I looked in that sweater? Cleavage, collarbones, angular shoulders. My neck at fifty, a work of art. Most women never look like that once in their lives. I felt powerful in it because it was lab-grown angora and the green of it grew right out of the flesh.

You were already in advanced classes and were such a good girl (unglamorous, granted, but fresh and clean and perfectly presentable) and I liked to be seen with you just then. I wore that sweater one day to a fancy lunch. That cute advisor of yours had just told me the big news about you getting into your program, and he'd let me be the one to tell you.

Did you ever even think about your children? I think about them, how old they'd be now, how accomplished. Maybe they would have brought some light to the 'dark dark dark'.

You ask how the treatment might be affecting our emotions. I must say it has brought me to a great sense of sympathy for you. Everything you say, the blackness of your world and the hurtling away from true Eden, your sad little flirtation with the man at work, all of it breaks me. I feel for you, having a mother like me, having a husband like Pero. You're always being eclipsed. I feel how that hurts, now.

I know you aren't going to be back for my birthday. The naïve me of three weeks ago, I feel for her too. My birthday doesn't mean anything, dear, compared to your woes. Don't think of it again.

Pero is right about why a man speaks of his dead wife. You're saying I never approved of him anyway, and I have always thought Pero is a bit too much of a Ferrari to your Subaru and all of that, but he's also smarter about people than you are. How could he not be?

My Anthony, early on, sobbed to me about his wife. It sets off something animal in us, doesn't it? I read that section of your letter, I can't see anything but sex imagery, what with the 'melting' and 'his everything' and the 'f—ing'. You'll have been in his bed before you get this letter. You know what I'll be hoping, so I don't have to mention it.

You are wrong, too, that men have anything to look with but their eyes – and hands. I'd have said Anthony connected with me soul to soul. I'd have said that, before he left me just as I was starting to be ill. At least he waited for that. I can't say the same for you.

You say I'd be mortified to know what I was like. I lived through every moment of it, shitting the bed, everything. Those memories are not gone.

So much more to say, but I am tiring you already and will let you go. I feel, though, that we are communicating for the first time equal to equal rather than one of us looking down her nose at the other. Do you feel this, too? Say you do.

Desperately missing and praying for you,

Mommy

★   ★   ★

Paradiso Mission Communication
Elapsed Time: 12:06:01:21:22
Distance from Earth: 4317.05799673 AU

Another dream last night. A brief flash before I woke again after having sunk halfway into sleep. I dreamed your face – nothing more. But the expression on your face told the whole story. You were looking down at me, your eyebrows raised toward the middle. Not enough to crease your brow. Only a mild disappointment. Pity. It's the expression my mind has held in some deep recess all these years, created from a composite of disappointments. The face which looked down on me the night of the Irvine evacuation. With the wildfire closing in around us, I looked up and saw – almost simultaneously – 2016FZ2 flash across Earth's atmosphere, and your look of condescension.

Upon waking, I realized this was impossible. 2016FZ2 never made it as far as the exosphere before it was harvested. That asteroid I saw as a child was not so large or significant. Just a shooting star upon which I probably made some desperate wish while walking the shoulder of that smoking highway. I don't remember.

I remember you were wearing running shoes. Rubber soles melting into hot tar. In some miraculous last-second decision you decided not to wear the gold patent pumps, but carry them. Which meant I hauled my own suitcase out of Irvine.

How did we survive? The trees bug-infested tinder. The ocean a cesspool. Mutated cyanobacteria in the aquifers. The blood of the Earth is septic. No amount of inoculation is going to fix this mess. What are we doing? They sent us out here for the answer. For the fix. But there is no original state. Not out here. Not anywhere.

★   ★   ★

Something is going on with Pero. After he spent the day in the lab, he crashed. He slept for three days, save for the fifteen minutes each diurnal cycle where he stumbled down the hall, feverish and sweating, to check the monitors. I let him be. I worked longer hours.

"I like to keep a routine as much as possible." That's what Rob said when I told him I was skipping dinner to stay on at the lab, keep sifting through rocks. "It's what saved me after Ani." He added that last part as I was nodding my acknowledgment.

"Pero's not dead," I said, gulping the words back even before they passed my tongue. How could I have said that? Lips pressed, Rob invited me to share a meal with him. I followed him down the hall, tail tucked.

We ate, Rob mastering those food packets in a way Pero never had. He'd added some kind of green leaf to the sauce. He told me the name, but I've forgotten it now. You remember my black thumb. I never was good at keeping green things alive. Rob's growing all kinds of plants in his cabin, on a shelf with timed spectrum lights. When I glanced up from my examination of a veined leaf, I found him looking at me.

"Do you love him? It seems like maybe—"

I felt something in me shift then. It wasn't a release, or a giving in, as you sometimes hear about with these things. It was as if I suddenly found myself inside a fortress, a thick wall between me and the world. But the wall was porous, the spaces between cells enough to let the infection through, to hold it safe and warm, to let it grow into the mortar.

"I do," I said.

He turned away from me with a look I saw then as anguish, a look which triggered my placating impulse. It's the impulse you planted, nurtured, grew.

Now, Mother, you harvest it.

As he turned, I reached around his body. Thicker than Pero. Solid. He relaxed against me. I slid my hand into his pants, felt for my grip. He stiffened, blazing against my palm. His body heaved forward. He braced himself against the wall.

"Veronica," he said. He used my full name. Invoked authority. But the tears were already in his voice. As his shoulders collapsed under the weight of a sob, I saw the photograph of his dead wife on the wall in front of us.

"Rob, relax. Let me—" I started, but he grabbed my wrist, already breaking away from me.

"I'm going to be sick."

He ran to the washroom, the stain blooming on the seat of his pants. I listened to the sound of his purge. The stink of sickness filled the cabin. But when I called out to him, looking through the crack of the open door, I found him gray-faced, slick with sweat, tears running into the hair at his temples as he arched against the back of the toilet. He gripped and pulled himself furiously, breathing through clenched teeth.

"Let me—" I said, ignoring his rolling eyes.

I kicked his soiled clothes aside and knelt between his legs.

★   ★   ★

Dear sweet darling Veronica,

"How did we survive?" you ask. I'd say it's debatable that we did.

You must be happy to tell me you've done something so disgusting. I'm not shocked, though. I think you forget how much I've lived.

And how vividly you've described it all! I read your letter to Millie, by the way. We peed ourselves over it. She is a jolly woman (heavy-set, you know). We love a laugh, so we thank you.

Am I glad to have never creased my brow over-hard for you? You bet. I would be a Shar-Pei. Every day of yours is a tragedy, isn't it?

I remember the first time you got your period, you bawled. You'd wrap the pads in layer on layer of toilet paper so that the trash filled up in a day. It still smelled. You washed your hands until they cracked and bled. Your body and the whole disgusting world were never good enough for you. You want me to help you with this — what? perversity of yours? this infection — but I can't.

I looked at myself in a full-length mirror this afternoon, curtains open and full daylight coming in from the courtyard. I can remember the movements that led to each mark and wrinkle. Isn't that curious? I still wear a pearl-colored bikini, and the rest is an appaloosa-spotted travesty folding and melting toward the floor, but you're right, it is rewriting even as I watch. I think in time I'll have it all back. Tell me if that's not so — or don't. I don't want to know.

Just tell me that the treatments will continue no matter what happens with the mission. I need this.

Missing you, praying for you,

Mommy

★   ★   ★

Dear Veronica,

I don't remember if I mentioned this before: A woman named Claire, elegant woman really, came around when I was waiting in the lobby for my treatment. You see, she is a reporter. I'm not going to mention the paper's name because you'll scoff, but she left a few issues for Millie and me, and we think it really is a serious paper.

She'd like to have your story — our story. She's going to call it 'Trouble in Eden'. Isn't that clever?

Millie and I have had such a good time reading your letters. I'm sure you won't mind Claire reprinting them. Just excerpts. We haven't discussed the amount, but she'll pay a pretty penny, you can bet. You should have seen the watch she wore.

Expect good news very soon,

Mommy

★   ★   ★

Paradiso Mission Communication
Elapsed Time: 14:02:14:44:03
Distance from Earth: 5001.00000029 AU

Haven't read your two previous letters.

Keeping this brief. I'm voice recording. Remaining vertical results in what's left of my insides finding the nearest emergency exit. I ran some tests. The microbe we've been looking for. We found it. It found us. A slow bug. It found a nice habitat here despite the cycling. I've compared it to the fossil record and can see little development from previous forms. Nothing like what took place on Earth. Environment out here is static. More tests are needed, but I wonder if it will be enough. Or too much? Can you travel too far back in time to fix your mistakes?

Each cycle reset us as hosts. Rebuilding the perfect home. Before there's a chance for mutation, we're reset to defaults. To our original sample that promised us a round trip. Our return. The treatment was built for a closed system. For quarantine protocols. Every time we reset we're vulnerable again. I knew this going in. I knew it.

The treatment is keeping us alive. But each time it cycles back to the original it simultaneously recognizes the microbe as a foundation of human life, and rejects the exobacteria as environmental, as external to us, and steps in for our immune systems. The paradox. It's a part of us. It changed us.

At the beginning of the cycle this morning, feeling not too bad, I did Pero's rounds for him. As much as I could. Checked for alert messages. Not sure what I would do if there were any. Pero's never been great with illness. But we go on. How far? Not too far. Then we reset. We return.

When fever set in again, I remembered the heat of the drive room. There the sweat of my skin evaporated in the cyclone. Felt like nothing could grow there. I crawled up into the ducts above the reactor. Imagined myself thermophilic. Mutating. Each cell drawn out into the long rod forms of Escherichia coli. Familiar but foreign. I am stretched taut. Bursting blood, shit, vomit until I don't remember being human.

Then, I reset.

I am three years old, strapped into a moving stroller. The damp wad of my diaper is held tight by the harness between my legs. The shade is lowered, but I can hear the click click click of your heels on the sidewalk behind me. I squirm sideways, reaching for the shade. I push it back. You come around to the front of the stroller, smiling. You are looking over my head, smiling.

"Oh yes," you say. "Bright children can be such a handful." A male voice laughs in response. You pry my fingers from the shade, place my arms at my sides, and tuck a blanket tight around me. You do not replace the shade. The sun blazes. It reflects off the gold buttons at the shoulders of your navy wool jacket. When you straighten, pulling the wool smooth, you are still smiling. I watch your face, hoping for that brightness to turn to me. But as you step around behind the shade, laughing at something flattering the man has said, I am left only with the impression of the impossible cut of your jaw.

Reset. Reset. Reset.

*   *   *

Veronica,

Are you reading this? Are you ignoring me? You are scaring Mommy, now.

Tell me you are reading my letters.

Mommy

★ ★ ★

Dear Veronica,

I do not accept this behavior. I think you are only trying to frighten me.

I look in the mirror now, see the skin of my throat moving upwards. It reminds me of skin crawling on a scrotum. Have you ever seen that, dear? I am feeling sick. I swear I am.

★ ★ ★

This afternoon, I swept myself away from my mirror and the endless rereading of your letters. I went into the common room, saw a raging fire on the news. The rest home far up from ours, the one like a palace, is burning. Tight, greedy smiles on everyone's faces. We loved watching it.

Could I walk through a fire and see the scarred flesh smooth as I walked away? Could I sit through the whole conflagration and still reset? I'd like that.

I'll walk through fires and the floods and reset back to myself each time. I'll be beautiful. If I find people, I'll tell them my daughter was an astronaut. That will be as good as having you here.

Life will go on as it is, as I like it. Won't it?

I don't need you to answer. I know it will.

Judy

WATERSHAKERS

Mom screamed at me to do something about the horse trough. When I went out there, the mosquito larvae's herky-jerky dance hypnotized me. Algae, seedpods, and grass showed all bright and clear in the sun.

I considered pouring in some bleach, but that's no good for horses. I imagined finding a hose and suck-starting to pump the water out, imagined the horses dancing around, all joyous to have clean water. The idea of sucking that water kept grossing me out, though. I didn't see a hose right away. Then I got distracted.

I happened by about a week later. The larvae herked and jerked like before, but they were large enough I could see their little insides. The sun wasn't lighting up the water, and it didn't smell particularly bad. I wandered off again.

The water was low, and it was darker by the time I came around again, but the sun shone in like before. I thought, *I really do have to do something about this.* The larvae did more of a belly dance now, sinuous hip shakes instead of the jerk. I lifted out a handful of water and saw three little transparent women rolling their hips in my palm. I just about screamed. Even as I held them, two slowed and stopped moving. The center one kept on.

She was clear like mineral jelly, her skeleton structure like a human's but made of silver wire, her pale organs more or less like ours, as far as I know.

A jelly head but no face, no skull, a little pink brain floating on its stem.

I dropped her in a big tumbler of water on my nightstand. She stood and moved her hips in swift circles again. I watched – too long. When I returned, Mom had managed to tip over the trough. I cried seeing what all was scattered on the ground.

The one in my water glass seemed to be all right, though. She twitched and twitched her imaginary hula hoop all that night. I woke up several times to flick on the lamp and check her. I knew she needed food because she was moving more and more slowly each time, and by morning she jerked barely at all.

I guessed they'd been eating algae and leaves, but every pet I've had has loved raw hamburger, so that's what I tried. I impaled the ball of meat on a toothpick and lowered it in to her. The blood aura wafted toward her head, which stretched up to meet it. It was gross. I could see what would happen: the dimple in the top of her head would deepen to engulf the meat, which would suck into an esophagus opening above her collarbone.

I didn't get to stay and watch. I had chores, school. When I returned, she'd grown an inch and shook at full speed. I thought she must be happy.

She was half as tall as a Barbie when I finally had the epiphany: minerals! I held the tumbler to the trough. She leaped out and swam to the rusted edge. Her head opened and took in a large flake of metal. She came back to the tumbler and shook her hips like, *OK, let's go home.*

After that I fed her staples along with the hamburger, which really helped. Her skeleton grew sturdier, and a little chrome skull began to grow. I watched it form, as much of it as I could. It started thin as a spiderweb, like a sketch in fine-line pencil. Day by day, the lines grew wider until one day it was a perfect skull with perfect little silver teeth. It had all the cool of a heavy metal album cover. The jelly outside the skull formed a pleasant profile, too: upturned nose, firm chin. She would have been pretty if she'd had skin.

Her movements enthralled me, as you might imagine. I fantasized sitting on the bathtub's edge and sliding in to dance with a full-grown version of her. I was afraid, though. Her jelly might sting. Her head might open again.

Or might I harm her?

She had to squat now to stay submerged in the tumbler. I was feeding her stranger and stranger things, and at night I had terrible dreams about what would be the outcome. This couldn't continue.

I knew I would release her in water, but I couldn't see her being happy in a river and couldn't get to the sea. I settled on the neighbor's dark, smelly pond. Fish to eat, if she grew large enough. If not, snails and insects.

I felt stupid carrying the Kool-Aid pitcher, relieved I didn't run into anyone on the way. Once there, I pushed the pitcher down into pondwater before I could change my mind.

She lay shaking her hips in the shallows. Suddenly she tensed, plunged her arm into mud, and pulled out a worm. She held it up, which made me smile. It was like she was saying, *Victory!* She slurped the wriggling thing, then jerked her head toward something else. She bolted. I couldn't see her anymore.

I tucked big stones around the pitcher so it wouldn't float away. I thought if she got homesick, she might go back, or maybe I just didn't want to carry it home.

I was awfully sad walking away. It was like when we put Sam to sleep, or the night we got the call about Dad. Everything lost.

The pitcher was still there the first couple of times I visited, then it was gone.

I got back to routine: Mom screaming about chores, me being distracted, video games, a field trip to the state capitol. Things really were normal by the time I thought of her again. I was at a friend's house watching a movie where a woman gives a lap dance on a dare. I thought it was one of the most moving scenes in any movie I'd seen. The woman's upturned nose, her grinding. Sexy and sweet and sad.

I went out to the pond that night expecting to mope around the edges like before. I got to the place where the pitcher had been and looked across the water. Something moved in a group of scrubby trees, and I approached.

Her chrome teeth flashed in moonlight. She was chewing a great big frog, legs sticking out of her mouth, skin and blood on her lips.

When she saw me, she stood her full six feet and shimmied, in greeting I suppose. I was proud to see silver hairs starting on her head and new marbled skin, like the skin of a plum frosted over with blue. I could still see through to organs but just barely.

Was she full grown? I couldn't say. I didn't think so.

I reached for her shoulder, and she shuddered back a few feet. She squatted there a while and ran her fingers in the mud, looking up at me every so often. Then she jumped up, went behind a tree, and came back, offering the pitcher. I smiled and handed it back. *It's yours to keep.*

She misunderstood. She went down to the pond's edge and filled it with water. She offered it again. I didn't take it.

She shimmied slowly. She looked inside the pitcher and shimmied at the same time. When I took it, she went down on all fours and slid into the pond.

I was thinking how we were really connecting, right up until then. She didn't swim back, didn't surface. I started to get sad, but then something occurred to me.

The pitcher vibrated in my hands, you see.

It kept shaking as I walked home. I couldn't wait to get it in light. I'd see silver women, surely, but in my imagination there were little golden men in there too, jeweled horses, dragons in red and in green.

VIRIDIAN GREEN

Trevor, younger than the other workers in his division, had long assumed they found him charming. Weren't they always asking about his community theater roles, encouraging him to put up posters in the kitchenette area? Promising to remember to come to the next one.

Weren't they always implying he was handsome? But in the first day of remote work, he had the wool pulled from his eyes. He was profoundly unattractive on-screen. The asymmetry – one eye higher and larger than the other, the uneven jawline – and the gray tint to his skin. All their faces were placid while his contorted into strange expressions.

That very evening, he set about changing things. After finishing his work with the spreadsheets, he put in an hour practicing calm and fluid speaking, another hour analyzing the recording, another rearranging the bookshelves behind him and then moving the bookshelves into the cramped entry so that there could be a plain white wall behind him to facilitate smooth edges on a computerized background.

It did not take another hour to find the background. His initial search brought up the perfect thing, soft leaves (or were they feathers?) in viridian green. Subtle enough for business but a little nod to his supposed creativity, just the thing to bring out some warmth in his skin.

Sleep was short that night, but the morning meeting went well. Before official business started, Trevor had compliments on his background and in a private message, Margie said, "Glad to see you looking so well today! I was a little worried...."

The supervisor spoke for a long while. Trevor had time to study the picture he made and was pleased. As long as he didn't speak, all was well. And yet he had to be visibly engaged. He practiced reducing his expressions – smaller nods, smaller smiles.

The meeting, then paperwork. Trevor fell asleep on the couch and woke feeling certain that the meeting had never ended and would never end.

Another morning, another meeting. The face in his rectangle was not his own. It had a cleft chin. Trevor had always wanted a cleft chin, but not like this. This was wrong.

When Trevor moved, this new face moved, but never in exactly the same way. His small nod at a colleague's recommendation was translated to a thoughtful, slow, deep nod, chin on the knuckles.

Then the Trevor on the screen began to speak. Not agreeing but challenging the colleague, challenging the idea in a snide, arch, winning way.

"You're on fire," said Margie in a private message.

"I think I've been hacked," he typed back, but the face on the screen was his own again, now. He didn't hit send, only gave small nods while the supervisor, beaming, said, "Trevor has a great point there."

Still worried there'd been a hacker, he couldn't focus on work that afternoon. All was given over to internal debate about what had happened and what he could do. He couldn't say, "I wasn't me for a moment there," could he?

Just before five, a complimentary email came from the supervisor. Trevor was being considered for an important new project and had to write up a prospectus, ASAP.

But he didn't. Once he'd taken a walk and had dinner, he fell asleep on the couch and dreamed of the theater, a big musical production with Trevor as the lead. (He was never the lead.) On an opening-night high, they all went bar-hopping, singing in the streets. He landed in a cozy back booth with the female lead and the handsomest man on crew. They seemed in competition for him. The woman leaned in close and said, "Trevor, you're muted."

Trevor sat up. The laptop was open, the morning meeting about to start. For an instant he saw the handsome, cleft-chinned face, heard it saying, "I *could* write a prospectus, sure, but wouldn't it be better to just…" but then the sound was gone. The others still seemed to be listening.

The face faded. As though the green leaves were darkness and this other man had stepped back from the light, he dimmed until Trevor saw only the beautiful field of flowing green.

"I'm here. There's something wrong," he said. He typed it into the chat and hit return.

It didn't appear in the chat. He re-entered it, but it did not ever appear. There was nothing to do but watch the others watching, smiling, nodding, admiring. After a while, there was applause.

PROMISE

Brochures fanned across the lace tablecloth in Grandma's dining room. Up close, I saw the recruiter's immaculate makeup starting to crack, the silver showing against auburn at the part in her hair. She slanted forward with briefcase on knees and weight on the balls of her feet. I was meant to think she'd bolt and that I'd lose my chance, which made me wonder why she was so desperate.

"An innovative, community-owned academy." The paper was thick, graphic design on point with a subtle white font over a background of the canyon at sunset. The recruiter dropped names I only pretended to know, graduates who were making waves in the gaming industry, townspeople treating academy kids like a semi-pro sports team. I tried to trust the images on the brochures and turn off the signals I was getting from her.

Grandma's eyes welled. To her question of how many from my class, I told the truth: "Just me. I think I'll be the first from town." It wasn't just the town. I'd be the first from our state.

I signed, spent the next six months sure that it was a scam. Then I had two weeks after graduation to shop and pack and part from Grandma, nearly weeping. I fit in a few last dates with Jack before it was all over. Then it was the bus to the plane and the wait in a tiny airport until all of our planes had come in and the academy shuttle picked us up in the dark. Each leg of the trip was like another six months.

★   ★   ★

The dormitory just about burst my heart when I entered: wide pine floorboards, wide dark ceiling beams, and chains of cut-paper flowers strung across the beams. Twelve beds were organized like a muffin pan in four rows of three, each one made up with beige sheets and a patchwork quilt. Each bed had a round nightstand with a stained-glass lamp on it. I chose the one with lions on it. One girl's lamp had a dragonfly, one girl had a little more brass in her hair, and other than that we were all the same and seemed to know it. There was some talk around how excited we were and what a pretty place.

We hadn't seen the place yet, to say that it was pretty, but for a cobblestone parking area and a series of dark walled gardens crossed en route to the dormitory. Some of us waited turns to wake our loved ones with calls from a corded phone in the corner. I did. I told Grandma how fine the trip had been and repeated inane things I'd already said to the girls.

A sleepy girl brought a cart with salad and homemade bread with butter, glasses of warm spiced milk. We sat on hard chairs on the patio and balanced our plates on our knees.

We joked about the outhouse on the way down the path, but inside it we found modern toilets and sinks, a good strong shower. The counter held deep stacks of unbleached cotton towels and a glass bowl of travel-size toiletries with European names. Still, I dreaded the time I would have to come down the dark path alone.

★ ★ ★

It is midnight now. I find my bed soft and sweet smelling. Patterns play before my eyes, just thin gray static that morphs into lines and swoops, then sleep comes hard. It can't be more than five minutes before my blood calms and I'm out.

I've dreamt of a school like this, a chance like this. I wake to the smell of windows standing open all night. The morning lights the distant canyon and edges in to pastures of sheep and of cattle, the closer fences of grapes, and opposite the canyon the lava stone of all the campus walls and buildings. One of the pamphlets had a story about the people who salvaged this stone. It was heartbreaking.

A girl barely older than us arrives, saying she's to be our mentor. She wears a soft work shirt and tan duck pants. Her body is healthy, skin peach tinted. We sit in an arc before her on the patio where she tells us how our first week will go. We're to keep lists of what we want from town, observe classes, and get adjusted. She asks us how we're going to feel being disconnected from our phones and such, and now I see that this meeting is some sort of counseling session. One girl voices our apprehensions about being away from technology.

"We have technology," the mentor says. She lists the appliances and gym equipment and all the rest, but of course that is not what we mean. She talks at length about our healing.

At the end, she gives us bundles of clothes like her own, all stiff and sharp smelling from drying in the sun, and for each of us a leather-bound journal. Mine is emerald and has a tree of life tooled into its cover, pages of creamy, thick unruled paper.

I make calls to Grandma and to some friends. My news is happy. The other new girls and I sit in on classes in drafting, architectonics, calligraphy, drawing, a class where a dozen girls discuss the plots of books I haven't read. The professors do little more than cross their arms and lean back, pleased.

Only the life drawing class gives me pause. The tableau vivant at the center of the room, the man and woman posed in a desperate nude embrace. I've never seen a nude man except in pictures. I haven't even looked at a video if I knew it might have something like that in it, and yes, it was hard to get through high school so innocent.

I think this is part of why they took me. I suspect it was also something about my body, my face. Our mentor could be my sister. Most of the girls could, and there are other things common between us.

Not one of us seems to like games. We're told we're going to form the next wave of creative talent in the industry, but in the week we share the dormitory, no one takes a board game down from the shelves or spreads a hand of solitaire. In the few hours between work and sleep we will sample old books from the shelves or, more often, we will withdraw to our beds to sketch and write in our journals.

Our mentor says that the goal of our education will be to show others what we have seen – though first we have to see something.

For now, we visit classes and cook and clean and learn some of the work of a farm. In the evening we take long walks on a cobblestone path that weaves through fields. It always seems like we are going to go to the edge of the canyon, but the path loops away just before. At the furthest point, we sometimes see animals in the wasted acres of sagebrush between us and the canyon. Jackrabbits, foxes, distant deer.

When I see the fox, my hands still shake from a chicken whose body I held as she died, a chicken I wouldn't touch at dinner, but then I see the fox and have that little animal shock and realize I am so hungry I could kill and eat another whole chicken.

At week's end, we pile into the academy shuttle and ride the half hour to town. We dress in street clothes, but we are already different from the locals. They seem course-grained, like they are formed of swarms or static, surrounded by beeping and buzzing and the ubiquitous screens.

In the stores we run into three or four couples who have our academy crest embroidered on their polos and sweatshirts. The men are very old and the women somewhere in middle age. We're made to stop and briefly greet them. They say they just happened to be out shopping. No one has told us to, but we have a haughty stance with them. We are aware of our long legs and our sharp jawlines as we stand beside them. They have a little bit of regional dialect and don't seem like very serious people, somehow. And there are boys our age and older looking at us like we're meat. I've never caught someone looking at me that way before – or maybe I *just* caught them and they looked away embarrassed – but these boys and these men do not stop when I meet their eyes.

The people are harried, even the kids, all of them profoundly unattractive to me. On the street our mentor says that it wasn't true that they just happened to be out. "No?" one girl says, and the mentor mumbles, and I think it is only I who hear: They received mailings telling them the date in case they wanted to be the first in town to see us.

We've been told to charge purchases to the academy, but the things for sale interest me no more than the people. I return to the shuttle early with some of the others. I think ahead to the evening. We will have a fire out on the knoll if it's cool enough. We will look out over the canyon in one direction and the sun setting in the other. If I can stay awake, I'll watch the stars. I write about this in my journal. I smile to myself with the sun warming my face and feel content with what I have.

Three of us have come back empty-handed, and it is to those three that our mentor makes her visit late in the night.

She guides the loud luggage cart over cobblestone paths, through walled gardens to a building with high lava-stone walls. I am the first to lift my bags and go with her while the others wait. We pass through an arched doorway and up a staircase to a nine-by-nine room paneled and floored in pine. It has a door, a bed, a large cedar trunk and three pegs for clothing, nothing else. No window. She gives me my class and chore schedule on a slip of paper.

"Will you be all right?" she asks.

I've passed a test and know my rank and am secure. I gush some of this to mentor. She hugs me and says I *will* be all right, and she goes back down the stairs to cloister the others.

In the morning, I am off to classes like the ones we visited as a group. In the afternoons I'm shoveling compost, picking peaches. Muscles torn in the evening heal stronger by morning. All of the spaces are pleasant, clear and open. The light is good.

The other students and I do not talk except in the classes requiring discussion. We debate or we ruminate when we are asked to do so and only then. The tennis court stands empty and in common room after common room, the decks of cards stay still in their wrappers.

★　　★　　★

I'm asked to focus on images, but words still occupy me as I lie in my little cell before sleep. *Splayed*, I think now, *flayed*. The words make me think about touching myself, but I do not. The image of a white lion flickers at the edge of some wall or boundary.

I have a memory of a book I must have once read, where a man always pictured, at the moment of orgasm, a show dog jumping through a hoop in triumph. I seek in vain for the title of the book or for anything else about it, but then the images begin their strobe, lines at first and then mosaics and paisleys and cutwork waves of the sea in aqua and navy, then flowers and glossy fruit, intense patterns this time.

I've been taught to name this effect on the way to controlling it: hypnagogia. This state might normally last a few moments, but I have learned to stretch it to an hour or two before a deep and restful sleep finally comes. I will wake during the watch and see more imagery in the dark before I open my eyes.

I go down my stairs to my little outhouse in a long pale gown. I am no longer afraid of the dark because I see so clearly at night. Everything lit is silver and blue. The dark is true black where it was once gray static. I see a lizard on a rock outside the outhouse, stars, burst roses, the cobblestone of the path. I can see some of the distant way to the canyon. A figure moves far out in the fields, blue-white like my gown but so far away, dim and swift.

The humming in my ears is gone. I hear the last crickets and the rustling of sheep and everywhere, leaves touching leaves. When I piss, it is loud.

Back upstairs in my little chamber, the imagery is back before my eyes as I sit, then slump against pillows. It is on its way to being a game. Viewed from the side it is like an ant farm, the structure of tunnels building themselves in flat cartoon colors, blue and tan and chalk red. There are ruptures in the walls of the tubes, allowing glimpses inside. Fast-moving patterns within the tunnel give way to darkness and a crescent of light on a horizon, and I approach the light, which reveals itself as a rupture looking into a little lighted cave. I look inside to see a pair of lovers gripping one another and whipping around in the wind. They are animate, though flat as paper cutouts, stroking each other's backs and making angry, confused faces toward me. A paper banner beneath them reads 'Paulo and Francesca'. I feel there has been a little breakthrough.

I mention this to a professor after class. He does not think anything of the names but says it sounds like I'm beginning to render game architecture, which is encouraging.

"I've never played games. I don't know how they're supposed to go," I say.

"That's why you're going to be a great designer," he says.

As he leads me out into sunlight, he passes me stale, worn books of Gaudi buildings and M.C. Escher drawings and a stack of pages cut out of magazines. "To think about before sleep," he says.

★   ★   ★

Mentor has asked me to have a conversation with myself. She says it is simpler than one might think. There is a large screen beside my bed now, which I am to think of as a mirror. There is a hard shell to cup my head.

I stare at the screen until my eyes fall closed. I jolt out of sleep as a half circle of chairs appears before me, then settle again. There is a clamp of the aperture and the chairs are peopled, another shutter click and then a single figure only, plainly myself, sits before me.

The image of her is neither flattering nor horrifying, as photographs tend to be. She looks like someone on the cusp of great fortune, a girl who's gotten a chance. Her skin is clear and golden toned, lips full, long hair streaked from sun. She does not offer conversation. She smiles and says, "Go ahead" and will not say more.

It's an easy slip from here into reverie. Looking at her until I tire, my eyes close and I see patterns. There is no sense of time passing. The imagery is no more or less intense than usual. When it is over, she is holding my journal so I can see the white page, which says, in my hand:

Chalk red, tan, butterscotch, cross-hatch. Galaxies, violet and purple-white Hubble imagery. Art Nouveau imagery. Bas relief chevrons, gray iridescent rainbow obsidian, fish bones. Western lines, arabesques, psychedelic Art Nouveau. Klimt, cloisonné, Celtic knotwork, fractal patterns. Galaxies, Hubble imagery blue and gold. Golden swoops and aqua, more Art Nouveau, ancient Egyptian flat colors. Cabbage roses. Gold filigree on deep red. The layered geometries of a red tile. Orange topographia on black background.

And it goes onto the next page and the next, the handwriting growing tighter and looser, nearing illegibility by the end. I feel the cramp deep in my hand. Though the words are insufficient to describe what I saw, I can account for the general order of the list.

I see why mentor recommended this exercise. If I can take notes or sketch during a reverie, I am a step closer to building my game world, though it remains to be seen if the words will be written there once I am fully awake. The list *is* sensical, except for one thing.

"I don't know 'Art Nouveau'," I say.

"You've heard the term," she says.

"Maybe, but I don't know why I'd use it if I don't know its meaning."

She takes the notebook back and finds the references.

"When you said, 'psychedelic Art Nouveau', that would be like a sixties poster, Jimi Hendrix or the Grateful Dead. There's all this scrollwork, bright colors, maybe flowers…."

She doesn't have to keep talking. I can see the posters she mentions and others like them strobing, superimposed over her face while she speaks. I linger on a bright orange blacklight poster that says, 'The Burden of Life is Love' with a long-haired girl drawn in flowing black lines. I can see the rest of the room where the poster hung, the television playing in that room. I recognize the show on the television and the people sitting before it, my ninth-grade boyfriend and his brothers in their basement, me trying to hear the show over their talk. At the same time, I see the me in front of me giving a lecture on Art Nouveau. These images layer on one another on the screen.

"This is too much," I start to say, but I cannot speak. My mouth feels forced closed. It is not until now that I feel fear.

She is still speaking. "Now, when you mentioned Art Nouveau the second time, you probably meant something like one of those Alphonse Mucha calendars, all these double-chinned ladies. I had one calendar of them with iridescent glitter, and…." The pages of the calendar display, and I am sure I've never seen this hideous imagery before. The women are crusted with scales of glitter like fish, the paper shiny and cheap.

Through the veils, I am seeing other scenes from my life, just glimpses of corners of rooms and of expressions. They are discernable only because they are all of them so familiar.

She says, "It makes me think of the wall of calendars in *Let Us Now Praise Famous Men*," and an image comes before all of the others of a black and white photograph of a poor person's house a long time ago. There are pictures hung on a wall, and she is lecturing again about how they were all sharecroppers in the Great Depression and they couldn't afford to buy anything pretty but would hang old calendars for decoration, and how when you read the book you feel this overwhelming guilt for the way that you live and the way poor people the world over are forced to live and the guilt is part of the beauty of the book. She talks forever, and I become more and more frightened because I have never read or heard of this book, and then I must sleep deeply because the next thing I know, I am standing against the wall, shrieking and clutching at my mouth to stifle the sound.

Mentor is a few feet from me, calming the air with her hands, saying, "I'm sorry. I didn't mean to startle you."

She is only dimly there and still followed by a comet tail of copies of herself that are dimmer still and at the very end disappearing, an arc of figures moving sideways toward me in a way no human moves.

"Oh my God," I say when my mouth will move again voluntarily. "I was so scared."

She comes to me and holds me, but mentor and I do not talk further. I'm made to understand that I'm supposed to be talking to *her* from now on, let her become my counsel.

★ ★ ★

"Did you think you saw a Tralfamadorian?" she asks.

I think, *again* you say words I do not know. You've brought fear back to me. Why? "Who are you?" I say.

"I am you," she says. "I couldn't be anyone else. If I say words you don't remember, it's from books you read in passing."

I let her keep talking though I hate her bitterly for making me fear this little room that has been such a comfort to me. Before her, I felt so safe locked inside.

Is she an enhancement of me? Is she the me who is unbounded, or what I would be if I were a machine? Mentor tells me she is there to enhance my aesthetics, enhance my erudition.

I open my green journal to read the handwritten words again and see that the paper has been replaced with a small tablet, all my pages scanned in and the new pages indistinguishable from the previous ones. I keep turning the virtual pages and see that she has written many new thousands of words in my style.

*   *   *

I'm learning to render from memory.

"Imagine the junk drawer at home," she says. "Imagine the contents of your hope chest at home," "your closet," and so on. I draw out whatever she says in detail. Drawing the hope chest unnerves me. My mother left me soft dresses in deep earth tones and jewel tones and snarls of silver and stone jewelry. I remember how she romanced the past.

She says my healing is complete. She says what I've been cured of is a disordered relationship to objects.

All the time I draw she is talking to me about the contents of a chest in a little-used room of a sharecropper's house, the little baby's gown with lace on it, worn and kept as a memento, a piece of past finery not to be given up to time. I draw the cedar walls of the trunk, every fiber of the fabrics within the suitcase within the trunk. I can see it all, render it all.

She shows it on the screen just as it was. Breathtaking detail. I have gone to another level, I am sure.

*   *   *

I attend classes and do chores as I like now. Nothing is asked of me. The other life with her, I think of as the *demimonde* because that is what she called it once.

Trips to town are rare and painful. The people barely look like people anymore. I see black and white rectangles and know they are screens. I wish I could wear blinders, but that would not stop the terrifying noise.

I return to correspondence with Grandma. She asks for news of my world and sends news of hers. Laws are changing, and while I once might have agreed with what she says about it all, I find I am now indifferent. The upshot of it is that if things had been different and I'd gotten pregnant with Jack's baby, I couldn't have gotten rid of it, and maybe I wouldn't have needed to go to school at all. I'm surprised to find I'm glad to hear of the changes. I think in someone's life something like that did happen and turned out nice. I spare one brief moment to think what might have been, then tear up the letter and put it in a fireplace on my way to chores.

I am scheduled to paint an outbuilding, already savoring the way it will feel to cover pitted lichen-spotted clapboard with a fresh robe of white. The day, when I make my way out across the pastures, is as clear and real as ever.

Grandma writes that the world is like something out of science fiction, people now handled like crops and everything precious growing fragile. She is thankful that I am where I am and tells me never to leave unless there is word from her or a relative. She lists the names I am supposed to trust. I don't know if it is really all so bad or if the problem is in her mind. I write back to let her know that the sun will rise and set and the gardens will be beautiful like always.

I still have dreams. Sometimes I am in a big disordered house I am trying to make livable but it has too many bathrooms and though they all have expensive jetted tubs, all of the tubs are stained with rust and algae and some are even filled with stinking piss.

She tells me these are architectures out of Kafka or Borges or Saramago, but when I ask for more, she says she never read them.

She tells me I am close to finding out something about Yeats' gyres, and about the *Origin of Consciousness in the Breakdown of the Bicameral Mind*. She is turning her hand to show me the movement of a gyre. It starts with broad swoops of the wrist and narrows down to the tight wave of a single finger before broadening out again. She says that consciousness once narrowed down on itself and realized – or mistook – that it was part of us and not a god, but that now we're gyrating out again and the god is simply becoming un-conflated from the consciousness.

I do not know the books she speaks of or the word *conflate* and, as always, I think of my journal and myself writing and know that the words will be there in the morning.

I am no closer to trusting her. She strikes me as mad, and more than that, reckless, always flaunting her pseudo-intellect. Always when I ask for more on the books she references, she says she never read them.

When I initiate, it is only ever about this plateau I seem to ride. I am getting no further in game rendering. Perhaps a spatial disorder is the next thing in me to cure, if it is indeed a disorder and not a structural flaw. I say, "I heard this story about...tribal people? I feel terrible. I don't remember their name or even what continent."

"It's all right," she says. "Tell me."

"These people never get lost. They think of themselves as a dot on a map and always know where they are because they have a mental image of the map and an image of where they are within it. But I always get lost and when I do, I'm not intrigued. I'm panicked."

"You have to think about the winning if you're going to play a game."

"I never care. If I do win something, I think it couldn't have been that hard."

"Except one time."

"Coming here. Yes, well."

"And another?"

I smile remembering it. "A costume contest."

"I remember," she says.

I say it anyway. "Grandma and I stayed up drawing fur on a white sweatsuit and braiding a yarn tail so I could be a lion, and in the morning we painted my face and ratted my hair. We sprayed all this white in it and silver glitter and multicolored iridescent glitter, so I had a big wild shimmering mane."

"It was like the calendar, the Mucha women."

"Yes." I see this. I was glittering all over like fish scales. I say, "I remember when I came home that night after winning the costume contest, I took off the sweatsuit. My skin was so dark against my white hair. My belly button was high on my stomach and my ribs were just heaving."

"Your first erotic memory."

"No, of course not."

"Too early for that?"

"Too late."

"The first time you thought you were beautiful?"

"Not that either," I say. I'm too ashamed to admit it, but I have never questioned my beauty.

"The first time you thought you were powerful?"

"Yes."

"You want to go into a game with that in mind."

★ ★ ★

I don't know. I guess I'm a senior. I imagine it's like what a sports star must feel, to enter the flow, to not think of time or care for other things. I live in my lab overlooking the canyon, far from campus. I have powerful computers, sleek black work surfaces, a bank of windows looking out over the rocks.

I can render not just how a memory looks but how it smells, how it feels, or we can. We render Jack, and he is perfect. Soft eyes, soft hair on his face. He smells like him but stronger. Within my thesis game, I embed a memory of getting to the point on the last night when I stopped him, when I stepped down from his truck, the kiss. We render fictional backstory to add to the feeling. I might have been, perhaps, a little bit bad and now was being good being with someone like him, and by stepping down from the truck I was being even better. In the game, the pounding in my groin is like the pounding on a thick wooden door.

Thesis project, dissertation, whatever: a game. I know it is pretentious, uneven, but it is so vivid. The player is the girl with promise. You can look into her every drawer at home and her friends' homes. You can look into every corner of her mind. You can do whatever you want with her grandma, her friends, and then you can take the trip to school and learn design, though this part is vague because I must not sell out secrets. It's rare a senior project finds distribution, but even so. And then once the player is in school, it all becomes more fantastical. The lion lurking like the minotaur in the maze of school buildings, the gods with heads of foxes and chickens and sheep. There is a sequence lifted from the start of *The House on the*

Borderland, which *she* claims not to have read. She tells me to tell mentor and the panel that the game is a *Künstlerroman.* I tell them that without feeling I need to know the word. I trust her implicitly now.

I keep thinking it's finished. She says, "No, you're going to spend your life on this. Can't you feel it?"

The panel gives me accolades, far as they ever do, I'm told. On graduation night, mentor leads me out to a patio lit with Christmas lights for the first dance and then the others join. None of us are dancers. We have a live band and for the first time in years hear the songs of our youth and get just a little stupid on champagne.

Sponsors dine at tables on the dark edges of the patio. We will circulate and speak with them as the night wears on. I focus on the dinner jackets' academy crests and try not to see the faces.

Late, late into the mingling, mentor approaches me, eyes welling. I've gotten an offer.

★ ★ ★

The room looks like a sound studio. Where singers would stand, I construct the inside of Jack's truck cab. All of it is there, at once accurate and ornamented with sworls of pattern, the spangled X-ray diagram lifted from a book of Alex Grey paintings, swirling paisleys and floating jewels, the empty shape of a man where the player will be and the empty shape of a woman cupped against him.

I am starting to enter the space for her body. It feels like the player is pouring in all around me.

"Yes I said yes I will. Yes," *she* whispers with a dry cough of a laugh and is gone.

I am alone in that space where he straddles my knees. The player's thumb sticks up between my top button and the fly. It's pulling up the seam, cleaving me. The player, whoever they are, is about to pull off the button. The pounding like someone knocking on the door of my cell, it doesn't end.

ACKNOWLEDGMENTS

This, my second fiction collection, is dedicated to my writing friends, writing groups, mentors, and mentees. The Codex Writers Group, in particular, exposed me to many wonderful science fiction and fantasy writers and spurred several of these stories with its various writing contests. Special thanks to Eileen Gunnell Lee. Our story 'The Orbital Bloom' was developed in the Codexian Collaboration Challenge in 2017, and the first story here, 'Cocooning', showed in that group's Codexian Idol contest in 2018 – a proud moment! (Another of my stories would go on to win first place in a Codex contest in 2021, but it will appear in a later collection).

I remain inspired by my fellow Moanaria's Fright Club, Sawtooth Alliance of Women Writers, and HOWL Society members. Thank you to my critique partners who read many of these stories, Samuel M. Moss, J.A.W. McCarthy, Ken Hueler and the late Scott Wheelock. I also want to thank the mentors and mentees I have met through SFWA and HWA, along with the participants of my workshop class The Art of Dread: Crafting Contemporary Horror, which is sponsored by Idaho's literary center The Cabin.

Many thanks to the readers and editors of the periodicals, anthologies, and podcasts in which many of the stories first appeared, and special thanks to those who published more than one of the included stories: *The Arcanist, Fusion Fragment, Tales to Terrify,* and *Dark Matter Magazine.*

I am also grateful to Don D'Auria, Mike Valsted, Kirsty Parkinson, Zoë Seabourne, and the rest of the Flame Tree Press team for bringing my story collections out into the world.

FULL PUBLICATION HISTORY

'Cocooning', *Three-Lobed Burning Eye*, 2020. Reprinted in *Tales to Terrify*, 2021 and *Dark Matter Magazine*, 2022.

'Laurel's First Chase', *Humans Are the Problem: A Monster's Anthology*, 2021.

'Finishers', *Dark Matter Magazine*, 2020 and Dark Matter Ink's *Zero Dark Thirty*, 2023.

'A Fully Chameleonic Foil', *The Arcanist*, 2017 and *Sins and Other Worlds*, 2018.

'What Do You See When You're Both Asleep?' *The Arcanist*, 2019 and *Manawaker Studio Podcast*, 2020.

'Flexible Off-Time', Original to this collection.

'A Game Like They Play in the Future', *Etherea*, 2022.

'Paper Dragonfly, Paper Mountain', *Apparition Lit*, 2019.

'An Account'. Original to this collection.

'The Laffun Head', *Speculative North*, 2020.

'Guesthouse', *Orca*, 2022.

'Lovey', *Haven Spec*, 2022.

'Every City a Small Town', *Nonbinary Review*, 2021.

'Cubby', *Portable Story Series* podcast, 2016.

'Fables of the Future'. Original to this collection.

'Substance', *Fusion Fragment*, 2020.

'The Earthly Garden'. Original to this collection.

'The Orbital Bloom'. Co-authored with Eileen Gunnell Lee. *Fusion Fragment*, 2021.

'Watershakers', *PULP Literature*, 2020.

'Viridian Green', *Tales to Terrify*, 2021.

'Promise', *Escape Pod*, 2018. Reprinted in *SYNTH: An Anthology of Dark SF 3*, 2019 and *Fusion Fragment*, 2022.

CONTENT NOTES

These notes were not included with the first publication of these stories, but I provide them here in hopes they might be of some help to readers:

- 'Cocooning', 'Laurel's First Chase', 'An Account', 'The Laffun Head', 'Fables of the Future', 'Substance': contain body horror. I would consider it mild.
- 'Flexible Off-Time', 'Paper Dragonfly, Paper Mountain', 'The Laffun Head', 'Lovey': deal with aging, death, and grief.
- 'Cubby': contains a somewhat naïve treatment of what it means to be nonbinary, as I wrote it in 2015 before I had become more informed.
- 'The Orbital Bloom': contains more pronounced body horror, sexual situations, narcissistic abuse.
- 'Promise': deals with sexual situations and sexual exploitation.